CROSSED SWORDS

A Classic In Every Way!

The legendary tale of mistaken identity is being brought to the screen in a multi-million dollar spectacular featuring the star-studded cast of Oliver Reed, Raquel Welch, Rex Harrison, Charlton Heston, George C. Scott, Ernest Borgnine, David Hemmings, and Mark Lester.

While no author today could possibly hope to improve on the classic novel, Tim Warnak has faithfully brought to you the novelization of the contemporary film version, and David M. Petrou and Berta Dominguez D. have provided a fascinating insider's look at how the film was made—and what the stars did when they weren't before the cameras!

There are *thirty-two* photographs, too, that help make this edition of *Crossed Swords* (based on *The Prince and the Pauper* by Mark Twain) a contemporary classic of its own!

ALEXANDER SALKIND
Presents
A RICHARD FLEISCHER FILM
OLIVER REED • RAQUEL WELCH • MARK LESTER
ERNEST BORGNINE
Guest Star
GEORGE C. SCOTT

CROSSED SWORDS

REX HARRISON as Duke of Norfolk
DAVID HEMMINGS as Hugh Hendon
HARRY ANDREWS • MURRAY MELVIN • SYBIL DANNING
CHARLTON HESTON as Henry VIII

ORIGINAL SCREENPLAY BY BERTA DOMINGUEZ D. AND PIERRE SPENGLER
FINAL SCREENPLAY BY GEORGE MACDONALD FRASER
DIRECTED BY RICHARD FLEISCHER EXECUTIVE PRODUCER ILYA SALKIND
PRODUCED BY PIERRE SPENGLER
MUSIC BY MAURICE JARRE DIRECTOR OF PHOTOGRAPHY JACK CARDIFF TECHNICOLOR PANAVISION
AN ALEXANDER AND ILYA SALKIND PRODUCTION
From Warner Bros., A Warner Communications Company
Printed in U.S.A.

ALEXANDER SALKIND
Presents

Novelization by Tim Warnak

Special section on The Making Of *Crossed Swords* by
David Michael Petrou and Berta Dominguez D

ace books

A Division of Charter Communications Inc.
A GROSSET & DUNLAP COMPANY
1120 Avenue of the Americas
New York, New York 10036

CROSSED SWORDS

Introduction and Photographs Copyright © 1978 by Film Export
AG

Ace Books Novelization Copyright © 1978 by Ace Books

All rights reserved. No portion of this book may be reproduced
without written permission of the publisher, except for brief
quotes to be used specifically for reviews.

Published simultaneously in Canada

ISBN: 0441–67865–3

First Ace Printing: March 1978

An ACE Book

Printed in U.S.A.

The Making Of

CROSSED SWORDS:

Fantasy to Film

ACKNOWLEDGEMENTS

There are a number of people to whom I am deeply indebted and without whom this book would not have been possible. First and foremost, I wish to thank my friend Ilya Salkind, who gave me the opportunity to write this log and whose creative genius is largely responsible for the success of *Crossed Swords*. Naturally, I wish to extend this appreciation to my co-author Berta Dominguez D.; Alexander Salkind; Producer Pierre Spengler; Director Richard Fleischer; Director of Photography Jack Cardiff; Assistant Director Nigel Wooll; Production Executive Almos Mezo; the Production Supervisor in Hungary Basil Keys; our Unit Publicist Al Hix; our Hungarian assistants Janos, Akos and Peter; Jim Aubrey and Amy and Paul Berkowitz; the staff at Mafilm in Budapest and, of course, the people of Great Britain and Hungary, as well as the entire international cast and crew. I would also like to thank my editors at Ace and Tempo Books, Harriet McDougal, Susanne Jaffe and Robin London, whose advice and criticism were invaluable assets to me. Lastly, I wish to add some very personal acknowledgements: to my dear friend Susan Ann Melnicove, who typed this manuscript and always had a soft shoulder to cry on; to my brother-in-law, for Xeroxing all those screenplays; to the English Department at Georgetown and the University of Maryland and, most importantly, to my mother, father and sister, who believed in me even when *I* didn't and who had me paged at the Polo Lounge when no one else would.

—DAVID MICHAEL PETROU
Budapest, September 1976

Editor's note:

At the time this introduction was prepared, the title of the film was *The Prince and the Pauper*. It was subsequently changed to *Crossed Swords*.

1. ORIGINS OF A CLASSIC

SOPRON, HUNGARY. August, 1976. "It may have happened, it may not have happened, but it *could* have happened," Mark Twain wrote in his preface to *The Prince and the Pauper*. But even Twain himself could never have imagined it happening quite like this.

In a seven hundred-year-old Hungarian village, tucked neatly in the westernmost corner of the country, smack on the Austrian border, a thousand local extras—most of them card-carrying members of the Communist Party of the Peoples Republic of Hungary—are milling around, lavishly arrayed in early 16th century Tudor dress; laughing, smoking, talking Hungarian at a mind (and ear!) boggling pace, munching on kaposzta (a sausage and cheese concoction) or scurrying in and out of the shops —twentieth century clothed children in tow—trying to get some early morning marketing done before the shooting starts. Over to the far right of this chaos which looks as if it were taken straight from an Hieronymus Bosch painting, Raquel Welch is making some final adjustments on her period headdress (a pearl encrusted snood) while a phalanx of hairstylists and makeup attendants hover about her. Costume designer Ulla Soderland (she won an Academy Award for *Barry Lyndon*), is busy putting last minute tucks and folds in Raquel's satin gown to better display the bosomy, voluptuous, world-renowned shape within. Nearby is Oliver Reed and his friend-companion-bodyguard of fifteen years, Reggie Prince. They are sitting in the sun squinting, smirking and drying out from last night's stint in the night club at the Hotel Claudius in Szombathely, while cameramen and grips, prop men and sound mixers are efficiently shuttling the trappings of movie making from their caravan of cars and trucks into the cavernous warehouse where the filming will soon be underway again.

An incongruous scene, in an unlikely setting, yet here in Hungary, and earlier, on locations throughout England, producers Alexander and Ilya Salkind and Pierre Spengler had assembled an enormous all-star international cast and crew for the mammoth nine million dollar production of Mark Twain's immortal *The Prince and the Pauper*.

Now you will learn the whole story of how the movie was made—for the most part, a thousand miles from its English setting, 6,000 miles from Hannibal, Missouri, Twain's hometown, and nearly a century later from when the great American humorist first set down what was originally to be a simple children's story for his favorite daughters, Susie and Clara Clemens.

It wasn't too long after the book was first published in 1882, however, that readers and literary critics alike began to theorize that beneath the surface of this supposedly innocent fantasy was a scathing satire and high comedic mockery, as well as a stinging assault on the realities of social injustice.

Yet regardless of the interpretations, *The Prince and the Pauper* remains one of the most popular and widely read stories of all time. The fantasy, the timeless appeal of the adventure and romance, the pomp and pageantry, the intrigue and the innocence are ingredients that blend beautifully to make it a true classic.

In 1937, Warner Brothers, recognizing the universal appeal of the story, produced a swashbuckling film adaptation of *The Prince and the Pauper*, starring Errol Flynn as Miles Hendon, Claude Rains, and a pair of twins —Billy and Bobby Mauch—who, incidentally, were never heard from in films again. The movie was a great critical and commercial success, as had been predicted.

Other productions of *The Prince and the Pauper* have been made in the years since 1937, including a smattering of theatrical attempts, a Walt Disney special and a BBC "made-for-television" feature. Though the obvious incredible potential of the story was always seen, a significant, big-budget, all-star production had never been made.

For that to happen, it took the foresight, imagination and talents of Alexander and Ilya Salkind and Pierre Spengler.

For the last several years, the team of Salkind and Spengler had been purchasing and producing properties which to them best represented entertainment in its purest form for every age group—their most notable recent accomplishment being the hugely successful *Three* and *Four Musketeers*. To these three men, the prospect of mounting a first-class, expanded and updated production of Twain's enduring classic was too enticing a challenge to ignore. In fact, Spengler, along with noted Mexican authoress Berta Dominguez D. (who also happens to be Mrs. Alexander Salkind as well as co-author of this special piece) had written an initial screenplay for *The Prince and the Pauper* nearly eight years ago.

So early in 1975, the probing and planning began in earnest, and tentative pre-production got underway for what was soon to become the most important—and costly—production of Mark Twain's "simple children's story" in motion picture history.

2. THE PRODUCERS SPEAK

At Budapest's Hotel Gellert, slouched on sofas in Suite 223—a veritable battleground of scattered papers, photographic contact sheets, overflowing ashtrays and empty caviar tins—Ilya Salkind and Pierre Spengler talked about the genesis of the entire production.

"The whole *Prince and the Pauper* project began about eight years ago in Paris at a very low point in our film career," Ilya reflected in his heavily accentèd English, toying with an empty Marlboro pack. "You know, the Salkinds weren't always making multi-million dollar pictures. My grandfather was a real artist, but he had absolutely *no* concept as to what would be commercially successful.

"Anyway, during this period, we were running around from hotel to hotel, living out of suitcases, and one day we found this book that Berta had boughten . . . . had bought?" (Ilya Salkind is acutely conscious of his less than total command of English syntax.) "I looked at the book. It was Twain's *The Prince and the Pauper*. Berta and I stared at each other at the same time—right out of the movies, you know?—and we both said 'This would make a marvelous film.' So I reread the book, suggested that we simply expand the possibilities of an already terrific story by making the two boys sixteen instead of nine, and after Alex's approval, I hired Berta and my best friend Pierre Spengler—for very little money, mind you—to do the screenplay.

"In about five weeks, they came up with a good script. Berta was truly the guiding inspiration at this point. I had the script printed and nicely bound and went to London to see George Cukor, who was already involved with my father on several other deals. Cukor read the screenplay and decided that he preferred the original concept of the two boys being only nine or so. Naturally, this depressed us because he seemed adamant on that point, so I guess we all just lost enthusiasm. We shelved the script and moved on to another project—*Light at the Edge of the World* with Yul Brynner and Kirk Douglas—and thankfully, we started making profits again.''

Because of Ilya's enthusiasm, Alex's interest was roused; and *Light at the Edge of The World* was made. And with this picture the tide changed. *Bluebeard*, starring Richard Burton followed. Then after a few minor cinematic disasters, Ilya, Alex, and Pierre became known as ''The Three Musketeers'' due to their success as the producers of the films *The Three* and *The Four Musketeers*.

A little background information would be useful now. Mikhail Salkind or ''Don Miguel'' as he was lovingly called by all those who worked for him, was known as ''The Quixote of the Cinema.'' He had also made a classic film *Don Quixote* with the great Russian Bosso Chaliapin which, although it left him penniless, was applauded and rewarded by a gold medal by the then King of Belgium, Leopold I.

Alexander, Don Miguel's son, became no less a legend in classic cinema history. Alex, as he is called by all, was described as ''The daring young man on the flying trapeze'', or ''Le poet de l'argent'' (the poet of money) by *Paris Match* in 1963, when he astonished the entire film world by assuming the task of producing Kafka's famous book *The Trial*. Single-handedly, magically, and backed by what seemed non-existent invisible monies, the great classic was made. With daring and forsight he took the risk of engaging "The Colossal" Orson Welles to direct, and the film became a classic like its literary counterpart.

During that epoch, the youngest of the dynasty, Ilya, then thirteen, was trying to concentrate on school mathematics while carrying a satchel full of dreams and films. He was in a most profitable position—being Alex's only son and the only grandchild of Miguel. So, during his teenage years, Ilya dropped school and joined forces with his father and grandfather. The trio of Ilya, Alex, and Miguel Salkind became *The* Salkinds with the international success of their *Musketeers* films. (Not long ago, Ilya married Skye Aubrey, daughter of former MGM chieftain, James Aubrey, Jr. They have a daughter, Anastasia Mikiala, who will probably be the *fourth* generation of movie-making Salkinds!)

Then *The Prince and the Pauper* came to life, and with it the saga of the making of this spectacular film and its spectacular cast.

"A lot of people have asked us about the wisdom of remaking a classic," Pierre now said. "We proved our point with *Musketeers*. Dumas's story had been made thirty-two times. Ours was the thirty-third. The real challenge is to take a popular story that people know and love and bring new perspective to it; to do it in a way that's never been done before. This is just what we've accomplished with *The Prince and the Pauper*. Never has there been so lavish a production of the story, with so many distinguished contemporary stars. And on top of that, as Ilya already pointed out, we've made a few minor—though significant—twists in the plot, so this gives the whole story a brand new dimension while still adhering to the Twain classic. Hopefully, our film will surpass the previous versions.

"Beyond that," Pierre went on enthusiastically, "we've filmed it using some great new techniques that Wally Veevers has been working on. He's the one who did *2001*. In using the split screen—with Mark (Lester, the star of *Oliver!*) playing both title roles—(Richard) Fleischer has gone well beyond anything that's been done before. We have the 'two' boys facing each other, completely walking around one another—even touching! This is all a first."

"That's the whole point," Ilya added quickly. "With most of our recent successful pictures, we've done something different, gone one better. We now have an established image of producing a successful product. Successful artistically, yes, but even more so commercially. Also, the three of us have found a way of operating together—a certain recipe, I will almost say—which wasn't always the case."

"Did you know that Ilya and I were boyhood friends?" Pierre interjected.

"Playmates," corrected Ilya.

"Yeah, and we're *still* playing with each other!" Pierre deadpanned.

"Anyway," Ilya went on, "now we're very realistic commercially and by making all the decisions ourselves, we can control the quality of our pictures."

Ilya stopped for a moment to pour himself some already flat mineral water before continuing.

"Of course, we all exchange ideas and criticisms, but we have our specialties. Alex is the financial wizard; Pierre is the chief administrator—he *hopefully* keeps the costs down; and I more or less handle the creative end: the selection of properties, casting, publicity, all that sort of thing."

Then Ilya glanced at his watch (with two faces; one for

European time, the other with Los Angeles time) and decided that he and Pierre had devoted enough time to answering questions.

"Look, we can sum it up by saying that out style may be unique, even a bit unorthodox," he said, "but whatever the formula is—if, in fact, you can call it a 'formula'—it works for us!"

And with a little bit of luck and a great deal of money, effort and talent, hopes were running high that it would work again with *The Prince and the Pauper*.

3. "MORE STARS THAN THERE ARE . . ."

Whether or not there exists for *any* producers a "formula" to guarantee box office success (and, one must assume, if there were, every picture would be a hit), a key part of the Salkinds' packaging has always been to feature a first-rate, all-star cast. And as plans started to evolve, it soon became apparent that *The Prince and the Pauper* certainly would follow this rule.

"The initial casting of *The Prince and the Pauper* was very painful," Ilya explained once after production had been completed. "From the outset, both Pierre and I wanted Mark Lester for the dual role. We screen-tested him and we both thought that he would be fine. Unfortunately, for various reasons, the test was on videotape—not the best for a strong impact—directed by a London theatre director, and Fleischer (the producer's choice for director) was, quite honestly, not convinced. So at that point—in London, New York and Los Angeles—we tested tens, hundreds of boys; twins, everything. It was great for publicity. You know, 'Salkinds Conduct World-Wide Search for Prince/Pauper.' But it became a bitch of a problem.''

''We still were convinced that Mark had the best potential for the part,'' added Pierre, ''so we again asked Fleischer to see him . . . this time, personally. They spent about an hour and a half together just talking and after their meeting, Fleischer was impressed enough to request another screen test. So we scheduled the test for a day or so later and this time, Fleischer too was convinced.''

''Mark gives a smashing performance,'' Ilya said. ''Do you realize that, actually, he plays *four* roles—the prince, the pauper, the pauper *as* prince and the prince *as* pauper. That's really quite an achievement.''

Naturally, it was the principal roles that commanded the greatest attention and efforts of the producers.

After locking up award-winning director Richard Fleischer (whose track record includes *Tora, Tora, Tora, Doctor Doolittle, Fantastic Voyage, See No Evil,* and *The Incredible Sarah*), the first major star to be signed was Academy Award-winner Charlton Heston. Heston had worked for the Salkinds before in the *Musketeers* films and of course, his considerable talent and box office appeal were all a matter of record. Beyond that, Heston's commanding adaptation of biographical roles was a major factor in his selection for the part of the legendary Henry VIII. Because of his commitments, Heston's work on the film spanned only the first weeks in England. But as he does for all historical pictures, Heston did a voluminous amount of research before the cameras started to roll and it was soon apparent that Charlton had become one of our resident authorities on Tudor England.

A warm yet introspective man, Heston demonstrated

abundant patience as he daily submitted to several hours of Peter Robb-King's superb makeup which literally transformed him into Henry.

During his stint on the picture, Charlton's awesome physical presence could be seen early each day in a baggy sweatsuit as the health-conscious actor jogged for several miles through the English morning mist. And much to his amusement, he came to be known affectionately as "Hop-a-Long Heston" when the cast and crew learned of his grueling world-wide schedule after *Prince*, during which time he would be plugging his new film *Midway* and officiating at Bicentennial ceremonies back in the States.

The next major star to be set was another Academy Award-winning actor, George C. Scott. Scott and his lovely wife, actress Trish Van Devere, had already been in Europe for some time working on a new adaptation of the fairy tale *Beauty and the Beast*. Scott's obligations in the intervening months seemed certain to preclude any serious consideration of his involvement in *The Prince and the Pauper*. But when his long-time friend Dick Fleischer met with Scott in Vienna to persuade him to play the part of the Ruffler, Scott agreed to read the screenplay, liked it, and soon after signed for the role. Like Heston, Scott's contribution to the film spanned only a short time in Budapest. A rather shy and evidently private person, the impact of Scott's towering acting ability nonetheless added a major contribution to the film.

At about the same time Scott was signed, another renowned motion picture performer agreed to play, by his own admission, his "first cameo appearance in any film." Rex Harrison was cast as the Duke of Norfolk, the crafty elder statesman who became a threat to King Henry's own power.

"I enjoy doing historical features," Harrison remarked

soon after accepting the part. "And I'm pleased to see that *The Prince and the Pauper* is being made on such a grand scale, like the swashbucklers of the Thirties. I honestly hope that it will signal a return to films that everyone can enjoy . . . you know, real entertainment."

The selection of someone to play Miles Hendon became one of the crucial decisions in the making of *The Prince and the Pauper*. For months, such talents as Michael York, Sean Connery and Alan Bates were all seriously considered. Michael York had been very engaging as D'Artagnan in *Musketeers*, and Connery was fresh from receiving critical acclaim for his rousing performance in another classic period film, *The Man Who Would Be King*.

Eventually, however, the names were knocked off for one reason or another, and the producers finally settled on *l'enfant terrible* of films, Oliver Reed.

Reed's casting as Hendon marked another major plus for the picture. A dynamic and incredibly intense performer, the British actor had achieved a major critical and box office reputation in such films as *Oliver!*, *The Jokers*, *Women in Love*, *The Devils*, and both *Musketeers* films. As Miles Hendon—the only role other than the Prince/Pauper requiring an almost continuous on-screen presence—Reed, so the thinking ran, would unquestionably add prestige and power to what was already shaping up as an unusually strong cast.

Reed's notorious reputation as a rebel and a reveler created some anxiety among the growing production team, even though those who had worked with Ollie firsthand were quick to point out that the actor's personal hell-raising had never interfered with his professional commitments. But at the time Ollie was cast, he was reportedly in the midst of another of his highly provocative public squabbles—this one with Raquel Welch, who had just been signed to play Hendon's leading lady.

How can one describe Raquel Welch? There was a newspaper article in October, 1976, dateline Budapest. Raquel and Oliver Reed stood eyeball to eyeball in a very nice Hungarian restaurant, shredding the air with obscenities.

The effect on the multitude was adrenal.

Producer Pierre Spengler, who had just spent millions of dollars to make a movie with Reed and Welch, paled visibly.

Director Richard Fleischer shuddered.

But suddenly the scene switched.

Oliver and Raquel fell into each other's arms, their bodies now limp with laughter. The crowd breathed.

Raquel was surprisingly blunt in voicing her reasons for accepting the relatively small part of Lady Edith.

"The Salkinds sent me a copy of the script—which I liked—accompanied by a nice fat offer!" she remarked when we were several weeks into production in Budapest. "So I said, 'Why not?' But I wanted to do the film anyway because I think it's going to be an excellent picture; it's a great classic. I mean, what a cast and I wanted to be part of it.

"Now as far as this so-called 'feud' with Ollie," Raquel smiled, tossing her chestnut hair away from her exquisitely tanned face, "it's all Hollywood bullshit! I think the stories say that Ollie once told a reporter that he'd rather go to bed with my hairdresser than me! And then he supposedly cabled Richard Harris to be his stand-in for our love scenes. It's ridiculous, isn't it? Ollie *never* said those things and even though we've had our share of misunderstandings, we're getting along just great. I think he's a fine actor and one helluva interesting person. Now *that* should set the gossip peddlers straight!"

Another Academy Award-winning American actor

who was lined up for the picture was veteran film star Ernest Borgnine, who would portray the scoundrel ruffian John Canty, the brutish father of the pauper.

Ernie's reputation as a character actor made him a natural for the demanding role of Canty. And his attitude of complete professionalism and personal warmth easily made him the favorite performer in *The Prince and the Pauper*.

Ernie arrived in Budapest with his fifth wife Tove, a Norwegian-born beauty who quickly became the Perle Mesta of *The Prince and the Pauper*, organizing the evening activities for the cast and crew, even when we were stuck in some tiny village far out in the Hungarian provinces. And when she wasn't planning parties, Tove, a professional cosmetician, and Ernie were both busy pitching her forthcoming line of wonder cosmetics made from the fleshy parts of Mexican cactus plants. Despite the enthusiastic claims of the Borgnines as to the powers of these creams, soaps and lotions, most of us remained highly skeptical . . . *until* we used them! We were amazed to find that they did everything from cure blemishes and dry skin to heal cuts and bruises; they even brought a tingling warmth to sore muscles. Happily, we all predicted a revolution in the cosmetic industry once Tove began mass-marketing her "prickly" panacea!

Despite the documented stories of Ernie's volatile Italian temper, we all found him to be an engaging, unpretentious, lovable guy who spent most of his off-hours with Tove, fraternizing with the crew, drinking Austrian beer or shopping for the exquisite hand-painted Herend china he and his wife loved.

With most of the major casting done and much of the pre-production work well underway (location scouting had already been going on for months), the producers were ready by the time of the Cannes Film Festival to project a tentative starting date in England for mid-May. The remaining casting was accomplished in the few weeks before filming began, with one or two key roles carrying over until after we were into production.

David Hemmings was set for the part of Hugh Hendon, Miles's dastardly brother. And another veteran of *The Four Musketeers*, Sybil Danning, was signed to play Mrs. Canty, the pauper's oppressed mother. The shapely Austrian-American actress provided a real challenge to the "magic" of movie-making, requiring hours of painstaking makeup to have her look sufficiently haggard, wizened and gaunt for the part. And then a few miraculous hours later, "old Mother Canty" would be in the nightclub of our hotel, sans makeup, dressed in a form-fitting leather jump suit, doing the Bump with Mark Lester!

The final remaining roles were mostly filled by distinguished British actors. Harry Andrews, a venerable veteran of the English stage and screen, was cast as the Duke of Hartford, Julian Orchard, another veteran, became St. John. The delightfully foppish Murray Melvin was slated to play the delightfully foppish De Brie, young Prince Edward's attendant. The cameo role of King Henry's jester was filled by a talented British performer with innumerable screen credits, Graham Stark.

With the casting essentially resolved, Ilya Salkind and Pierre Spengler totally immersed themselves in the last minute problems inevitable in any multi-million dollar production of such scope and stature. Working at a furious pace to see that every detail was in order, the producers cautiously set a start date of May 17 for production to begin at the 16th century English palace of Penshurst.

4. "THIS EARTH, THIS REALM, THIS ENGLAND"

As far back as six months before the start date, Richard
Fleischer and others had begun scouting authentic historical locations throughout Europe; locations that would
firmly adhere to the historical integrity of Twain's story
and yet would provide modern accommodations with a
minimum standard of clean sheets and indoor plumbing!
One of the people who worked closest with the director on
this is a remarkable character who has become something
of a fixture on most Salkind productions.

Eddie Fowlie is a jovial, robust Englishman with a
heavy cockney accent and a thick, flowing mane of
snow-white hair. Although Eddie held the rather amor-
phous title of Property Master (which made him sound like
some kind of overseer), he actually was more of a jack-
of-all trades ombudsman, who saw to it that everything
needed for each day's shooting was where it should be at
any given time. And, along with Fleischer and our U.K.
location manager Chris Kenny, it was Eddie Fowlie who
was largely responsible for choosing the location sights
throughout England and Hungary.

One of Fleischer's (and the producers') most important
and distinguished selections was that of Oscar-winning
cinematographer Jack Cardiff. Cardiff, whose film credits
include *The African Queen, War and Peace,* and *Black
Narcissus* (for which he won the Academy Award), has an
international reputation in the industry as (according to the
highly respected *Films in Review*) "the greatest master of
color composition in British and—some would say
—world cinema" and his signing for *The Prince and the*

Pauper was another indicator to the trade that something big was in the works.

Apart from Fleischer, the man most responsible for the success of each day's shooting was our First Assistant Director and Production Manager Nigel Wooll. In addition to being an experienced film craftsman despite being only thirty-four, Nigel is unquestionably one of the best-natured, fiendishly sarcastic and totally lovable taskmasters this side of Simon Legree! Nigel quickly became the most instantly conspicuous crewman on the set, with his ruddy English face, his natty racing cap and his designer blue jeans. Throughout the more than fifteen weeks of shooting, Wooll's relationship with the crew was an on-going (benign) battle in search of the best "wind-ups" (the British slang for "put-on" or "tease"). Before each take, Nige would give his own unique interpretation of "Quiet on the set!" by shouting through his megaphone—in his most posh, upper class English accent (which invariably became more pronounced when he talked to any of the Americans)—"All right now, let's cut the cackle!" And then, later in the evening, after a few logger and limes had dispelled the daily tensions and had affixed an appropriately silly grin on his face, Nigel would suddenly launch into a little tirade we'd all be mimicking by the end of the film: "My ears may be a bit *woolly*, but who's got all the cackle!"

Working closely with the producers and Fleischer, Nigel made his own recommendations to complete the crew list with the best people in the British film business, so that by the time our starting date had arrived, we were fully crewed with a crack production team numbering just over eighty people.

With the production offices headquartered at Twickenham Studios in Middlesex (about twenty miles outside of London), facilities there as well as at Pinewood Studios in Iver Heath would be used in addition to the predetermined location settings.

The first day's shooting was at Penhurst Palace, about forty miles from London. We had an early call for that day (most days, in fact, we would be up by 6:00 A.M.) because Fleischer had been out several times prior to the start date and had carefully planned the first shot, which involved Mark Lester as the pauper, fleeing from the constables of Offal Court, climbing the palace walls and then falling into the king's garden.

A mock wall—complete with mock portal through which Mark was to fall—had been constructed, as well as an elaborate English garden below. The portal was several feet above the ground and mattresses were stacked to break the fall. Unfortunately, Fleischer suddenly decided that he didn't like the final set-up, so the mattresses were removed (in the interest of achieving a more realistic fall sequence), replaced by additional shrubbery and Mark's stunt double, Graeme Crowther, was called on to do the take.

Surprisingly, everything clicked and the first scene was in the can by ten o'clock. We remained at Penshurst, in Tumbridge, for about two weeks, completing those sequences which involved the exteriors and grounds of Henry's palace (which included the first scenes with Heston and Harrison together) as well as some interior shots of the King's chambers. (These fantastic interior sets —including the ornate, gilded bed—had been painstakingly designed by Wilfrid Shingleton under the direction of our production designer, Tony Pratt. Tourists who visited the palace while the picture was located there thought the reproductions were incredibly well-preserved pieces of authentic Tudor furnishings.)

After completing the shots at Penshurst, we moved into Pinewood Studios to film one of the most visually spectacular scenes from *The Prince and the Pauper*, the masque and ball. The huge set occupied an enormous sound stage and was carefully constructed to approximate the ornate banqueting halls of Hampton Court Palace, an actual residence of Henry VIII. To further the period realism and heighten the visual impact, the scene was to be lit by hundreds of authentic double-wick church candles—an effect which proved dazzlingly impressive but which soon became an infuriating nuisance for our usually high-spirited props man, Mickey Pugh. To get ready for each take, Mickey would first scurry around lighting the myriad of candles, only to find that the heat from the candles, coupled with the high intensity movie lights, caused them to droop and drip hot wax on the extras even before the principal actors and actresses were in place. And snuffing them out between takes proved an impossibility because the entire set would fill up with thick white smoke! Finally, Mickey enlisted the help of six full-time assistants whose sole job was to madly replace and relight the drooping candles as soon as Dick Fleischer yelled ''Cut''.

The masque and ball scene was one of the dramatic high points in the script, when Tom, still in pauper's rags, is mistakenly presumed to be a cleverly costumed Prince of Wales and is escorted off to be presented to King Henry at a lavish ball given in the prince's honor.

The costumes for this sequence were among the most ornate and opulent ever seen on any movie set. Judy Moorcroft—a costume designer with an impressive list of film credits in England—had created colorful, diverse and historically authentic wardrobe for the entire picture and throughout the filming of *Prince*, it was Judy and her wardrobe mistresses (Dorothy Edwards in Britain and later, Betty Adamson in Hungary) who were awake a good hour and a half before the rest of the crew, seeing to it that the eight hundred extras needed for that particular day's shooting were clothed and coiffed according to plan.

"Doing a period picture is always a challenge," Judy said once later in the filming, "and particularly when you are working for practical producers who are being careful to keep the costs from absolutely sky-rocketing—especially when you're already working with a multi-million dollar budget, like this picture.

"Pierre went to Berman's in London—the best costumers in Europe, if not the world—and they hammered out an acceptable arrangement. And when I was hired, I was obliged to work within the framework of that budget.

"Of course, every designer would like to be madly creative and say 'Oh, screw the damn budget!' and then just do as he wildly pleases," she continued, "but then, the *real* talent comes in creating a first-rate wardrobe *within* the framework of your financial limits.

"I became particularly involved with *Prince*. For months before we started shooting, I must have pored through just about every important book on sixteenth century Tudor dress. I made preliminary sketches for each one of the principals and then I worked closely with Berman's—choosing colors and fabrics, selecting thousands of accessories and saving money where I could by using existing costumes. We're using many of the costumes that were in *A Man for All Seasons* and *Anne of a Thousand Days*.

"I'm enormously pleased with the end product. I'm seeing something the audience will never really see, but *I* know it's there—the fine detail, the intricate workmanship; it's all a hallmark of Berman's and something that pleases me. Mark's coronation costume alone was over twenty-five hundred pounds which is about five thousand dollars! But when you think that all two thousand sequins and gems and all the gold thread stitching were done by hand, then you realize that it's the *extra care* —that going one step further—that makes your costumes special.''

One of the main sequences in the masque and ball scene involved a series of dances by the elaborately costumed courtiers, including a stylized period dance called a galliard and a lively peasant jig (introduced by the pauper) entitled ''Jenny's Gone to Smithfield Fair'', both of which were brilliantly executed by Sally Gilpin (wife of the outstanding British dancer, John Gilpin), our choreographer. As Mark and Felicity (Dean, a lovely newcomer cast as Lady Jane Grey), and hundreds of extras in satins, silks, ostrich plumes and ermine whirled around the ballroom, a sound-system was blasting a play-back of the appropriate lute and recorder musuc while on a specially constructed balustrade overhead, an ''orchestra'' of mute extras—complete with actual period instruments— ''played'' along in accompaniment.

After about a week at Pinewood Studios, we packed up the entire production and moved north to Stratford-on-Avon, birthplace of England's most famous bard. Here in the beautifully restored Shakespearean village (complete with Anne Hathaway's thatched cottage), we spent two days doing pick-ups (a series of brief sequence shots) by a lakeside. The scenes involved (Prince) Edward tending Miles's wounds after his duel with Hugh and subsequent escape from Hendon Hall. We finished up in Stratford without any problems, and headed back to Pinewood to crate and load our gear for the move to the Continent in early June—right on schedule.

By the time we were ready to depart England, the crew had already begun to fall into an efficient and comfortable routine of working on the set and relaxing in the off-hours. (Because a film schedule is so erratic and because the story line often necessitates, much of the production may involve night shooting—from five in the evening until three or four the next morning—and frequently, filming on a Saturday or Sunday as well. Such was often the case with *The Prince and the Pauper*.)

Our work day schedules followed a pleasantly predictable order. After being jangled out of bed anywhere between 5 and 6 A.M. by a "wake-up" call, we'd dress in jeans or shorts or whatever, and the more stalwart among us would sleepily stumble out in front of the hotel to join the "Over-the-Hill Club." (Although most of the English crew lived in or near London, commuting distances were far too time consuming, so we were all together in hotels on location.) The "Over-the-Hill Club" was organized by our focus puller, Frank Elliott, a big, burly, bearded man who looked like he'd be a perfect "Little John" in *The Further Adventures of Robin Hood*. Frank was also a hold-over from the *Musketeers*, in which he played a bit part under the stage name of "Tyrone Cassidy". He also played a royal guard in *The Prince and the Pauper*—under the same pseudonym—and can be seen in the final print, booting Mark, as the disguised prince, out of the palace grounds. He immediately established himself on *Prince* as the master prankster nonpareil and it was with his usual mien of mock-seriousness that Frank would be out most mornings in his sweatsuit, urging a motley group to do one or two quick laps, a few push-ups and about *three* deep knee bends.

Our order of departure was worked out the night before by our Second Assistant Director, Michael Green, who would assemble all the pertinent info onto the daily "call-sheets" (our assignment schedules for each day), which he'd distribute the preceding evening. Then, in the mornings, our two French "tea boys" (the "gophers", whose names, believe it or not, were *Laurent* and *Olivier*!) would see to it that we were put in the right cars or trucks to be transported to the set.

Once on location, after the hours of preparation—Jack Cardiff and his assistants setting up the arc and mini brute lights; Jose-Antonio Sanchez, Paqueta Nunez, Pepita Rupio and Pepe Quetglas, our Spanish makeup team, getting the principals ready; Eddie Fowlie, making sure every extra was in place—we'd be ready for rehearsals. And then, after we'd run through a scene two or three times, Nigel's familiar litany would signal the start of shooting:

"All right, let's clear the set. Everybody *absolutely* quiet, please—cut the cackle! Shooting this time. O.K., Alec?"

And after a nod from our cameraman, Roy Charman would reply with his distinctive "Sound speed!" to indicate the sound taping system was in operation.

Then, after Miki Thomas, the camera leader, would strike the clappers with something like "651—Take 3", director Fleischer would shout "Action" and suddenly, all the efforts of dozens of people during months of preparation would coincide in one moment and the incredible fantasy that is filmmaking would be underway. And magically, that art form most clearly a product of the modern age would transport a myriad of lights and cameras, a mountain of wires and props, and hundreds of performers and technicians from a sound stage in London to a throne room in the palace of King Henry VIII in the year 1547.

In the evenings, the entire production team would unwind in the hotel bar or a local pub, gathering in small, familiar groups. In a cozy, warm atmosphere, we'd drink and talk and kid each other until exhaustion simply caught up with us—or we were too drunk to move!

The little more than three weeks of shooting in England had progressed without a serious hitch. Miraculously, the weather had been with us, our equipment had worked, even Oliver Reed stayed sober—but now the fascinating, arduous and often surprising twelve weeks of filming in Hungary were about to begin.

5. BACKLOT: BUDAPEST

As soon as the entire cast and crew members who would be moving on to the Continent were packed and ready to go, it became apparent that the plans to fly to Budapest on a small BAC-111 plane would have to be scrapped. The Salkinds and Spengler quickly made arrangements to charter a British Airways Trident-Three to transport the more than 150 pieces of equipment—weighing in excess of four tons—along with forty-three of the nearly 100-member cast and crew.

The producers had chosen the seemingly improbable choice of Budapest and the surrounding Hungarian countryside to shoot extensive location scenes for a number of crucial reasons.

First, the Salkinds and Spengler had successfully produced a picture (*Bluebeard*) in Hungary a few years earlier and were thus familiar with the advantages of filming there. Secondly, after exhaustive scouting in England and throughout a good part of Europe, Fleischer and the producers had agreed that some of the best examples of existing fifteenth century structures anywhere to be found were in Hungary, and equally important, were *available* for use in a motion picture. Finally, whatever construction, or embellishment to existing edifices which might have to be done (as with the building of the mammoth Westminster Abbey set), could be accomplished in Hungary at a significant economic savings.

The thought of making a lavish, multi-million dollar picture behind the Iron Curtain made a few of the less imaginative, adventurous and knowledgeable among us more than a little apprehensive. But soon after our arrival in the Hungarian capital, any apprehension that was felt quickly dissolved into curiosity, enthusiasm and anticipation.

Budapest, the largest city in Hungary with a population of about two million, is situated on both banks of the Danube River (called the Duna locally). The city is an amazing amalgam of its fascinating past, where the glory of the Austrian Empire and its last Emperor Franz Joseph seems just as tangible as the scars of the brutal Nazi occupation of thirty-five years ago. And undeniably, while the Russian "liberation" of Hungary (which has been on-going since 1945) has cast a repressive pall on the city, the vestigial remains of the indomitable Hungarian spirit and gypsy gaiety of what was once the most vibrant city in central Europe is still—at least for the visitor— alive today.

From the moment we arrived in this Eastern bloc nation, however, we knew we were quite a distance (at least philosophically) from England or the United States!

On the ride in to our hotel from Ferihegyi Airport, the driver of the cab in which David Petrou (with a stack of American magazines on his lap) was riding suddenly swerved over to the roadside, screeched to a halt and grabbed the top magazine, practically panting, "Americanski sex magazine!" and proceeded to frantically thumb through a June issue of *Newsweek* before tossing it aside in disgust!

It is important to note that despite what the travel brochures may tell you, the language problem for a tourist in Hungary is a *very* real one. Few people in Hungary speak English; because of proximity to Austria and the

high influx of East Germans, German is the closest thing
to a second language for *some* Hungarians. Those of us
who made an effort to learn the language rarely got much
further than *tessék* (please), *köszönem* (thank you), *igen*
(yes) and *nem* (no).

The drive through downtown Budapest revealed a surprisingly Western city, complete with discos, rock music
and America's legacy to the world, Coca-Cola, although
the immediate impression was of a city in the U.S. in the
early 1950's. Sidewalks were clogged with shoppers,
streets were jammed with traffic and Budapest's famous
trolley cars, and except for an occasional Red Star atop
some official-looking building, we might have been in any
attractive city in north central Europe or perhaps Scan-
danavia.

Our hotel in the Buda or residential section, the Hotel
Gellert, was a famous edifice, an architectural hodge-
podge built about fifty or sixty years ago. Overlooking
the Danube and three of the city's eight bridges (which
were rebuilt after being destroyed in the war and which
connect Buda with Pest, the commercial district), the
Gellert is so named because it abuts Gellert Hill, a famous
landmark now topped by the Hungarian version of the
Statute of Liberty, commemorating the Russian liberation
of Budapest from the Nazis. According to legend, the first
Christian crusader to Hungary, St. Gellert, was taken to
the top of the small peak by some barbarians, placed in a
barrel studded with huge spikes, and then rolled down the
hillside.

The Hotel Gellert has been host to shakers and movers
from Adolph Hitler to Richard Nixon, certainly because of
its reputation and ambiance and partly because the entire
building is constructed on top of one of the city's most
popular public thermal springs and health clinics.

After settling in and doing some preliminary sight-seeing, shooting resumed in early June at a location about forty miles outside of Budapest, at a place designated as the Ruffler's (George C. Scott) cave. The first day of filming in Hungary—working with the requisite number of Hungarian crew members—was a nightmare of misunderstandings (the names for certain equipment we needed—arc, brute, boom, etc.—simply had no Hungarian equivalent and, of necessity, we all became accomplished pantomimists that week!), malfunctioning equipment, unavailable accoutrements and unbearable heat. Thankfully, most of our initial problems were eventually ironed out by our Production Supervisor in Hungary, Basil Keys, and his assistant, Barbara Back. Basil and Barbara oversaw the logistical "heart" of the production: ameliorating the language difficulty, coming up with needed supplies, and generally coordinating the frequent comings and goings of most of the cast and crew.

Of course, the language barrier was never totally breached, but thanks to our lanky Hungarian Assistant Director Vilmos ("Willy") Kolba and his own aide, Susie Szemes (a diminutive sprite who spoke near-perfect English and boomed commands on the set in a voice that belied her petite size), that problem at least diminished. The producers had initially pared back the crew somewhat before we left England in the hopes of economizing. But the difficulty in communicating with their Hungarian counterparts forced Nigel to send for several of the technicians who had been left behind, even if it meant duplicating some jobs.

The Ruffler's hideout, to which the unfortunate Prince is taken by John Canty, was a mammoth natural cave winding and descending deep into the side of a mountain. One of the many interesting aspects of the location was the fact that carved into the sides of the mountain itself were a vast number of niches covered by small, locking metal doors, like hundreds of tiny vaults. These, we were told, were used by the local villagers as natural wine coolers for their homemade wine and their use has been passed down through families for generations. There was certainly no question that the damp, dark cavernous mountain kept things incredibly chilly, because even in the midst of 90°-plus June heat and humidity, most of us needed heavy coats and jackets in order to work inside the cave for any extended period of time.

The scenes in the Ruffler's cave went well, despite the crowds of often bewildered extras, the extremes in temperatures and the dust and mud and filth of the location. Scott's brief performance in the film, as the leader of a rag-tag band of misfits, thieves and cutthroats, was an electrifying spark which literally "charged" the entire production. Off-camera, he would talk and joke with the crew, looking relaxed and comfortable despite the surroundings and a considerable amount of undoubtedly uncomfortable makeup (one entire eye was covered over with putty and flesh-toned plastic to form a hideous series of scars).

After a hard day of filming—sometimes ten hours or more—our drivers would race us back to the Gellert (Hungarians, like many of their counterparts in the West, are maniacal speed demons behind the wheel), which by now had become a bastion of comfort and convenience for most of us. Fleischer, Scott, Ollie and Reggie Prince preferred the air-conditioned comfort of the more modern Duna Intercontinental.

If it wasn't too late after wrapping the day's shooting, several of us would head for the clinic and baths beneath the Gellert. Use of all the clinic facilities (including the nude sun roof, segregated by sex) was included in the price of our hotel bill and we could be steamed and soaked and massaged for just a few *forints* in gratuities, a *forint* worth approximately five cents.

Going to the baths at the Gellert was an incredible experience. On entering the cavernous, blue-tiled baths beneath the hotel, both men and women, decorously separated, are given an exceedingly skimpy, cheesecloth-type loin covering which one puts on after doffing their clothes. (If you planned to have a massage, a small metal token, which was always ice cold, was attached to your Tarzan garb. This "functional" attire was *mandatory* for entering the baths. Once exasperated members of the crew had to strip down in order to simply dash in and search for Harry Andrews and Julian Orchard, who were late for a call to the set!) Once properly "dressed", we'd meander through the steamy subterranean rooms, trying out the saunas, swimming in the soothing mineral waters, getting massaged. Oliver Reed and Reggie Prince used to frequent the famous Rudas Baths, barbarically opulent with its dome of stained glass dating back from the Turkish occupation. On one occasion, Reg—a bruising hulk of a man—got a particularly "enthusiastic" masseur and ended up having the toenail literally torn off his previously injured big toe!

Most of the crew would split up in small groups for dinner, which in Hungary was always something of an event. The food in Hungary is generally excellent—our major complaints were the lack of fresh vegetables and the obvious dearth of such high-cost imported items as citrus fruits, melons, etc. Our meals often consisted of such specialities as *csirke* (chicken paprikash), *Hortobágyi palacsinta* (meat-filled crepes, which became our favorites), and stuffed cabbage. Everything in Hungary, except the fantastically rich desserts—is covered with paprika (it's on the table in lieu of pepper), and we all quickly found out that what *we* usually refer to as goulash is in reality *not* meat stew but a hearty peasant soup called *gulyás* (pronounced "gooyash") consisting of a spicy paprika broth seasoned with dill and rye, all simmered together with generous portions of meat and potatoes. Any of us who yearned for the more simple fare of home could always go over to the Intercontinental for the Hungarian version of a hamburger: a highly seasoned combination of ground pork and building mortar served on one-half of an impenetrably dense roll!

For Hungarians, lunch is the main meal of the day, but for the crew (and most visitors), dinner became the big event. Budapest features a number of expensive (largely for the tourists), medium and low price restaurants, with the better establishments featuring the ever-present gypsy violinists, whom, we were assured by Janos Pataki, one of our Hungarian assistants, *never* play "the real muzik of the Hungarian peoples!"

Two of our favorite haunts were the gilded, baroque Hungaria, once a hangout for journalists and show business types, and the dining room at the Gellert, which featured great food and the *worst* gypsy band in Hungary. Many evenings, Ollie and Reg would come over from the Duna Intercontinental to join us for dinner and then a few drinks in the nightclub. When Ollie did join us for dinner, he would smile as the waiter jabbered in Hungarian, thinking he was asking, "Are you ready to order, sir?" to which Ollie would always reply, "Sure." The waiter would suddenly stop, go into the kitchen, and return immediately with a huge pitcher of beer, obviously fostering the rumors about Ollie's penchant for booze. It wasn't until some weeks later that we found out that the Hungarian word for beer is *sör*, pronounced "sher"!

After a hard day, a heavy meal and a few drinks, we'd be ready for sleep. The beds were something of an amusement, rock-hard and narrow, with, in place of a top sheet, a muslin ''envelope'' with a round opening in which a heavy woolen blanket had been tucked. Naturally, we all removed this ''device'' from our beds in mid-June. But when we were back at the Gellert in mid-August and needed some sort of covering, quite a few of us spent several infuriating late-night hours trying to squeeze ourselves into this envelope or cover ourselves with it width-wise, only later discovering that the whole affair had to be unfolded, turned around and used lengthwise.

The bathrooms in Europe—and especially in Hungary—are usually alien, archaic chambers of horror, particularly to Americans. Central heating is an anomaly outside the States, as must be, some of us conjectured, hot water. So the colder mornings of late August more often than not guaranteed the rudest of rude awakenings.

The plumbing itself offered another series of novelties. Of course, most European bathrooms have bidets (douches) as standard equipment. The showers were mostly the hand-held types, and in Hungary, even the toilets were unusual, the bowl being an empty (*no* water) receptacle with a small opening towards the front into which the waste was washed after flushing—an economizing measure that amazed Ernie Borgnine and the more fastidious among us.

If our rooms were often less than plush, this was more than set off by the ambiance, style and overall graciousness of the Hotel Gellert. And even more importantly, the people who staffed the Gellert were genuinely warm, hard-working, and friendly. Despite the inherent barriers and the frustrations yet to come, it was the Hungarian people who would play a key role in the carefully planned-for success of the long weeks of location shooting ahead.

6. IN DAYS OF GYÖR

Towards the end of June, we completed the shots in the Ruffler's cave. George C. Scott and his wife returned to their work on *Beauty and the Beast*, while the rest of us moved *The Prince and the Pauper* into Mafilm Studios, the state-operated film production headquarters in Budapest.

Mafilm is a small operation, with just a few large sound stages and ancient equipment dating back to the earliest days of motion picture production. Luckily, most of the equipment we used on the film was sophisticated machinery which had been shipped over at great expense from England and the United States.

The scenes we would be shooting at the studio included the Guildhall banquet (during which Tom, as the Prince, learns that Henry VIII is dead so that he, at least for the time being, is now king), as well as the Prince's apartments (in which De Brie, the Prince's attendant, urges Edward to choose a costume for the ball and more critically, where Tom and the Prince first confront each other).

Under Tony Pratt's guidance, the elaborate sets had been constructed in advance. Painstaking effort was taken to duplicate in detail—complete with royal escutcheons, suits of armor and rich wood paneling—the original interiors of Guildhall and the royal apartments at Hampton Court Palace in England.

The scenes in the Prince's dressing room presented an elaborate and quite technically involved challenge for director Fleischer as well as for the cast and crew. As called for in the script, De Brie, along with Princess Elizabeth and Lady Jane, is attempting to persuade the petulant Prince to select a costume from one of his four splendidly arrayed attendants: Mars, in surrealistic Roman armor with a fiercely painted red face; Adonis, a handsome youth in golden laurel wreath, leopard skin and massive buskins; Tamurlaine, king of the Turks, wearing brightly colored Oriental silks; and finally, the fourth lackey in an undefined confection of silver gauze and gold cloth, heavy with jewels. Immediately following this sequence is the first direct meeting between Edward and Tom Canty and, according to our shooting schedule, the first scene to make use of the impressive split-screen effects. To fully perfect the quality of the split-screen shots, Fleischer had two special technicians—Ian Henderson on focus and Trevor Rutherford on audio—flown in from England.

Richard Fleischer had some of his own distinct thoughts about the split-screen technique after shooting most of the major sequences.

"The process has been part of the film makers' repertoire for some time," Fleischer reflected. "But the style of film making is so very different now from what it was thirty, forty . . . even *ten* years ago. And beyond that, the technique of split-screen which we're using in *The Prince and the Pauper* has never been used before. Usually, you have two characters who cannot cross a mat line in the shot, so theoretically, you can only bring them up to a certain point. Well, in this film, we have them shake hands—often considered an impossibility; we have them walk around one another; we have one character put a prop down and the "other" character pick it up—all in the same shot! Up until now, that simply hadn't been done.

"Of course," Fleischer went on, "shooting these scenes is extremely complicated and costly because both pieces have to be done separately, the timing has to be exact and you've got to work to a play-back for your second version—with the ''second'' character—of the scene. This puts extreme pressure on the actor, because he's got to do the scene to beats and to counts, so that if one character is walking around, the *other* character has to be following him with his eyes, and yet, of course, the *other* character is not there. So he'd better be looking in the right place at the right time and it's my job to see that he is!''

The delicacy required to film these split-screen sequences obviously required absolute quiet (the set was always cleared to a mimimum of people), and, above all, Fleischer's absolute control of the shooting. During these scenes, the atmosphere was charged with a palpable tension and pressure, and it was during these extreme conditions that we witnessed those rare occasions when Fleischer's epithet as ''The Iron Butterfly'' took on a real meaning. If someone talked or made an abrupt movement that would in any way jiggle the camera, the normally soft-spoken, gentlemanly director would suddenly let loose with a momentary outburst of rage that made everyone freeze in their tracks.

Happily, these important scenes in the Prince's chambers proceeded with only minor problems, and by the middle of July, we were finished at Mafilm, for the time being. After some quick night shots at St. Matthias Cathedral and Fisherman's Bastion—which served as additional palace exteriors—we were ready to move on to location, right on schedule.

However, while events *on* the set were going according to plan, things started happening *off* the set which had our efficient producers in a sweat and sent minor shockwaves through the entire production.

Just before the whole cast and crew was scheduled to depart for Sopron, a small village on the Austrian border about two hundred and sixty miles from Budapest, it was discovered by one of the full-time physicians assigned to the picture that a young member of the crew had all the symptoms of secondary syphilis. When the tests proved positive, the first order of business, was to order blood tests for the entire cast and crew to make sure that the disease had not spread.

We all received a clean bill of health, and our friend returned to his native country, well on the road to recovery.

As soon as things had apparently calmed down, we were all immediately involved in another imbroglio which few of us had the audacity (or guts) to laugh at . . . at least not at the time!

July 15, a few days before we were set to leave for Sopron, was Mark Lester's eighteenth birthday. Up until then, as required in his contract, Mark had been accompanied on the film by a combination chaperone-business manager, much as Felicity Dean—under-age and the daughter of a British peer—was under the watchful eye of Marilyse Morgon, her "duenna", in Hungary. Now that Mark would be reaching his "majority", he would be on his own.

To celebrate the event, the producers had planned an elaborate private dinner party at the Gellert for most of the cast and crew. About forty or fifty people showed up, relaxed, casually dressed and looking forward to a fun evening. Things progressed nicely, with everybody apparently enjoying themselves, laughing and eating and getting mildly *brahmsed* (a British euphemism for "polluted"), when suddenly, in storms Oliver Reed with a young girl in tow and Reggie Prince not far behind: shouting, swearing, and chugging from a bottle of wine. Everyone tried to act casual as Ollie—dressed in his usual rumpled jeans jacket and trousers and muddy cowboy boots—hopped up on the huge banquet table and proceeded to march up and down, kicking an occasional glass, directing insults at a few people and demanding more wine, which a terrified waiter quickly brought him. Ollie pitched his empty bottle in the direction of set publicist Al Hix, who foolishly insulted Ollie back.

As Pierre and Ilya nervously huddled over how to handle the situation, Ollie motioned to his female companion—a "lady of the evening"—and then presented her to Mark Lester as a birthday gift. When an embarrassed Lester didn't respond and the poor girl fled from the room in tears, Ollie started ranting and raving again, yelling suggestive profanities at Mark. (It should be noted that when he was sober, Reed—who played "Bill Sykes" to Mark's "Oliver"—and Lester got on famously.)

Reed then leaped down off the table and started marching around insulting people (including big Ernie Borgnine, who was one of the few people who Ollie couldn't intimidate). When he got around to Ilya, the burly actor seated himself on top of the startled producer—with such force that the entire chair splintered underneath their combined weight. It's fair to say that *brahmsed* or not, everyone was genuinely horrified. Reed crawled away under the table laughing and a couple of us helped the stunned producer to his feet.

Ilya Salkind is an incredibly proud individual, and turning absolutely white with rage, he screamed at Reed (who by now was seated across the table from Salkind) to apologize that instant. Reed chose to ignore the outraged producer, but Reggie Prince, sobering up enough to sense the seriousness of the situation, offered *his* apologies to Ilya in Ollie's place.

Anxious to quell the disturbance, Salkind appeared momentarily mollified and when Reed, smiling at Reggie, extended his muscular arm across the table in an apparent offer of friendship, Ilya foolishly replied in kind, at which point Ollie grasped the producer's hand and dragged him across the table, preparing to punch him! The completely stunned, now disheveled and thoroughly enraged Salkind tore himself away and challenged Ollie, screaming that he had a black belt in karate and that if Reed made another move towards him, he would break his neck!

This clever bluff was enough to temporarily startle Reed so that Reggie and a few of the larger, and wiser, crewmen were able to escort Ollie, staggering, shouting and laughing again, out of the room and back to the Duna Intercontinental. Needless to say Al Hix quashed this ugly episode, and this is the first time, to our knowledge, that the *whole* story has appeared in print.

Luckily, Mark's birthday came immediately before our departure for location, so there was fortunately precious little time for any recriminations.

The producers, Fleischer and Art Director Eddie Fowlie had chosen Sopron for the principal reason that it is over seven hundred years old and offers incredibly preserved structures. Beyond that, because our shooting schedule called for the Westminster Abbey scenes to be shot while we were in Hungary, we needed an enormous facility suitable for the construction of the elaborate set. Mafilm's sound stages were far too small for the task, and nothing else was available in Budapest. In Sopron, the ideal facility was found: a mammoth warehouse, which was originally a riding academy and stables and was now being used to store huge bales of wool. And it was here that Tony Pratt, Maurice Fowler, Rosalind Shingleton, and John Oldnow had, for months, been secretly supervising the design and construction of the spectacular Abbey set.

Unfortunately, hotel accommodations had obviously not been scouted with the same degree of care. For a number of reasons—its age, its out-of-the-way location, its tiny size—Sopron didn't have any hotel facilities large enough to put up the entire cast and crew, so the production office had booked us into a hotel in Györ (pronounced "gyour"), a small village about twenty-five miles southeast of Sopron.

Right from the start we knew we had hit bottom. It was hot, dirty; there were no private bathrooms and some floors had *none*—and to use the elevator, you had to send for it by ringing up the front desk. Needless to say, our few days in Györ was the low point of filming. But even there, with Tove Borgnine as our social director extraordinaire planning little parties, dinners and get-togethers, we were able to grit our teeth and tolerate a situation made bearable only by our shared misery.

Fortunately, our stay was brief because Basil Keys found a large, modern, air-conditioned hotel, the Claudius, about sixty miles in the opposite direction in the town of Szombathely (pronounced "zombatay"). Of course, the commuting time would mean getting up even earlier each morning, but we all agreed that a shower and a decent night's sleep more than made up for it.

Popular as a weekend resort for visiting Austrians and East Germans, the Hotel Claudius provided perfectly suitable accommodations, with private baths, good food, a small nightclub and the most incredible huge, glass-enclosed public phone booths any of us had ever seen!

During those first few days while we were staying in Györ and later, in Szombathely, most of the filming involved scenes in the authentic Offal Court set, which was also in Sopron.

Offal Court, the London slum dwelling of the Canty family, was largely the work of Maurice Fowler, who essentially embellished and rebuilt a series of decaying vacant houses, shops and alleys which had actually been built centuries ago. By adding a minimum of the appropriate Tudor characteristics to the façades of the buildings and then filling the narrow streets with refuse, raggedly dressed extras, brimming vending carts and roaming pigs and ducks, Offal Court became a most impressively realistic movie set.

While we were getting settled on location, back in Budapest the producers were getting ready for the much-publicized arrival of Raquel Welch the last week in July.

The superstar reputation of the actress had obviously penetrated the Iron Curtain, because here in Hungary, where she had worked for the Salkinds before, the media now prominently acknowledged the arrival of "Miss Raquel *Velch*," as they referred to her.

Raquel arrived at Ferihegyi after a fifteen hour flight over the North Pole from L.A., with a brief stopover in Copenhagen. She was accompanied by her personal secretary, Merrillee Waterstone, and her makeup artist, Charlene Roberson. Her British hairdresser, Stephanie Kaye, arrived a day later. Raquel was also accompanied by over $1,500 in excess baggage, which required a separate minibus to transport it all to the hotel!

Raquel disembarked looking radiant and tanned, though just before her departure, she had been hospitalized for exhaustion after her uncompleted cabaret tour. Tragically, she had also lost her father one month earlier.

Wearing her soon-to-be familiar tight French jeans and décolleté "Oui" t-shirt, Raquel was greeted by Pierre Spengler (Ilya Salkind was on his way back to Rome at the time), and a carefully limited number of European press people.

Before leaving for Sopron, Raquel spent the night in Budapest, catching up on her sleep and preparing for the four weeks of shooting ahead.

Much to the chagrin of several show business muckrakers, two dozen red sweetheart roses were waiting for her in her hotel suite, with a simple note: "Much love, xxx your Hendon."

7. "IT'S A WRAP!" (ALMOST)

Raquel's arrival on the scene created quite a stir with most of the production team. Only a few of the crew had ever seen the celebrated sex goddess in person and the thought of spending an entire *month* living and working with her was, to say the least, titillating.

Raquel checked into the Hotel Claudius on a Saturday, just two days before the main Westminster Abbey shots were to get underway.

To almost everyone's surprise, Raquel seemed relaxed and friendly, although in fairness it must be said that like many major screen stars, Raquel's mercurial mood changes became something of a legend on *Prince* and when she was prone to ill-humor, the best advice was to avoid her. To help keep tabs, we'd usually check with one of "her girls" to forecast whether we'd be having a productive day's shooting or a washout—filming often hinges on temperaments and whims.

Naturally, we were anxious to see how she would greet Ollie, because despite the disclaimers about the feud, there undoubtedly *had* been friction between the two performers. To almost everyone's relief, particularly the producers, Reed welcomed her with an affectionate peck.

With the principals assembled, shooting resumed August second on the impressive Westminster Abbey set, painstakingly recreated in Sopron, Hungary. "Mankind was never so happily inspired," wrote Robert Louis

Stevenson, "as when it made a cathedral." No doubt the writer would have equally admired the inspiration which made possible our Abbey set.

The huge warehouse had been cleared of its enormous store of wool bales, which had been piled right up to the ceiling and would now have to be stored in various locations around Sopron.

As the largest and one of the most elaborate sets built for *The Prince and the Pauper,* the Abbey had been under construction for nearly eight weeks. One of the benefits of being in Hungary, as mentioned earlier, was the availability of a large, highly skilled and economical labor force. Because of this, the complete frame of the set—including the entire length of massive viewing galleries through which the coronation procession would pass—was built of solid wood beam construction, which gave it a more substantial appearance and provided an extra margin of safety for the anticipated 1,000-plus costumed extras who would be packed in during the filming.

Most of the lavish set dressing had been prefabricated in England, with some of the larger pieces being done in Hungary. The set was carpeted in rich, royal red, edged in gold and the seating galleries were a riot of greens, blues, silver and vermillion.

The tremendous columns of the Abbey were actually pillars of Styrofoam which had been cut into huge blocks, shipped from England and then spray painted and reassembled to exactly match the massive columns of the actual Abbey.

Naturally, Mickey Pugh was kept busy with all the props needed for these scenes—including the fabulous, glittering regalia. When they weren't being used, various members of the crew (English and Hungarian) would sit around in their dusty shorts and sweaty t-shirts, wearing a gem-encrusted replica of St. Edward's Crown!

The only accoutrements that caused any problem were the elaborate royal insignia which festooned the set, emblazoned with the legend "DEO ET MON DROIT." Of course, the purists among us protested that the actual French motto, as it appears on the Royal Seal of England today, reads "DIEU ET MON DROIT." Hearing of our protestations, however, Maurice Fowler was quick to point out that according to his research, in Edward VI's time (1547–1553), the seal, in fact, read as it did on the reproductions.

To make sure more serious conflicts didn't arise and to assure correctness and continuity (as well as demonstrate the producers' sense of historical integrity), one of England's leading authorities on Westminster Abbey, in addition to Edward's reign, was brought over from Cambridge solely for the coronation sequences. Charles Knighton was everyone's caricature of the contemplative scholar, wearing his blazer and "school tie" and toting his battered briefcase stuffed with essential papers to the set each day. Charles was a real pip; his actual name was Stephen Knighton, but he introduced himself to everyone by saying that his name was "Charles, by preference." So, of course the name "Charles Bypreference" stuck.

Despite all the excitement and preparation, the twelve days or so of shooting in the Abbey set were long and often tedious, with Fleischer ordering several retakes of the delicate split-screen shots (which meant *hours* of work under the hot arcs for Mark and his lighting double, Julian Peters. As it was, poor Mark had to contend with getting frequent permanents and having his hair put in rollers every time he played the Prince). As usual, work would begin early, with most of the actors having a call on the set for seven-thirty. Considering the distance from the Claudius to Sopron, that often meant being up by five or five-thirty. (Out of deference to Raquel—the only female lead—most of her calls weren't until nine-thirty or ten. But it took her nearly *three hours* to have her hair done and her makeup applied, so as it turned out, she was up at six most mornings anyway.

Raquel's makeup artist, Charlene Roberson—a delightfully earthy woman whose ''deep from the heart of Texas'' temerity *always* guaranteed she'd say what was on her mind—operated out of two huge footlockers filled with oceans of blush-on and boxes and boxes of false eyelashes. Raquel's hairdresser, Stephanie Kaye, had three enormous crates of hairpieces and equipment, which came to 190 pounds sterling in overweight baggage duty!)

Of course, the extra effort and preparation always paid off, because when Raquel arrived on the set and was fitted into one of Ulla Soderland's stunning period costumes, she looked gorgeous enough to turn *any* head—even Henry VIII's!

Preparing for a shot in the Abbey set took even more than the usual amount of time, not only because of the vast size and numbers involved but also because of Wally Veevers' added special effects. To duplicate the spectacular vaulted gothic ceiling of the actual cathedral needed for the critical distance shots, an elaborate, detailed photograph of the original was taken and enlarged. Then the photo was dry mounted on mat and cut and angled in front of the camera in such a way so that the cut-off point of the stone columns in the photo *exactly* matched up with our Styrofoam pillars on the set. Mat shots have been used in film making for years whenever reproduction of mammoth location backdrops are called for.

When the mat shot had been perfectly lined up, which often took hours, and the actors and extras were on the set, Nigel Wooll would launch into a new last-minute litany (since we were now in Hungary): ''Smink! Maquillaje! Makeup!''—calling for our Spanish makeup team in all three languages! Then, after a final fleck of powder on Raquel's nose, the more familiar "Alec, yes?" and "Sound speed!" would signal that the cameras were rolling.

Though none of us were permitted by Fleischer to see the rushes (which were literally rushed back to Budapest each night to our brilliant film editor, Ernie Walters), the actual takes in the Abbey gave us some indication of the quality of the final cut the producers would be offering. To watch the awesome coronation procession slowly wend its way through the Abbey—the crimson-robed clergy and peers of the realm, bearing the sacred regalia; a reverent looking Richard Hurndel as the Archbishop of Canterbury, in jewel-encrusted mitre, carrying the crosier of his high office; and Mark, draped in ermine and scarlet—was to briefly be a part of some splendid event from a long-vanished past. And few among us with any sense of history were not momentarily transported in time, as we hoped our audiences would likewise be.

Of course, not all the events during the Abbey scenes progressed with quite so much solemnity or smoothness.

Each day, we were subject of the vagaries of the electrical generators in Sopron and many mornings were lost waiting for the lights to come on.

Also, those first days of dealing with over 1,000 extras was like a comedy of errors. The procession would enter, Mark would come into view and his loyal subjects would just sit there, not knowing to wave unless they had been cued. When they finally did react, they'd frequently look in the wrong direction, stare at the camera, carry on little conversations among themselves or suddenly pull out a local newspaper or put on a pair of sunglasses! When a livid Nigel would ask Willy to "quiet 'em down and keep 'em still," the loquacious Hungarian would begin a half-hour harangue always followed by little Susie Szemes shouting into her megaphone *"Csedes! Döda! Döda!"* which implied, in essence, "Shut up!" None of us ever really determined what the "doo-da" meant.

Our "choir" was made up of about twenty or thirty cherubic-faced Hungarian boys, who were told by Susie to "lip-sync" some song they all knew so that there would be continuity when the film was eventually dubbed. And to our amusement, as the coronation of King Edward VI of England got underway, it was to the tune of the Hungarian national anthem!

Perhaps the single most amusing incident during the filming in Sopron occurred one day when little Mason Cardiff was on the set. Jack's family—his engaging wife Nikki and children Jane, Fergus and Mason—joined him in Hungary for a few weeks, and six-year-old Mason (with a freckled map of the British Isles on his face) quickly became the impish mascot of everyone on the production, Hungarians and British alike.

On one particular occasion Mason, who was usually quiet and well-behaved on the set, obviously decided that he wanted to take a more active role in *The Prince and the Pauper*. Just as Fleischer was ready to start a difficult shot that had taken hours to set up, Mason screamed "Action!" at the top of his lungs! For a moment, while Dick turned purple, no one dared react. But when the director burst out laughing, everyone simply cracked up, despite the costly reality of a ruined take. Needless to say, Mason's future visits to the set were severely monitored.

After finishing a lengthy day of shooting, we'd pack up our gear and race outside so that Helena Toth (from the Hungarian production office) could assign us to a driver and we could start the trek back to Szombathely and the Hotel Claudius.

Time off at the Claudius was deadly dull, with little to do but talk and drink and sleep. Television offered little diversion. There was one TV in the lounge, but after the Olympics were over there was little of interest during the short hours of broadcast on the two state-controlled stations. Radios (which we had in our rooms) weren't much better. Sometimes we could pick up other countries, but Radio-Free Europe was usually jammed. Naturally, English reading material and news of the West was limited, and any of the American crew members who wanted to keep up with the political conventions back home had to depend on copies of the *Herald American* (a twelve-page excerpt of the *New York Times* and the *Washington Post*) which Al Hix passed around.

Most nights, after dinner, we'd gather in the small disco. The weather had turned wet and dreary and *much cooler* by the second week in August and a few people got really miserably colds (Mark Lester was coughing and sneezing for weeks). So we'd sit around in the nightclub sniffling and drinking tea and Irish coffee to take the chill off.

If it was particularly quiet, Ollie was always around to launch into one of his burlesque routines.

One Saturday night in Szombathely, Ollie challenged Nigel to a drinking match, which our playful First Assistant surprisingly accepted and, even more surprisingly, *won!*

To break the monotony in a more decorous manner, our Spanish makeup team, along with Andres Fernandez of wardrobe, arranged with the hotel dining room to have a paella dinner at *their* expense for the entire cast and crew staying at the Claudius. Apart from being a wonderfully generous gesture, the dinner proved to be a delightfully welcome—if not gastronomically authentic (the Hungarians aren't too familiar with paella)—break from *palacsinta* and *paprikas*.

Most of the group attended, including Dick Fleischer's

lovely wife and daughter who were traveling around
Europe at the time, and after a few liters of red and white
wine, everyone was in fairly high spirits. Frank Elliott,
our resident prankster, was "brahmsed" enough to even
try a "wind-up" on Pierre Spengler, who was on location
as much as possible.

While Pierre, elegantly dressed and puffing on a
Gauloise, was deeply engaged in conversation, Frank
filled his cupped hands with water, crept up behind the
unsuspecting Pierre and, pretending to sneeze violently,
showered the producer with water. When everyone who
was onto Frank's bluff started howling, even the normally
dour Spengler cracked a smile.

The paella dinner was also a welcome change from the
culinary fare we had been getting each day on the set since
we had been in Hungary . . . in other words, it was
edible.

The formal catering—if you can call it that—on the
picture had been arranged at the last minute, and became
the only real source of friction between the crew and the
producers.

According to their union contracts, the British crew was
entitled to a hot meal or, in lieu of that, adequate monetary
compensation to buy one. Because the Hungarian technicians had separate arrangements with Mafilm, Salkind
and Spengler figured that giving the rest of the crew an
extra daily allowance would simply be the easiest and
most practical way of feeding them.

However, when this didn't work out—because of the
dearth of restaurants on location and, as always in Hungary, the amount of time involved—the unprepared producers had to find some other answer. Unfortunately,
local cooks, unfamiliar with the idiosyncratic demands of
the English palate, wasn't it.

And this is where the unsung hero (or, more correctly,

heroine) of *The Prince and the Pauper* appeared on the scene.

Jill Marshall got her job as caterer on *Prince* when she was hitchhiking from her home in Bristol to London. A university student, Jilly (as she was known on the set) had planned to spend her summer traveling through Europe, hoping eventually to wind up in Israel. But when an attractive gentleman in an expensive sports car—who happened to be a close friend of Nigel Wooll's at Twickenham Studios—told his adventurous and equally attractive young passenger that a major motion picture production was desperately in need of a caterer and would *she* be interested, naturally Jilly was hooked. (Those of us who've come to be enormously fond of her can imagine Jilly, wide-eyed with anticipation, sounding just like Eliza Doolittle as she probably said something like "Cor, that sounds super!")

Whatever Jilly lacked in experience, she more than made up for in enthusiasm. Having been told before she left England that she would be given an adequate budget, an English-speaking assistant and available transportation each day, Jilly arrived on the set without *any* of these prerequisites.

Instead, with a lovable old Hungarian woman who didn't speak a word of English, Jilly set out with the crew every morning and waited around until Helena Toth could assign her an available car and driver. (One of Jilly's favorites was Steve, a self-styled Don Juan who kept picking up girls and disappearing between stops for a quickie assignation—while Jilly plaintively waited with her arms full of groceries!) Then she'd start scurrying around to the nearest markets so that she'd be ready in a few hours to feed nearly eighty people!

Jilly was totally without equipment, and had to start from scratch tracking down—with her meager budget

—everything from plates, cups and eating utensils to warming trays and two huge buckets to serve as makeshift tea kettles.

Of course, one of Jilly's biggest problems was the lack of refrigeration which, in the summer heat, meant buying food fresh each day. Typical meals featured a variety of cold meats, tomatoes, cheeses and bread (which is excellent in Hungary). Occasionally, Jilly would be able to purchase hot, already-prepared dishes like roast chicken or sausage-like patties which posed as hamburgers.

Setting up each day also presented a problem for Jilly, because most times we were either in huge, dusty sound stages or out at some remote exterior location, far from any proper sanitary conditions. (In Sopron, we had to set up within about 50 yards of an enormous trench that served as open toilets for the extras.) In any event, the luncheon buffet was usually swarming with flies and wasps (the Americans kept insisting they were bees) and lunch was, more often than not, an unpleasant, unappetizing battle with the elements.

In addition to feeding the crew, Jilly and our "tea boy," Laurent Perrin, had to prepare separate trays for most of the stars who ate in their private caravans. The trailers, however, were cramped and hot and offered little refuge from the insects, so that Mark Lester and a few of the others wisely came to eat with the rest of us.

When we were finished, Jilly was faced with cleaning up, usually without the benefit of sinks or running water, and then had to pack everything away in boxes for the next day.

Cleaning up after one particularly long day, Jilly found to her horror that although her equipment had been picked up, *she* had been *left behind* on location some forty miles from Budapest! After walking in the dark for hours, someone stopped to offer Jilly a ride and she got back to

the Gellert around midnight, *just* as people were beginning to notice she was missing.

Whether the whole dietary debacle was simply the
result of the producers lack of adequate planning or was,
rather, the result of their efforts to economize, it was
perhaps the only real gripe any of us had against the
production. And even so, eventually we were still more
than willing to laugh about it—particularly once we were
home!

By the time we finished up on the Westminster Abbey
set in mid-August and prepared to head back to Budapest,
we were close to completion on *The Prince and the
Pauper*. Much of the most demanding work had been
accomplished and it now appeared that barring any major
unforeseen difficulties, Fleischer would be able to meet
his September first wrap date.

8. "BACK TO AMERIKAI EGYESÜLT ALLAMOK . . . AND ENGLAND AND FRANCE AND SPAIN. . . ."

After nearly three weeks on location, getting back to
Budapest and the Gellert was like getting back home. We
were all familiar with the many fine restaurants near the
Fisherman's Bastion; the night spots, the "walking
street" for shopping known as the Váci útca, the ballet
and opera house on St. Margaret's Island, the best local
folk bands ("Sebö"), and even the two or three movie
theatres.

Then it was time for the huge press party that had been
planned.

The press coverage of the filming of *The Prince and the*

Pauper had become a major event, with trade anticipation getting hotter by the minute and public interest growing with all the talk of an all-star production of Twain's classic. Newspapers, magazines and trade journals in the United States, Great Britain and every country in Western Europe had been seeking coverage. Now their representatives were flying in as guests of the producers to interview the stars and bring back stories about making a major motion picture in a Communist bloc country.

Because of the significance of the journalists' visit, Alex Salkind arrived in Budapest for two full days to meet with the press and mingle with the cast and crew of his multi-million dollar production. And since our self-styled social director, Tove Borgnine, had already returned to Los Angeles, Berta Dominguez served as hostess at the lavish Saturday night dinner for the press at the Intercontinental.

The producers had planned an active four days for the reporters, including press briefings, parties, luncheons, interviews with the stars, visits to the set and even tours of the city. Since the total number of reporters who came to Hungary numbered over forty, Al Hix had arranged for them to be brought from the Gellert to the studio in small groups of eight or ten, primarily so as not to distract the working members of the cast and crew.

At the time of the press doings, we were working on Hendon Hall, another elaborately authentic set complete with all the trappings of a Tudor manor home. Of course, like every set designed for *Prince*, Hendon Hall, despite the look of realism, incorporated the best of movie make-believe, with massive andirons "forged" in plastic and banisters "carved" from balsa wood.

During our shooting in Hendon Hall (the ancestral home of Sir Miles, where he confronts his villainous brother Hugh), one of the major fight sequences in the film between Oliver Reed and David Hemmings took place. One of England's and America's best known fight directors, B. H. Barry, coordinated and staged the lightning-paced duel sequence, developing some honestly innovative parries and working with all the litheness and lyricism of a ballet dancer—much to the delight of the journalists present. (Ollie was especially intense about his preparation for *all* the fight scenes, going through the rehearsals in slow motion, as if he were doing stylized Chinese exercises.)

For the more curious and untutored among them, Barry explained to the reporters how each twist and turn was carefully worked out with the actors and stuntmen in advance, all within the framework of the chivalric rules of the period. On our last day in Hendon Hall, the visiting journalists witnessed the dramatic climax to the duel, with Hugh at the top of the great staircase, attempting to flee, and Miles and his brother's henchman plunging over a shattered banister. Setting up for the scene took Barry and the crew the better part of a morning, piling the floor beneath the staircase with carefully placed cardboard cartons and layers of foam to break the actors' fall. With an anxious press contingent gathered around, Fleischer completed the dramatic sequence on the first take. Actual time elapsed for the scene in the final print: about ten seconds!

Of course, most of the press interest centered on the film's stars, particularly Mark Lester, Oliver Reed, and especially Raquel Welch.

While Mark was friendly and made himself available to reporters, Ollie and Raquel were not quite so amenable. On the day of the press reception and dinner, Ollie Reed effectively *disappeared,* causing a minor uproar among the producers and their publicists. By coincidence, three crew members stumbled upon Ollie's little hideaway, an offbeat bar near the "walking street." Reed, in the perennial rumpled jeans outfit, was sitting by himself at a small table in the corner, already looking bleary-eyed, with several empty beer bottles on the table in front of him and a huge mound of cattail plants in his lap. He had just picked them from the banks of the Danube, we learned.

He asked us to join him, which we did, and after ordering us a round of beers, launched into a tirade on why he wouldn't attend any press party. Ollie explained loudly that he was already pressing several libel suits against reporters whom he claimed had slandered him, printing rumors and falsehoods, and that he had had quite enough of the ladies and gentlemen of the fourth estate, thank you.

Ollie then asked us if we'd like to be his guests for lunch at a nearby restaurant, the famous Hundred Years, and we accepted. Ollie went into the crowded restaurant shouting and laughing and slapping our backs—fortunately they already knew him there—and quickly settled us into a cozy corner booth. Suddenly remembering that David Petrou, one of the invited, was a writer as well as an American, two "qualities" of which Reed is not overly fond, Ollie focused his invective on the normally temperate author.

When Petrou was properly smashed, he decided it was time to answer the boisterous Reed back. So before his friends could stop him, he started waving his fork in the Englishman's direction, muttering insults of a sort. Reed then went into his Dr. Jekyll-Mr. Hyde routine, becoming deadly serious and staring at the ashen American with those incredibly piercing blue eyes. "Don't *ever* point your fork at *me*!" Reed said blandly and with that he reached across and grabbed the writer's left arm and jabbed his fork into it! Then, just as suddenly, he sat himself back in the booth and burst out laughing. Needless to say, the actor and the author never went drinking after that.

Reed's hiding from the press was causing consternation for just about everyone by this time, including Reggie Prince and Reed's younger brother Simon (who, along with David Reed, helps manage their unpredictable brother's career). After hours of searching in Ollie's favorite haunts in Budapest, they eventually found him "detanking" at the Rudas Baths. And much to the producers' surprise and delight, Reed made a grand entrance at the party that evening after all, wearing a smart, three-piece black suit (with his *boots,* of course) and carrying his armful of cattails (saying he had brought "the whole *reed* family"), which he playfully distributed to the guests.

Raquel proved almost as difficult—in some ways, more so. Originally she had the entire party delayed to suit her then boyfriend's, Paolo Pilla, arrival. Then got word to Al Hix that she wanted *no* photographs taken of her during the gala.

Since the whole shindig more-or-less revolved around Raquel, this presented the publicists with a terrible dilemma. Raquel, of course, had still photograph approval, but had been killing just about every photo Al Hix had given her. In addition, Raquel refused to look at contact sheets and so days were spent having color slides mounted for her approval.

Thankfully, most of the problems evolving from demands for photos of the star were solved when internationally acclaimed photographer, Terry O'Neill arrived. Terry spent a few days shuttling back and forth between Budapest and Vienna (where he was photographing another of his favorites, Elizabeth Taylor, who was filming *A Little Night Music*), and along with Raquel's personal press agent from London, Allen Burry, he got some stills together which Welch approved, and which Al could forward on to the waiting journalists.

The whole press trip was an unqualified success, with

all the reporters getting good stories and having a great time. The last night the press was in Budapest, most of us gathered in the nightclub at the Gellert for what turned into an all-night song fest. The French went into a few rousing choruses of "La Marseillaise", while the English countered with "Maybe It's Because I'm a Londoner" at least five or six times. The Americans held their own with Raquel and David Petrou going into a medley of Bicentennial numbers, including "I'm a Yankee Doodle Dandy" and "It's a Grand Old Flag" —before the press said their farewells and everyone finally staggered to bed.

After the journalists departed, the production moved to a location called Tahi Island, about an hour's drive east of the Hungarian capital. There we spent a week or so by the banks of the Danube, filming the ambush of Hugh and Lady Edith by Miles and the Prince and the frantic coach ride to the coronation, as well as a village scene, where Hendon is temporarily imprisoned in the pillory. The Tudor village which had been constructed was particularly realistic, with its geometric wooden inlays and leaded glass windows. Even more convincing were the extraordinary faces of the Hungarian extras we used here —like a Holbein or Dürer portrait come to life.

The scenes with Ollie in the stocks were great fun setting up, with Reg, as one of Hugh's henchmen, doing some fancy flogging of Hendon, and Terry Maidment, Graeme Crowther and even Reggie himself covering the helpless Reed with eggs, fruit and assorted garbage, all, they assured him, "for the proper effect." Ollie repaid them in kind later.

This was also to be the site of Reed's and Welch's much touted "love scene," when Lady Edith comes late at night to comfort the unfortunate Hendon. Raquel seemed especially on edge (perhaps because Paolo had left earlier in the evening), but luckily we completed the shot in one night, even though the fog-making machines kept over-heating. As it turned out, Raquel sensed her own tenseness and later requested a retake of the scene, which was done on a sound stage cleared of most of the curious crew.

Friday, August 20 was a national holiday in Hungary. Ilya's assistant Janos explained to us that it was originally a day honoring the Hungarian monarch as well as a cele-bration of the traditional harvest. Rather than obliterate it totally, the Communist regime had simply modified it into something less bourgeois called "The Peoples Festival of the Bread and the New Constitution". The bridges were all decked out with Hungarian and Soviet flags, the streets were mobbed with people, the river was clogged with boats and in the sky, the Hungarian Air Force performed dramatic air acrobatics. That night, there was a spectacu-lar fireworks display on Gellert Hill.

Then a real problem arose, totally unforeseen, which could have thrown the entire shooting schedule off by more than a week—and would have cost the producers thousands of extra dollars in overtime.

Ilya Salkind wanted to see the rushes of the coronation (he had been in Rome during filming) which had all *just* been edited and spliced.

After seeing the spliced version put together for the first time, both Salkind and Fleischer agreed that the moment of recognition in the Abbey—when the true Prince of Wales is positively identified—somehow had not been given enough dramatic build-up and now, undeniably, seemed to fall pretty flat.

The producers, along with the top technicians on the picture, met for two full days to thrash out some way to remedy the obvious crisis. Rumors began sweeping through the production that the entire cast and crew would have to be reassembled, people who had already gone back to England would have to be recalled, and the whole production would have to return to Sopron to shoot an entirely new ending!

Most of the crew—many of whom had approaching start dates on their next pictures—were horrified at the thought of returning to Sopron for an additional week, not only because of the extra time involved, but also because of the logistical nightmare of such a move. Over a thousand costumes would have to be packed and transported back to location, extras would have to be rounded up and rehired, and delicate camera equipment would have to be crated and shipped once more, not to mention renegotiation of high-priced stars' contracts.

Unquestionably, the greatest difficulty would be the Abbey itself, and Basil Keyes frantically kept trying to get through to Sopron to see if the entire set had already been dismantled by the Russian troops. Thankfully, it had not.

As it turned out, after a terrible three or four days, a more practical, less costly and equally effective alternative was reached. After lengthy confabs with nearly everyone involved, including the author of the final screenplay, George MacDonald Frasier, Salkind decided that returning to Sopron was out of the question. Instead, at the suggestion of original screenplay co-author Berta Dominguez, some key dramatic dialogue was added to enhance the suspenseful build-up of the pivotol scene and—without too many elaborate preparations—all the new material was shot in close-up in two days, requiring almost no new set construction (except for the immediate area around Edward's throne), and assuring the picture of a smashing new climax.

After this final crisis had passed, events seemed to speed up and miraculously, we were somehow still on schedule.

Our last days of filming in Hungary involved exterior

shots in front of St. Matthias cathedral, which doubled nicely as the Westminster Abbey porch.

While most directors ordinarily schedule relatively simple shots or pick-ups for the last days of shooting, Fleischer had, for reasons best known to him, set aside the final week for filming part of the arrival procession on coronation day, the recognition by Mother Canty of her son Tom, and the deciding, and most demanding, duel between Hugh and Miles Hendon. About the only thing that made a September first wrap date seem remotely possible now was the very minor fact that our final location was a convenient ten minute drive from the Gellert.

The entire centuries-old cobblestone square in front of St. Matthias had been cordoned off so that hundreds of curious tourists (and the taxis they arrived in) wouldn't interfere with filming.

All the buildings in the surrounding area had been (by prior arrangement) brightly decorated with royal banners, and colorful, multi-tiered reviewing stands had been erected at various strategic locations. Fortunately, because the area around the cathedral and Fisherman's Bastion is the oldest section of Budapest, very few changes had to be made by Tony Pratt and the art department.

By this time, author David Petrou had been effectively smitten by movie making to wangle his way into the picture in the only remaining scene he could possibly be in that was also guaranteed *not* to be cut because it involved close positioning with one of the film's principles, Sybil Danning.

David was set to play a local peasant who, along with Sybil, is thrown forward by the surging crowd. After being dressed in the costume department's temporary digs in back of the royal palace museum (a series of cold rooms each dimly lighted by a single bulb hanging from a cord), Petrou had to spend an hour or more in makeup having a false beard applied. He had a mustache, and in 16th century England, men either had both or were clean-shaven; Petrou refused to give up his mustache, even for art's sake. To the delight of the Spanish makeup team, he also had to have his teeth blacked out with colored pencil and covered with shellac.

Since Petrou, Sybil Danning and two stuntmen would be falling onto the stones as the mob pushed forward, Mickey Pugh wisely suggested that Petrou put on both sets of elbow and knee pads. (The headstrong writer decided on the latter only.) And of course, after *eight takes*, Petrou emerged from his role with bloodied elbows and—from the shellac—swollen gums!

On the last Saturday night in Hungary, Berta Domin-guez and the film's producers hosted a huge cast party for the entire production team of *The Prince and the Pauper*.

The bash was held on the patios and terrace of the Grand Hotel on St. Margaret's Island. Though just about everyone got ''brahmsed'', most people seemed surpris-ingly subdued and even a bit melancholy. We spent a good part of the evening hugging, kissing and promising our Hungarian ''comrades'' that we would keep in touch. That night the producers distributed our long-awaited pro-duction t-shirts, which read Mark Twain's *The Prince and the Pauper* on the front and the same thing—KOLDUS ES KIRIALFY—in Hungarian on the back.

For the final two days of shooting, the weather, for the first time on the production threatened to be a factor. It had become increasingly cloudy since Sunday, and Jack Car-diff had to keep compensating for the continually chang-ing degree of light.

In those last two days, everyone felt the pressure of that final effort. To no one's surprise, Monday came and went without completing the critical duel scene.

Tuesday dawned cold and damp and grey, and by the time filming resumed in front of St. Matthias, a fine rain had begun to fall—at which point the anxious camera crew considered packing up their delicate equipment. This time, though, everyone involved was in an almost fever pitch of readiness and the scene was in the can—and the film wrapped, exactly on schedule—just before lunch time. Of course, many months of intensive post-production work remained on *The Prince and the Pauper*: editing, looping, dubbing, scoring. In fact, Maurice Jarré, the Academy Award-winning composer, was signed to write the original musical soundtrack months after filming had ended. But for most of us, our work on the picture was done.

Today, it's fashionable among the new breed of actors, writers and directors to vehemently disclaim the myth about the glamour and magic of movie making. But this very lack of affectation is, perhaps, an affectation in itself.

For truthfully, in no other industry—no other profession—are a few talented people, *by their own choice,* permitted to pursue a unique career in which the reality of each day is a fantasy world of celluloid and dreams. And the glamour, the excitement, the intense stimulation—along with profound creative effort—is, despite the detractors, very much fact. Those of us who were fairly new to films and who worked on *The Prince and the Pauper* found that out for ourselves.

Without question, we had all labored long and hard on the picture, giving the best of ourselves and our diverse talents and abilities. But we had all worked together in our own way towards a common goal, a final end product—to make a motion picture that would entertain and in some ways perhaps enlighten, and of which we could all be proud.

AFTERWORD

My final night in Europe was spent in London as a guest of Nigel Wooll, visiting his local pub in Fulham and dining at his favorite Italian restaurant in Chelsea. We made it an early evening however because I wanted to weed through my mountain of notes and papers, and prepare for my trip back to the United States the next day.

Anxious to get started on this manuscript (and because my home in suburban Washington is close to Dulles Airport), I had booked myself on one of the new supersonic Concordes to Washington. Sitting on board the space-age aircraft, a technological masterpiece of man's achievement, I was jolted out of my euphoria by the pilot's voice crackling over the intercom, explaining that we were returning to the terminal because one of the plane's four "inertial navigation systems" was malfunctioning. As passengers started looking at their watches and muttering about the exorbitant premium we had all paid to cross the Atlantic in an incredible three and a half hours, a thoughtful stewardess—hoping to lighten the mood—remarked that although the problem wasn't a serious one (the plane could fly with only half its normal guidance systems operating), it was important to have everything in perfect working order because just think of the *bad publicity* for the airline if one of its new, sixty million dollar aircraft plummeted into the middle of the ocean!

Needless to say, the pert young lady returned to some other chore before noticing the horrified reaction of her passengers who didn't care a twit for the company's "bad publicity" but did value their own necks.

To me, usually a white-knuckle flyer, the remark had an extra tinge of irony, because I work in an industry for which publicity and promotion is the lifeblood.

And yet I had just finished up on a picture in which image making and "hard sell" really isn't needed. While the visiting press served a purpose, there is no need to educate and indoctrinate the public through some sort of media-blitz, though that, of course, will be left to the discretion of the film's distributor.

This is because our picture is based on a classic in American literature, the joy and wisdom and truth of which has endured the passage of the decades. It is a film founded on a tale that is known and loved the world over. A film with a story which may instruct and delight people of every age.

Of course, as a former publicist myself, I recognize and appreciate the value of publicity, especially in this business. Movies are truly the twentieth century's most representative form of expression, combining an unlikely mixture of art and entertainment with Madison Avenue hype. But in truth, publicity and hype can only carry a film so far. "Thunder is good, thunder is impressive;" wrote Twain, "but it is lightning that does the work."

Our picture rests on the story. And for that genius, that special spark of lightning, we are all especially indebted to Samuel Langhorne Clemens.

By the way, the plane landed fifteen minutes ahead of schedule.

CHAPTER I

On a splendid fall day in 1537—October 12th, to be precise—all of England exploded with joy as messengers fanning out from Hampton Court shouted the stirring news: a son had been born to King Henry VIII!

Not only did this mean that the succession at last was guaranteed (for Henry had only been able to sire two girls until then); it also meant the prospect of some peace and quiet. The failure of Henry's two previous wives to father a boy had been responsible in no small measure for a number of awful political, social, and religious paroxysms that had nearly rent the country asunder.

It can well be imagined that every Englishman high or low, rich or poor, dropped what he was doing and celebrated. Indeed, for many days after the event, scarcely anyone in the country did any work, unless it was the alehouse keepers, and the bakers and cooks who worked around the clock to satisfy the thirst and hunger of reveling Englishmen.

On that very same day, deep in the heart of ancient London, in the most squalid section of town just off London Bridge, another boy was born. Unlike his royal counterpart Edward Tudor, whose doting father had his little Prince of Wales swaddled in the finest silks and satins in the kingdom, Tom Canty was an object of distinct annoyance to his father. It was hard enough stealing to keep his tribe of five alive, but now the addition of this unwanted boy would stretch John Canty's resources to the limit. John Canty was a good thief, as good as there was in London, but more mouths to feed meant bigger risks.

He gazed down at the tiny little beggar gurgling innocently on his mother's breast, and cursed. If he had his way he'd drop the bundle into the Thames when no one was looking, and be done with it.

The only reason Canty did not do this was his realization that the boy might come in handy one day as a cutpurse. If he could somehow keep little Tom (as he named him) alive until the boy was capable of lifting pocketwatches or nicking chickens or fresh fruit from carts and shops, it might prove a worthy investment.

John Canty decided to give the boy five years, then Tom Canty was on his own—thieve or die. Five? No, make that four. If they're old enough to reach a tabletop they're old enough to grab what's on it.

Tom Canty did survive, despite the unfavorable conditions in which he was raised compared to the Prince; indeed Tom thrived somewhat better than Edward Tudor, who'd been sickly and whose sickliness was not helped by the continuous pampering he received at Court. But in due course Edward rebelled against the pampering and demanded to be treated like any other boy—or least, any other aristocratic boy.

And so, in addition to his regular schooling in Latin, Greek, French, Italian, poetry, music, physics, mathematics, astronomy, and a dozen other subjects, Edward also learned to joust, duel, hunt, and fish, just like his father. He also learned how to dance, though not as well as his father, who was considered the best dancer in the kingdom, and would have been even if he were not also the fearfully bad-tempered King of England.

In any case, despite the totally opposing circumstances of their birth and upbringing, despite the miles that separated their homes and the millions of pounds that separated their fortunes, Edward Tudor and Tom Canty grew up looking remarkably like twins. Had you stripped the two down to the skin, bathed and groomed and powdered Tom and dressed him in the silk pantaloons and embroidered tunic, jeweled chains and sword and feathered hat in which Edward was generally attired; and had you at the same time spattered some mud on Edward, matted his pretty blond hair, and draped him in the tattered rags that constituted Tom Canty's wardrobe, you would have been very hard put indeed to tell which was which.

Had anyone suggested that such an event might actually come to pass, that the boys might one day exchange not merely clothes but identities, he would have been the object of considerable derision. Yet he would have had the last laugh, for one day, against all odds, that very thing did happen.

CHAPTER II

In order to locate Tom Canty's house, you had to travel over London Bridge, itself no mean feat, for the bridge then was crowded with merchants and concessionaires, carts and wagons piled high with foodstuffs, flowers, produce, timber, livestock, cloth, stone, wool, and countless other goods on their way to market. Many people actually made their homes and established their shops on the bridge itself, giving it all the appearance of a narrow street like so many others in London.

Stepping off the bridge you had to make your way over many a narrow, crooked, dirty, and dangerous street, streets that barely saw more than a glimpse of sunlight from dawn to dusk thanks to the construction of the houses, whose second stories projected out over the first,

third even further out than the second, and so forth.
Garbage and slops were commonly dumped out of windows, and Heaven help the unwary visitor.

At length you found yourself on Pudding Lane, pressing a kerchief to your nose against the vile odors of unwashed bodies, rotting garbage, and slops. You shouldered your way through crowds of wretchedly dressed humans, toothless hags who'd burned out their lives at thirty-five, desperate men who eyed your finery hungrily, vendors and beggars chiding you for a farthing or ha'penny, and nasty little guttersnipes careering into you with their hoops and sticks. You asked if someone could kindly direct you to Offal Court, and invariably you got an almost incomprehensible reply in a language that scarcely had any connection with English at all: "Froo yon lyne, tun roight, an' yer'll foin' it d'reckly."

Trusting you understood correctly, you proceeded beneath an arch along a narrow lane, turned right when you could go no further, followed an even narrower alley, and at last came upon a square thronged with people so abysmally poor it was a wonder they had any flesh on their bones or clothes on their backs at all. Their houses, of a style we now know as Tudor, were of wooden crisscross beams and brick or wooden planks plastered over. The planks had once been gaily painted, but now were flaked and decayed, and the structures themselves rickety. Many were swaybacked like old horses, or bowed-out at the sides.

Despite these hideous conditions, the people of Offal Court were by no means thoroughly miserable. The women hobnobbing in little clusters cackled over some choice piece of gossip, the men over some ribald tale. The children played as hard as children anywhere, and their laughter was no less hearty for the ofttimes hollow belly it came out of.

In fact, in one corner of the courtyard, amid filth and garbage and squalor so gross that rats boldly feasted without fear of molestation, a little group of children sat raptly around a young lad reading them a story, and as far as they were concerned, they could have been sitting beneath a broad oak in the serene yard of a church in the country, so absorbed were they in the lad's tale.

The lad was Tom Canty, a sturdy youth with long, honey-brown locks that flowed around an animated face: a square jaw, a well-proportioned and slightly upturned nose, bright blue eyes with a vaguely dreamy cast, and an attractive mouth. He wore a dun-colored shift, almost as rough as burlap, tied with a string around the waist. The hem was all tatters and the cloth thin and frayed from innumerable washings that had still not managed to remove some of the deeper stains that spotted it. He was shod in rough leather shoes, but he wore no stockings.

The urchins surrounding him gazed open-mouthed as his sweet voice narrated a tale of a land that Tom had heard about but never seen, yet so convincing was he that not one of them doubted he had visited the places and encountered the lords and ladies who populated his stories.

"Once upon a time there was a young king," he said, gesturing with lively hands before the rapt children, "master of a glittering court and a great realm, lord of vast armies and innum . . . er, in-hoom . . ." He stammered over a word he'd recently heard but never pronounced.

" 'Innumerable', Tom," came a kindly voice from outside the circle of children.

"Thanks, Father Andrew," Tom said gratefully. A few of the urchins turned to see the contributor of the correct word, and observed a gentle-looking old man wearing the simple black habit and broadbrimmed hat of a priest. Of course, he was not a priest, because King Henry had gotten into a dispute with the Pope over the question of divorce, and in his rage had severed his land's ties with the Catholic church and turned out all the priests and closed down the churches themselves.

Father Andrew, supported only by a scanty pension, lived on the second story of the house in which Tom Canty, his father, mother, twin sisters, and grandmother lived. He adored children, and particularly loved Tom whose cleverness, vivid imagination, and decency stood out among the other ragamuffins who populated Offal Court. Coming from so wicked a father, Tom Canty had somehow managed to preserve something of his goodness and innocence, though in truth the boy still had to steal out of fear of the awful beatings his father administered to him.

At any rate, Tom was the apple of Father Andrew's eye, and the ex-priest had taken great pains to teach the boy how to read and write and even how to make out the rudiments of Latin. He had also secretly taught Tom and his sisters the ways of the church, for there were many in England who were certain that by one means or another, the papal religion would return to the land, and it was best not to be caught with one's allegiances facing the wrong way. Father Andrew was also a wonderful storyteller, and Tom absorbed the man's charming old legends about giants and fairies, dwarfs and genii, enchanted castles, and gorgeous kings and princes and lovely damsels and princesses. Indeed, Tom sometimes lost track of what was real and what was fantastic, and at night he frequently dreamed that he actually was one of the figures of his tutor's tales. It had gotten to such a point that Tom longed for nothing less than to see a real prince with his own eyes. He had spoken of this desire once to his comrades of Offal Court, but they had taunted him so mercilessly that he never uttered it again.

". . . and innumerable ships," Tom picked up his tale. "And the lords an' lydies of 'is court were like . . ."

"Oh Tom!" Father Andrew reproached him. "Not 'lydies'—*ladies*. And not ''is court', but *his* court. Has all my teaching gone for nothing? Try to speak properly, boy." Father Andrew rebuked Tom with a stern finger, but a gentleness around the priest's mouth showed how deeply affectionate he was of the lad.

"Sorry, father." Tom chided himself for this lapse into Cockney street-accent, for he did know the difference between proper English and the variety spoken by the poor of the city. Occasionally, however, old bad habits, like one of the evil demons Father Andrew always spoke of, took possession of Tom's tongue.

He took up the book again, taking great care to speak with the precision of a priest or nobleman. "And the lords and *ladies* of *his* court were like so many jeweled butterflies, flitting through the palace to pay homage to the young king. *He*, of course"——Tom looked up at Father Andrew for a nod of approval over Tom's emphasis of the letter H—— "far outshone them in beauty and wit and bravery and . . ."

"Wot was 'e loik?" asked a smudge-faced little girl sitting crosslegged at Tom's left. "Was 'e 'andsome?" She obviously was less scrupulous about the use of the letter H than Tom was.

Tom rose from the old cart in which he'd been sitting and closed the book, keeping his index finger inside it to mark the page. The little girl had posed a problem, for the book didn't say whether the prince was handsome, and as so often happened, Tom was obliged to supplement the book with information drawn from his own imagination.

"He was about my age," said Tom, "about my size. Not quite as good-looking, perhaps . . ."

The children groaned derisively, and even Tom's
mother, a worn, ragged, middle-aged woman pinning up
clothes in a corner of the court, turned and looked re-
proachfully over her shoulder at her charming little brag-
gart.

Tom leaped off the cart and caught the hand of the little
girl who'd asked the question. Looking romantically into
her eyes, he took up his tale, flipping open the book.
"And when, from all the beautiful maidens who were in
love with him, he singled out the damsel of his choice, he
said to her . . ."

"Ow yer doin', me old ducky!" shrilled a mischievous
little girl behind him. The other children exploded in
shrieks and hoots of laughter. Father Andrew threw up his
hands and good humoredly ambled away to attend an
ailing woman at the other end of the court.

"No, ducky, he didn't," Tom admonished his tormen-
tor. Then he turned back to the first little girl and dropped
to one knee with a courtly flourish. The little girl flushed
with embarrassment as Tom, book in hand, launched an
appeal worthy of one of King Arthur's legendary knights.
"Prithee, most sweet and gentle lady, thou must be my
queen for . . ."

All at once the book was struck from his hand, and even
before seeing his assailant Tom knew who it was. He
raised his hands instinctively to protect his face but it was
too late. A second blow with the back of John Canty's
rough hammy hand sent the boy sprawling in the dirt.
Tom's circle of children scattered, screaming, to every
point of the compass.

Tom rose to his feet, anticipating another blow, darted
and feinted but not quickly enough to elude his father, a
brutal-looking ruffian with a pocked face, bristly beard,
wild black eyes, and stained teeth. Canty seized his son by

the shirt and thrust him against the wall of a nearby house, rattling Tom's bones.

In an instant Tom's mother had put her laundry down and rushed to her boy's side, crying, "No, John!" but Canty thrust her aside as if she were a ragdoll. She stumbled and fell, scraping the skin on her hands and knees on the rough cobble of the court.

"Mother!" Tom called, squirming to get loose. But Canty held him fast. Pinning him to the wall, he cast his fearsome eyes on the boy, growling a question.

"Who's the best thief in London?"

Tom winced from the gust of foul breath from Canty's mouth. When he hesitated to answer, Canty gave the boy a shake that snapped Tom's head back and forth like the tip of a whip. "I am—father," Tom whimpered at last.

"And who made you that?"

"You did—father," Tom singsonged, as if reciting the catechism of a religion he did not believe in.

"And why did I take the trouble?"

"So . . . so I could keep the family."

"And?" Again Tom held back, and Canty slowly tightened his grip until his sharp dirty nails were beginning to pierce his son's flesh.

"And look after you in your revered and honored old age, when you'll be too old to steal yourself."

"Right!" said Canty with smug satisfaction. "So— you don't waste *your* time"—he emphasized the point with a slap—"and *my* training"—emphasized with another slap—"spoutin' bloody *fairy*-tales"—yet another slap—"to *kids*"—another—"or trying to talk mealy-mouthed like a gentleman!" This last he emphasized by flinging the boy down as effortlessly as he'd flung his wife a moment before. "Handsome king, is it? I'll show you who's king!" snarled Canty. "You'll cross my palm with five shillings come supper, or I'll flay your idle backside raw.''

Tom scrambled to his feet, ducked another vicious blow, vaulted over an old table and touched his mother's hand.

"Get away from him!" Canty bellowed at his wife, preparing to spring once again.

Tom skipped off across the courtyard, stopped, and, noting that his father's back was turned, made a gesture whose vulgarity might well be excused under the circumstances.

As an animal of the forest heads instinctively for a water hole, Tom headed for Market Square, for it provided the ideal conditions for a thief to work in: dense crowds, abundant purses, a plethora of goods with a dearth of vendors to watch over them, much noise and many avenues of escape.

Owing to the unusual makeup of his personality, Tom felt as much at home in this world as he did in the imaginary world of knights, princesses, wizards and dragons. He knew many of the merchants, and had helped himself to their produce and merchandise on many an occasion. Some of them knew him too, for there had been times when the boy's hands had not been quicker than the eye. These men and women watched Tom suspiciously or shook a finger at him warning him to go ply his dubious trade in some other part of the square if he valued his head—for in this dark age, the punishment for theft of even modest proportions was death.

Aside from its value as a source of profit, the market was a haven of amusement, entertainment, and wonder. In yonder corner an old puppeteer named Moreau had set up his Punch and Judy show around which pressed crowds of ragged children and not an inconsiderable number of adults as well. Further down the street, some clever ac-

robats in bright yellow costumes had stretched a rope
across a lane and were balancing upon it, spinning rings on
their arms and legs. Even the sight of a beggar being
whipped through the streets by a red-coated constable was
the stuff of great spectacle to the people, who cheered as
the King's policeman marched the poor wretch past them
crying, ''Behold a beggar and vagrant. Others take warning. Behold a beggar and vagrant. Others take warning.''

Nor was Tom totally unsusceptible to the allures of the
other sex, for though he was very young, one grew up fast
in that day, seeing and doing much by the time one
reached his early teens. Thus when a couple of pretty
sluts, leaning out of a window looking for men to spend an
hour and a few shillings on them, spied Tom and called his
name, he grinned, waved, winked, and proceeded to
swagger down the street like a cock of the walk. A pretty
lass in pigtails was bending over her stall assembling some
fruit for display, and Tom failed to resist the temptation to
give her behind a pinch. The outraged wench whirled
around red-faced and swiped at him with an open hand,
but he ducked, and when he found his feet again an apple
had miraculously found its way into his hand.

Ah yes, it was as his father said: Tom was (next to his
father, at least) the best thief in London. It was nothing to
be proud of, but unfortunately John Canty had not
schooled his son in any other trade.

Tom mounted a low wall and sat, munching his apple,
surveying the seething turmoil of the marketplace. It was
an amusing diversion, and the calls and cries of the merchants and mongers made a pleasant music to Tom's ear:
''Mussels!'' ''Fresh Fish!'' ''Bread, hot baked bread and
buns!'' ''Apples, two-a-penny!'' ''Lamb's wool, lamb's
wool soft as duck's down!'' ''Goose, fat goose!'' ''Cloth,
bright cloth!'' ''Vegetables, fresh vegetables!''

Tom's trained eye was casting about for trouble even as

his ear thrilled to the music of trading and haggling. He spotted a piece of gold flashing in the sunlight in exchange for a bolt of damask; a jeweled chain around a lady's neck glittered seductively; a fat purse swayed from a merchant's belt like a pear ripe for picking. The sum his father had demanded of him, five shillings, seemed like an easy goal, and indeed one he might achieve with room to spare, pocketing one or two bob against a rainy day. Of course, as Tom had learned to his regret, thieving is nowhere near as easy as it looks; one error and to the Tower he'd go, and perhaps from there to the scaffold, where an executioner's blade would sever his head from his shoulders in a trice. Tom gulped noisily, happy to have a throat connecting those two important parts of his anatomy.

But there was business to be done, and the sound of a familiar voice attracted Tom's attention.

Almost immediately in front of him, a pretty girl dressed in tatters was engaged in animated discussion—in truth, a rather heated dispute—with a thin, hawknosed man who looked somewhat like a rodent. The girl bore a basket of flowers on her arm, and the man was examining a handful of change.

The girl was Nancy, a blue-eyed little wench who'd always been a bit sweet on Tom and had abetted him from time to time in the conduct of his trade.

"It was only a sixpence you gave me, sir, truly," she said, injured that the man should think otherwise.

"You thieving slattern," he barked back, "it was a shilling. D'ye think I can't count?"

Tom noted a leather purse dangling from the man's belt, and the boy reached into his sleeve and removed a tiny but well-honed knife. Jumping gracefully off the wall, he quickly slid to the man's elbow. "I think your shilling is in your pocket, sir," Tom said. "I saw you put one there."

Startled, the man slapped his pocket. "Hey? I keep my money in my purse!" Nevertheless he thrust his hand into his pocket, and lo and behold produced a shilling. He gaped with amazement at the coin. "Saints be with us! What . . .? How . . .?"

Tom now appeared at his other elbow, shook his head in a high-sign to Nancy, then winked at her and melted into the crowd while the man surveyed his shilling as if some magician had produced it out of his nose. Indeed, it had been a magician of sorts, for Tom had dropped one he carried for the purpose into the man's pocket, and while he was stammering out his confusion, Tom was relieving him of his purse by means of his cunning little blade.

Suddenly the man discovered the ruse. "Well . . . my purse!" He fumbled with his belt and slapped his garments. "It's gone! My purse!" He whirled about seeking Tom but the boy was already well-buried in the throng and invisible to his victim. It had been as easy as rolling off a log, so easy that Tom threw caution to the winds and, instead of secreting the purse inside his garment and waiting to get clear of the crowd before opening it, he loosened the drawstrings and looked inside. He was thus occupied when he ran headlong into the red-clad belly of a constable rushing towards the baying victim of Tom's theft.

The collision knocked the purse out of Tom's hands and it fell to the cobblestones, coins ringing and bouncing and rolling every which way.

"Not so fast, cutpurse!" the constable said, clutching Tom by the sleeve. "You'll lose your ears for that!"

Cutting off the ears was the punishment accorded to petty thieves who, in the merciful view of the magistrate, were of too tender an age to lose their heads. This was the sixteenth century's notion of leniency. Somehow this notion of leniency did not correspond to Tom's. Tom was quite fond of his ears, and after quickly reviewing in his mind all the wonderful things one can hear with them, he concluded he was having none of the court's mercy, thank you. Accordingly, he brought the heel of his shoe smartly down upon the constable's instep.

The constable howled like a dog whose tail has been pulled. Tom broke the man's grip on his sleeve with a deft chop of his palm, broke free and darted through an arch. Looking behind him, he saw several more red-coated pursuers funneling through the crowd toward the arch.

The law had the numbers, but Tom had the geography, for he knew these streets intimately, and dodging up several lanes and alleys he managed to give the slip to the constables, at least for the moment. Before him was London Bridge, and if only he could plunge into that morass of humanity he could lose those constables once and for all. He made for it at top speed, and moments later breathed a deep sigh of relief as he mingled with the tradesmen and concessionaires, children, goats, carthorses, bullocks, shoppers, beggars, and—*constables!*

Tom had acquired some contempt for His Majesty's constabulary force, but Lord, these fellows were good, eagle-eyed, determined, and possessed of wind and energy unlike any that had ever pursued Tom before. He took off like a frightened fawn, nearly knocking over a wooden stall piled high with fresh bass and flounder, and emerged in a narrow lane flanking Westminster Palace. Panting heavily, he looked over his shoulder and—*there they bloody were!* Tom darted around a corner.

He came to a wall known as Fisherman's Bastion, boosted himself up on its stepped rampart, and ran along it a bit before leaping off, vaulting over another, and crossing a broad grassy space. Again he checked to see if he'd lost his pursuers. Not only had he not, but they'd gained on him. Cornered, Tom desperately looked about, and noted a window arch set in an ivy covered wall. Grasping the ivy and praying it would support his weight, he boosted himself up to the window arch, slithered over its sill, and blindly dropped to the other side, bracing himself for he knew not what, for it could be a courtyard, a parade ground, or a cloister, and it might lie a foot, a yard, or an eternity beneath his feet.

Fortunately the drop was short, and his fall was cushioned by a sward of muddy grass. He lost his balance, slipped and fell face down in the mud. When he opened his eyes and wiped the mud out of them, he looked about, but his vision was obstructed by a massive cylinder that looked like a flagpole, and in fact had the soft and yielding quality of—flesh! He examined the curious object a little closer, and noted that the cylinder of flesh terminated in a gaudy, rosetted shoe.

One need not be a brilliant scholar or a well-traveled man of the world to conclude that Tom had landed beneath somebody's foot. And not just anybody's foot, but obviously the foot of a man of some rank, for Tom had never seen a foot so magnificently shod.

It was time to follow the foot up to the rest of its person and discover what manner of man was its owner. But Tom's eye had traveled no further than the hem of a gorgeous ermine-trimmed robe than the foot stamped down upon Tom's arm, pinning him to the ground. Tears of pain sprang to the boy's eyes.

Had he known under whose foot his arm had the privilege of being crushed, Tom would probably have swooned dead out.

CHAPTER III

King Henry could scarcely credit his eyes. One moment he was sitting in his courtyard garden, trading quips and weightier discussion with his jester and several noble ministers, and the next he was using a muddy tatterdemalion for a footstool. Here was amusing sport!

"What! What wriggling worm's this?"

The boy tried to squirm loose but Henry exerted more pressure with one of his two famous legs (which he flattered himself were his finest feature), and the boy winced.

"Ha!" the monarch laughed, winking at his audience. "Is the weight of England too heavy for you? *I've* been carrying it this five and thirty years!" He leaned over and examined his captive a bit more closely. Splotched with mud as the lad was, it was hard to tell much more than that he was fair of face and had clever, shrewd eyes, eyes that were even now calculating an escape route. Henry kept the pressure on the boy's arm. "Who are you?" he demanded.

Tears of pain in his eyes, Tom whimpered, "No one, sir. Pray—pray you, let me go!"

"No one?" said King Henry, grinning cruelly. "Why then, if I break *no one's* arm, what's the matter?" He leaned a little heavier on his foot and Tom cried out in anguish. The king looked around with satisfaction at his ministers. Why, this *was* good sport! Better than dancing or jousting or the falcons. The noblemen, Milords Norfolk, Hertford, and St. John, laughed heartily with their liege, though one wonders whether they'd have laughed quite so heartily had they not been under obligation to humor the King of England.

The jester, clad in the traditional motley of his trade, threw himself down beside Tom and gazed at him, chin in hand. "That's true, gossip Henry," the effeminite fool said. "You'll have done harm to nobody. Break away, old Hal."

With this, Henry all but stood upon Tom's arm. The boy squealed and appeared to be on the verge of passing out, but the king felt no more sympathy for him than he would have for a rat beneath the heel of his shoe. Henry weighed over fifteen stone, and some said it was closer to twenty, or something around two hundred eighty pounds, and though the king bore these pounds gracefully and athletically, they had the same effect as the cornerstone of a building when concentrated on the bone of a mere boy.

The minister known as Norfolk, a slight gentleman whose jeweled chains seemed to weigh his head down, took advantage of His Majesty's play on words to make a lofty point. Leaning over, he said quietly, "And yet, sire, you may be crippling a hand that would serve you some day. Who knows, if you spare it, perhaps it will do good work for your majesty—cutting Scottish throats, for example?"

Alas, Norfolk's point flew back in his own face like a falcon stooping to its own master. "If he cuts 'em to no better purpose than you did, Norfolk, I may as well break every bone in his body," said Henry, glowering. "How many years did you lead my armies? How many years did you fail to settle the Scots for me?"

Norfolk gulped, and looked with distress at his colleagues, who were amused by his predicament. But Norfolk was clever, and he found a way out of it—by flattery. "True," he said to the king. "I might have done better if I had had your majesty to direct me—on the battlefield."

This exchange may have advanced the cause of state, but it did very little for the lad whose arm served as the metaphor for these quips. He groaned, reminding his oppressor of his plight. All at once Henry leaned over and glared at him, and Tom Canty found himself eye to eye with the King of England. It was a fair blue eye, and its expression seemed capable of violent change with the snap of a finger, from rage to amusement to mortal vindictiveness to mischievous merriment. At the moment the expression was one of cruel contempt and total indifference to the boy's pain. "Lie still, you maggot," roared the king, "or we'll have that precious hand of yours cut off, and the stump dipped in boiling tar. What d'ye say to that, Norfolk?"

Norfolk was certainly not going to risk his delicate relations with the king in order to beg for this wretched piece of refuse who lay whimpering beneath the king's heel. But he did venture, in a steady voice, "I say that he is some man's son, sire, and as precious to that man as your son is to you."

Norfolk gestured with his chin at a corner of the courtyard, where a boy of Tom's age was sparring with a burly guard, using quarterstaffs for weapons. The lad, stripped to pants and a loose shirt, aggressively drove back his opponent, adroitly using both the flat and the end of his staff to the confusion of his much larger opponent. King Henry gazed with intense satisfaction at his bonny son, who was turning out, for all the delicacy of his early years, to be as formidable as his father, and a worthy successor to the throne.

Henry's eyes traveled from Prince Edward to the detestable bundle of rags beneath his foot. "The Prince of Wales is not to be compared to this—offal. Up, vermin!" he commanded, directing a well-aimed toe at Tom's ribs.

Tom scrambled to his feet, clutching his throbbing arm.
"Aye," snarled the king, "crawl in my garden, will you,
and foul the king's foot with your lousy carcass. You're a
thief—I know the look."

Terrified, Tom dropped to his knees. "No, no master,
I'm an honest man's son. I . . ."

"Ha!" bellowed the king. "Even *my* son can't say as
much. Look you, worm—I give you ten yards; we'll see if
you can run as well as you can crawl. GUARDS!" he
bawled. "Run me down this rascal and thrash him back to
his gutter!"

It seemed that out of every cranny in the palace wall, a
guard materialized, pikes and shortswords glinting in the
sunlight. "Well," said the king, arms akimbo, "run,
fool! Your skin's at stake!"

Tom needed no reminder, but took to his heels, guards
hotly on the trail like hounds after a hare. Tom had
observed a nearby hedge that might lead to safety, and
dove for it. Even as he did, he heard the pitiless laughter of
King Henry, who looked upon the chase as a sport no less
amusing than bull-baiting or fox-hunting.

Tom emerged from the hedge, skin scratched and stinging, to find himself in the midst of a knot of shocked
courtiers, who gazed upon him as if he were a sack of
potatoes that had somehow fallen from the sky. Before
they could raise a hue and cry, Tom took off again,
through the elegantly dressed noblemen and ladies, and
dove under a bush immediately after rounding a corner of
the palace wall. He made himself small, held his breath,
and waited. A moment later there was a rush of footsteps
as the King's Guard hurtled past, snarling and snapping
like a pack of dogs.

The instant they were out of sight, he popped out of the
bush, assessed his situation, and, realizing he would be

captured if he attempted to cross the grounds, hoisted himself up the ivy clinging to the palace wall, towards the battlements atop the castle.

Muscles straining, he at last was able to fling a leg over the top of the wall, where he found himself on a slate roof punctuated by chimneys. For a minute he thought he was safe, and breathed the air of freedom deeply. Then a guard bayed, "He can't be far away!" That was enough to send the quarry into a frenzy again. He climbed into a large chimney and, trusting his fate to Providence, released his grip.

CHAPTER IV

Prince Edward Tudor paused in his quarterstaff combat to glance at his father to see if he was still watching him. The king's attention had been diverted by some brief activity involving the guards, but it was now focused on his son. Henry's eyes virtually blazed with pride, and his grin of satisfaction was almost fatuous.

Edward depended heavily on his father's approval, and under ordinary circumstances that was well and good. But in combat, even mock combat such as he was now engaged in, it was foolish to seek it, and it could be fatal. To remind him of that, his sparring partner, an old soldier named Grimly, fetched the prince a blow in the kidney with his staff. It was not as hard as it could have been, but sufficient to knock the wind out of the boy momentarily. It was a good lesson. Nevertheless, it enraged the prince, who launched an attack of surprising force and cleverness. He thrust at Grimly with the end of his staff, causing the soldier to fall back. Then Edward feinted twice with the flat of his staff, and when Grimly lowered his stick to parry, Edward quickly swung his staff with all his might at the man's neck. It was partially deflected by Grimly's elbow, but the old soldier stumbled, and when he looked up he faced the terrifying visage of the young Tudor, the very spitting image of the king, and it looked as if Edward was going to ram the end of his staff down the soldier's throat. The boy seemed to have forgotten it was a game!

"Mercy!" Grimly cried.

Edward scowled at him, then laughed, dropped his staff, and offered his hand to help the soldier to his feet.

Whereupon Grimly kicked the boy's legs out from under him. Edward landed with a thump on his behind, and in a trice the soldier was astraddle him, pressing the flat of his staff to the prince's throat. Edward's eyes bulged in terror, and Grimly snarled, "Say your prayers, little prince, for this is your last breath on earth." He leaned on the stick, crushing the boy's gullet.

Then *Grimly* laughed.

Extending his hand, he hauled the prince to his feet. The color had drained from Edward's face, and his hands trembled.

"I trust you've learned as much about human nature as you've learned about warfare, your highness," Grimly said, dusting the boy off. "Never give quarter on the battlefield—and never trust any but a dead enemy. You'll live to a ripe old age if you'll heed that advice."

"Thank you, Grimly. I shall certainly take it to heart," said the prince. "I need only touch my throat to remember it vividly."

The friendly combatants bowed at each other and Edward crossed the greensward to his father's side. The first to greet him was Norfolk, who was Edward's favorite, a decent and honorable man who had always treated the prince as man to man.

"Well, my lord of Norfolk," Edward hailed him, "would you take me to fight against the Scots?"

Norfolk beamed. "If I were twenty years younger, I'd be proud to follow your royal highness against the Scots." Then the Duke lowered his voice, so as not to embarrass the lad. "And yet, keep your hands closer together on the quarterstaff."

Edward, whose rump still throbbed from Grimly's surprise attack, laughingly acknowledged the Duke's suggestion. Norfolk bowed deeply before the king, pivoted, and marched away.

Edward turned to his father. "He was a stout old fighter, was he not?"

"Aye, stout enough," Henry said, grudgingly. Then, under his breath, he added, "A politician."

Edward looked questioningly at his father.

Henry put his hand on Edward's shoulder and they strolled around the grounds a bit, Henry limping slightly, for disease had begun to cripple those fine legs of his. "Beware of such creatures, Ned," Henry said, utilizing his favorite nickname for his son. "He is the Pope's man; he changes sides easily as you change your shirt, mark me. Aye, and he stands near enough to our throne to covet it; he has ambitions. But," the king added in an ominous growl, "I'll crop them before I'm done."

Edward gaped at his father amazedly. "Norfolk disloyal? No, father, anyone else but——"

"Oh, we're turned statesman now?" laughed the king, but humorlessly. There was only one thing the royal court feared more than Henry's wrath, and that was his laughter. Then Henry turned serious. "Wait till you sit on the throne. But in the meantime, leave vipers like Norfolk to me."

Edward was much vexed by his father's wrath toward Norfolk, which sounded much more serious than the violent rages his father sometimes developed and forgot in the span of a few hours. Henry's remark about Norfolk being a Pope's man—well, it was not easy to be anything else, for it was impossible for an entire nation to turn its back on everything it had been taught to believe, just because the king had decreed it. Nowadays, it was not so much a question of what you believed as it was one of how well you *pretended* to believe. Norfolk was apparently not as good at pretending as some others among Henry's ministers, such as Hertford.

As the king and his son strolled they saluted two charming young girls sweeping in long gowns along a path some distance from them. The girls curtseyed and giggled. One of them, hair as red as fire, was Elizabeth, Henry's second daughter. The other was Jane Grey, daughter of Henry Grey, marquess of Dorset, and his wife, Lady Frances Brandon, daughter of Princess Mary, King Henry's first daughter. Jane Grey had dark, teasing eyes that lit up at the sight of the young prince.

Edward looked up at his father, whose face was dark and brooding. Edward could only guess what he was brooding about, for under certain conditions either of these ladies could be a candidate for the throne of England. But as these conditions included the deaths of both Henry and his son, it was easy to understand why the king's natural affection (indeed, for Lady Jane it bordered on lust) for the two girls was tempered by distaste.

Finishing his thought about Edward's meddling in politics, Henry said, "You've better things to do, boy. A time for work, and a time to fight, and a time for . . ." The king nodded at Lady Jane. ". . . important things."

Edward followed his father's gaze to Lady Jane, who wore a long yellow satin gown, a jeweled comb from which depended a delicate shawl of Flemish lace, and another, embroidered shawl of French make, around her bare shoulders. The boy looked at her diffidently, even indifferently, and this disturbed the king mightily, for the king's goatish predilections for young women were famous throughout the land, and though his son might ride, dance, joust, compose poetry, and even rule as well as the father, Edward would always be a disappointment to him if he were not also as lust-crazed as the king.

"God, Ned," Henry exploded, giving utterance to the thought, "but you're cold-blooded! If I were your age . . ." Edward looked up at him, waiting for him to finish his sentence. But instead of articulating it, he gave the boy a shove in the direction of the two damsels. "Go to, boy, it'll do you good."

Edward gulped and reluctantly approached the princess and Lady Jane.

Henry shook his head, muttering, then ran a knuckle over his chin as two most trusted ministers, Hertford and St. John, sidled up to him. Henry appeared to be plunged in thought about his son's virility, but it was a tribute to the king's mental capacity that he could balance a dozen matters in his head at once. Quietly, and without turning his head, he said to them, "At the masque tonight, arrest the Duke of Norfolk. Take him to the Tower. The charge—high treason."

Hertford exchanged looks with St. John, looks that combined craftiness with satisfaction, for they had long calumnied Norfolk to the king, and at last their treachery had borne fruit: their power over the king would be consolidated with the removal of Henry's most faithful minister.

"Yes, sire," said Hertford. "And the substance of the treason?"

Henry smiled and waved his ringed, pudgy hand. "I do not like the color of his hat."

MARK LESTER as Tom Canty, the Pauper, with his mother, played by SYBIL DANNING, and his mean, miserable father, John Canty, played by ERNEST BORGNINE

CHARLTON HESTON as King Henry VIII makes light of the trespassing Pauper

The Pauper in trouble

King Henry VIII with
the Duke of Norfolk,
played by REX HARRISON

FELICITY DEAN (left) as Lady Jane Grey and LALLA WARD as Princess Elizabeth

MARK LESTER as Prince Edward trying to decide on a costume before the masked ball

Behind the
scenes with Director
Richard Fleischer
and Oliver Reed

The masked ball, and Lady Jane Grey never lovelier

CHARLTON HESTON
as King Henry VIII

Is it the Prince or the Pauper treating royalty
to a peasant dance?

REX HARRISON
as the Duke
of Norfolk

GEORGE C. SCOTT as
The Ruffler, villain
extraordinaire

ERNEST BORGNINE
as the thieving
John Canty

MARK LESTER
as the Prince—
or is this
the Pauper?

Executive Producer Ilya Salkind and Producer
Pierre Spengler on the set

DAVID HEMMINGS portraying
the evil Hugh Hendon

RAQUEL WELCH as
the lovely Lady Edith

HARRY ANDREWS as the
scheming Duke of Hertford

Royal diversion at a royal gala

Would a real prince eat with his hands?

The Duke of Norfolk and the deadly edict

Alexander Salkind with The Making Of authors
David Petrou and Berta Dominguez D.

Miles matching wits and swords with John Canty who
wants to reclaim the thieving services of his "son"

OLIVER REED as Miles Hendon, taking care of an evildoer

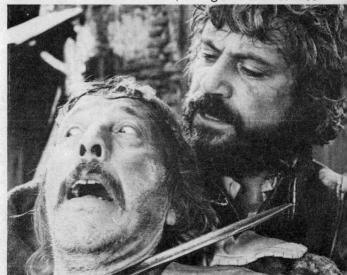

The king of villains, ruffians, scoundrels, and criminals—
The Ruffler, superbly portrayed by GEORGE C. SCOTT

The Prince jousts for his honor and his life inside the Ruffler's cave

John Canty is no match for one of the Ruffler's murderous men

Public shame for a hero and a prince

Miles Hendon finally
acknowledging
the rightful King
of England

RAQUEL WELCH as Lady Edith
at long last reunited with her lover, Miles

A mad dash to save the crown and the country

The true King of England with two of his
most loyal supporters

CHAPTER V

The palace was all aflutter with preparations for the masque. From King Henry himself to the lowest scullery maid, all attention focused on that evening's costume ball. It was as if all affairs of state—the continual Spanish and French plotting to restore Catholicism to England, the exploration of the New World, the incessant problem of keeping the royal coffers full, the perpetual conspiracies among Henry's courtiers to gain favor in his eyes—it was as if all these were suspended, declared null and void for one evening, in favor of the profound business of selecting a costume or preparing the castle for festivities.

In the tremendous kitchens below the castle, a dozen cooks and twice that number of assistants and apprentices rushed back and forth among the ovens and cauldrons with the geese, mutton, venison, larks, and even rarer victims of the gastly slaughter that took place whenever the king fancied entertainment. Soups and pies, vegetables and wines, cheeses and desserts materialized in quantities sufficient to keep a town contentedly fed for a season.

Tempers ran high over the vexing question of what to wear; Henry snapped at his groom, the noble husbands snapped at their noble wives, the ladies' maids snapped at each other, and in the hours of preparation, as anxiety filtered down to the lowest servant and least consequential guest, the castle sounded like a kennel full of hungry, jealous, snapping dogs.

It seemed as if only one rational head prevailed that day, and that was the one belonging to the prince. Edward stood in his dressing room, staring open-mouthed and dismayed at the ridiculous lengths that his fellow human beings, normally the most rational of souls, were going to in order to make fools of themselves. Standing by the mantle, fire to his back, he examined four young pages his own age and size who were modeling costumes for him. His sister Elizabeth and Lady Jane stood before the intensely uncomfortable lads, conferring in grave tones like a couple of surgeons determining the fate of a patient.

The first page, Richard, flexed his muscles in the leather and bronze armor of Mars, the ancient Roman god of war. Richard's face was painted a fierce red, and he effected a terrifying snarling grimace and rattled his shortsword to demonstrate he meant business.

Beside him stood another god, Adonis, as portrayed by John, a stablehand's son with whom Edward sometimes played. John looked absurd and distinctly uncomfortable in the effeminite costume consisting of laurel wreath, leopard skin, and massive buskins, and pleaded with his eyes for the prince not to tease him.

A third lad was dressed in the baggy trousers and gaily embroidered shirt of a Turk, and scowled from behind immense whiskers stuck on his cheek with a calvesfoot glue that would take two weeks to remove; and a fourth boy, glittering in an amazing confection of silver gauze and spangles, was apparently supposed to be some forest fairy out of Celtic legend.

De Brie, the Prince's chamberlain and an object of universal contempt around the palace for his womanly demeanor, fluttered about pinning this costume and tucking that, muttering and cursing and clucking under his breath, trying desperately to get the prince to make a choice.

Edward's manifest indifference was making the poor gentleman sick, and not a little worried for his head, for

these affairs were nowhere nearly as frivolous and incon-
sequential as they appeared to be. He had seen the king's
wrath come down quite awfully on the courtier whose
costume came close to His Majesty's own, and at least one
minister had lost his position for this atrocious breach of
manners. Duels were fought and friendships rent asunder
over seemingly trivial *contretemps* occurring at the king's
masques. Thus was De Brie frantically anxious that the
prince not displease and embarrass his father by appearing
in a costume unworthy of the boy's title, or indeed, by
appearing in none at all, which seemed to be the case at the
moment.

"But the masque and ball are in your highness's
honor," he pleaded with Edward, stressing his point with
a florid gesture. "If you do not wear a costume, all will be
spoiled!"

"If I wear one of those," Edward said with a sniff and a
contemptuous sweep of the back of his hand, "*I* will be
spoiled. Who are they meant to be, in God's name?"

De Brie minced over to the first boy, Richard. "This is
the spirit and embodiment of war, the pagan god Mars."
He moved to John, the stablehand's son. "And this is
Adonis, who was adored by Venus—simple, but fetching.
And this," he said, stepping down to the third lad,
"Tamurlaine, King of the Turks."

"King of the hairy apes!" Edward hissed. He glanced
at Elizabeth, who ill-concealed a smile. "Oh, laugh, big
sister! What are *you* going as?"

"*I'm* not heir to the throne," she said playfully. "I can
go in cap and apron for all anyone cares. But Jane is to be
Goddess of the Clouds," Elizabeth said, indicating her
dark-eyed friend. "All in cloth of silver."

Edward affected indifference. "Very becoming she'll
look," he said, not even glancing at Lady Jane, who
lowered her eyes with disappointment.

Edward glared at the four boys while De Brie, exulting in his handiwork, stood beside him expectantly. Edward tried to make a decision, but after closing his eyes and fantasying himself in each costume, he finally slashed the air with the flat of his hand, a gesture all too distressingly reminiscent of his father—and of the slash of the executioner's axe. "They're all monstrous. Take them out!"

"But Highness," De Brie protested.

Edward shooed him away. "I shall think of something myself. Or my clever sister Bess"—the family's nickname for Elizabeth—"will devise it. She used to embroider presents for me."

"I am a princess," Elizabeth said haughtily, "not a haberdasher. Stitch your own shirts, Prince of Wales." She curtsied arrogantly, then pivoted to leave Edward's chambers. Behind her, Lady Jane curtsied too, but with gracious sincerity and an affectionate smile for the prince. As they swept out of the room, Edward could hear Lady Jane say to Elizabeth, "Highness, I would be glad to sew something for the Prince."

Edward did not hear Elizabeth's reply, but for reasons difficult to explain to himself, he hoped that Elizabeth would accede to Lady Jane's desire. Just as the two trailed out of sight, however, Elizabeth took Jane by the ear and shoved her trippingly forward. Though it was an affectionate gesture, it probably spelled the doom of Edward's hope to spend some time alone with Lady Jane, in whose presence he invariably and inexplicably felt a tingle of warmth.

De Brie lagged behind, hoping that the Prince, as his father frequently did, would suddenly reverse himself and yield to the necessity of selecting one of the Chamberlain's costumes. But no, it was not to be. Edward darted a dark glance at him that seemed to say, "What?

Are you still poisoning my sight with your dreadful little presence?'' That was enough for De Brie, who rounded up his four models and hustled them out of Edward's presence. As it was an unforgivable breach of etiquette to turn one's back on the prince, the Chamberlain and his boys, looking like nothing so much as a mother hen and her brood, retreated in bumbling disarray, bowing and groveling and jamming out of the door like a troupe of clownish players.

De Brie closed the door behind him, and at last Edward was alone, a luxury he rarely enjoyed, for, from the moment he arose in the morning to the moment he retired, he was usually attended by countless servants whose jobs ranged from emptying his chamber pot to tasting his food, from dressing him to substituting for him when, thanks to some indiscretion or naughtiness, he was deemed by his father to deserve a spanking or whipping. Indeed, Edward said to himself, this constant fussing over me is one of the most irritating disadvantages to being heir to the throne. I've never really had an opportunity to get to know myself, to learn what sort of stuff I'm made of, for I'm always surrounded by flunkies all too eager to do for me.

The thought crossed his mind that one day he really must sneak away for a few hours where no one could find him. For a moment he deliciously contemplated what he would do if he could spring himself loose of all responsibility, but withdrew from the revery in anxiety. He would be caught and punished, so what was the use of even dreaming about it?

He was about to turn his thoughts to the odious matter of devising a costume for the masque, when he heard a sharp noise in the direction of his fireplace. He turned and looked curiously at it, noting a thin grey cloud of soot descending to the hearth. ''Must be a pigeon,'' he said to himself with a shrug.

But before he could investigate, there was a fearful rumble, a cloud of acrid dust, a shower of bricks, soot, and—arms and legs! This was no pigeon!

It was difficult to ascertain just what it was, however. The aspect was definitely human, but clearly this filthy jumble of limbs and tatters must belong to some sub-species of the human race, something a bit closer to the apes.

The figure wiped its eyes and rolled out of the fireplace, blinking and choking.

"In God's name! Who the devil are you?" the astonished prince cried.

Tom crawled out on his hands and knees, shaking puffs of soot out of his hair as his senses returned. The first to return was his vision, which took in the aspect of a pair of silk-clad legs, satin buskins, an embroidered shirt and fur-trimmed cape. A face gazed down at him with mingled apprehension, disgust, and curiosity.

Tom cleared the dust out of his throat and stammered, "Oh, cor, I . . . I beg your honor's pardon. I . . . I was up the chimney . . . and . . . and . . ."

"I know where you were," Edward declared, looking down upon him with cold contempt. "I asked who you are. Get up, fellow—what's your name?" The prince reached down to help the varlet up, but withdrew his hand in revulsion. God only knew what manner of plaguey vermin this ragbag might bear.

Tom scrambled to his feet, knuckling his forehead in a ridiculous approximation of a salute.

"Please, your worship. I'm poor Tom Canty, of Offal Court, in Smithfield. I . . . I was hiding from the guards—this great big horrible bastard in the garden made 'em chase me, and I crawled in your honor's chimney, meaning no harm." Tom punctuated his explanation with several bows, scrapes, salutes, and obeisances, each more awkward than the last.

The prince looked steadily at the pathetic creature. "Had the . . . great big horrible . . . um, gentleman . . . a crimson coat and a bandaged leg?" he asked, suppressing a smile.

"That's him, milord," Tom said eagerly. "You know him? Gawd, he . . ."

"Wait!" Edward barked, staring at Tom, who was so flustered he almost fell back into the fireplace. "Haven't I seen you befo . . ." He stepped closer to Tom, examining him with a frown. Then the prince glanced toward a mirror. Then back at Tom. Then back at the mirror. "Where did . . .? Turn your face this way," he commanded. "The *clean* side, man. Look in that mirror."

As Tom turned, Edward stepped even closer. They stared at their reflections, and despite the differences between hair style (if Tom's flaxen tangle could be said to have a style), dress (if Tom's miserable rags could be termed dress), and degree of cleanliness (on a scale of one hundred, Tom had no degree of cleanliness), one remarkable fact stood out, and it did not even escape Tom.

Brushing back a lock of hair, he gasped. "Gawd!" Their expressions were totally unalike. Edward's was cool and haughty, disdainful, aloof; Tom's was mobile, open, and friendly, and at the moment a host of emotions chased themselves around his eyes and lips faster than one could enumerate them, but they included amazement, disbelief, wonder, and amusement bordering on hilarity. "We . . . we look like each other!" Tom breathed.

"No," said Edward. "You look like me. Which is interesting, if rather impertinent. Do you know who I am?"

Tom shook his head bearishly. A little cloud of soot

descended from his hair, drifting past his face and settling on his shoulders.

"I am Edward, Prince of Wales. The gentleman who set the guards on you, very properly," Edward said, relishing the announcement with the faintest twinkle of a smile, "is my father, King Henry of England."

Tom's eyes rolled up into his skull, and with a moan he fell to the carpet in a hilarious parody of a courtly kneel. Head lowered almost to the floor, Tom exposed his neck as if it were inevitable that the executioner's blade would be chopping through it within the hour.

"So you can see you have blundered perilously, Master Canty," Edward pontificated. "You had better explain yourself."

"Oh, look, sire, your grace, your majesty," Tom blustered. "I couldn't help it. They were after me . . . the constables . . . and I ran in here, not knowing." He looked up at the prince, who suddenly seemed to tower over him like a goliath. Miserably, Tom continued. "It's like your dad said, I'm a thief. But I didn't come here to steal, I swear. I know my place. I wouldn't pinch from the likes of you, nor from anyone above an alderman!"

Needless to say, Edward's reaction to this explanation was not one of pure gratification. "A discriminating thief," he sneered. "But not a very expert one, by the look of you."

Tom looked at his shabbiness, then at the splendid young gentleman before him. "This is my best suit —clean on last August."

"You look like a scarecrow, or someone got up as a beggar for a fancy dress . . . ball." The words were no sooner out of the prince's mouth than his eyes lit up with inspiration, and he snapped his fingers. "Stand beside me again," he commanded. Tom did as he was told, and stood beside the prince, feeling foolish and self-conscious.

The prince stared long and hard for a minute, then clapped his hands. "Why not? Take off those rags." Edward began to strip out of his cape and doublet.

Tom looked bewildered and stood there, hands dangling limply at his side.

"Come on, man, get them off and give them to me." Tom began to fumble with the drawstring on his sackcloth garment, but still looked at the prince uncomprehendingly. Impatiently, the prince explained. "There is a masque and ball, and I must have a costume. Well, I shall wear your pauper's rags, and . . ." —another inspiration, another snap of his fingers—"and, by the mass, you'll go in *my* clothes! What will they say when we stand together? They'll not know which is which!" For one of the few times in his life, Edward laughed without restraint. "Here," he said, tossing his doublet to Tom.

Tom caught the garment and held it up. He had never touched cloth of such magnificent texture before. Why, it appalled him even to be soiling it with his filthy fingertips. "But . . . I couldn't put this on."

"My servants shall dress you," Edward said, misinterpreting Tom's remark.

"I don't mean that . . . highness," said Tom. "I mean, it wouldn't be fitting. What would your dad say?"

"My 'dad' will laugh until he splits," Edward replied, eyes glowing with anticipation. "He may be big and great, but he is not always . . . horrible. Cheer up, Tom Canty. Instead of a beating you'll go back to Awful Court . . ."

"Offal Court," Tom corrected him, realizing immediately afterwards that the penalty for correcting the

Prince of Wales was probably the loss of his tongue at the very least.

But Edward took it equably. "Offal Court, then, with a new suit and a pocketful of gold sovereigns."

Tom's eyes narrowed. "How many?"

Edward shrugged. "A hundred, two hundred."

Tom didn't hesitate a fraction of a second. "Done!"

Within moments, two piles of garments lay in the middle of the prince's chamber: one of elegant finery, delicate silks and satins, superb Flemish embroidery using threads of silver and gold, and furs of utmost rarity; the other, a noisome mound of sack cloth, stained, soiled, and tattered. The prince almost lost his enthusiasm for the prank when he raised Tom's shift to his eyes and examined it for vermin. Fortunately he found none, for however impoverished Tom's circumstances, his mother assiduously bathed him and scrubbed his clothes at least once every week, and kept their depressingly austere lodgings free of the lice and fleas that infested their neighbors'.

After his moment's hesitation, the prince sighed and wriggled into the pauper's shift. When his head emerged it was streaked with soot and dust. He stared into the looking glass and grinned, then turned to help Tom, who was struggling into the prince's silk stockings.

Tom had already managed to tear through the toe of one with his sharp toenails, but the prince eased him into the other, then showed him how the shirt went on, for Tom had donned it open at the front, when actually the fabric went to the front, and the hooks and eyes were fastened at the back. Then into the short pants, which made Tom feel naked and ridiculous. Then the jeweled chains around his neck, the velvet slippers, and the ermine-tassled cape. Finally, the hat, a sort of French-style affair with a magnificent plume in it.

Tom stepped before the looking glass and, though one could not detect it for the dirt and soot, his face drained of all blood. His eyes rounded and his jaw dropped. Cor! he said to himself. If this be royalty, send me back to my beloved squalor!

The thought of confronting a palace full of nobles dressed in this foolish costume filled him with abject embarrassment. The humiliation was so intense that not even the prospect of a hundred sovereigns made up for it. His only thought was, how much money he could get for it when he sold it to the first ragmonger he came across.

The prince took him by the shoulders and turned him around, studying the awkward boy, who stood with his hands dangling at his sides. "Nay, we'll have to wash your highness's face," the prince said. "Here." He took a towel from the lavabo, dipped it in a porcelain basin filled with water, and tossed it to Tom.

Tom touched the towel to his cheek, smearing a pink swath through the soot.

Impatiently, Edward snatched the towel from Tom's hand and scrubbed the boy's face till it gleamed. They stood again before the looking glass and Edward frowned. Something was wrong, still. Ah, of course! Edward took the sooty towel and smeared the muddy mess over his own face. That was the right touch!

A last glance in the mirror. The prince beamed. Tom looked miserable.

Edward crossed to the heavy oak door of his chamber, opened it a crack, and peered out. Then he snapped his fingers and beckoned to the mock-prince. "We shall try our disguises first."

They were about to step out of the chamber when Edward remembered something. He stepped back into the room and picked up the prince's seal, a raised brass dye bearing the prince's feather crest, with a gilt and jeweled handle, used for stamping the wax seals on the prince's correspondence. The prince hefted the seal and slipped its gold chain around his own neck. "To my clothes you are welcome, Master Canty, but the Prince's seal stays with the true prince."

He returned to the door and stepped into the marble corridor, looking both ways. Tom hung back, grimacing as if this were the last leg on the road to his execution. "Sir . . . your reverence . . . guvnor? I don't like it. Just let me go, and you can keep my clothes."

Edward glared at him, reached into the room and yanked the terrified boy into the corridor. For a moment they both stood there awkwardly, each in his own way, for Edward had immediately realized that he was probably no better at playing pauper than Tom Canty was at playing prince. Perhaps they should retreat to the chamber and coach each other on some of the fundamentals of poverty and nobility respectively. Edward knew not a word of street language, save one or two expressions he'd heard from his stablehand friend. Indeed, he had not even observed how a street urchin bore himself. Certainly it was not with the erect confidence and commanding swagger of a member of the royal family. He glanced at Tom and, taking his cue from him, rounded his shoulders and lowered his head in cowed fashion, as if awed and humbled to find himself in these magnificent surroundings.

At that moment there was a noise around the corner of the corridor, the familiar sound of guards snapping to attention as a nobleman approached. Tom gulped and dove back into the chamber, leaving the prince standing solitarily in the corridor just as his old friend the Duke of Norfolk strode around the corner, attended by a small page. The duke halted in his tracks and gaped in astonishment at the sight of the ragged figure.

"Good God! You—still here? Have you not had enough of kings and palaces?"

Ah, the prince smiled to himself, now we shall have some sport: if my disguise is good enough to fool the duke, who dangled me ofttimes on his knee when I was a mere princeling, and the page, who has served me my dinner too often to count, then surely no one at the masque shall recognize me, not even my own father.

But what to say? How about something like this: "Have pity on a poor pauper, me lord," Edward said, admonishing himself for not dropping the H, as Tom did. He'd have to remember that. He put out his hand. "Spare a copper . . ."

Apparently his accent, poorly rendered though it was, was good enough to fool the duke, for he glared sternly at Edward. "Your impudence will last longer than your luck, my lad. Get out while your skin's still whole. Guards!"

In an instant two burly red-uniformed guards materialized around the corner. The duke snapped his fingers at Edward, who smiled fatuously. Now he would reveal his identity. What a jolly good prank this was turning out to be!

But before he could open his mouth the guards had swept him up by the elbows and hustled him, feet flailing in mid-air, down the corridor. Suddenly the prince grew alarmed. Over his shoulder he shouted at Norfolk. "My lord, you are mistaken, I am . . ."

Before he could finish his sentence the guard at his right arm cuffed him brutally on the head, sending flashes of light through Edward's eyes and a high-pitched ringing in his ears. " 'Old yer bleedin' tongue!'' the guard barked.

Down a stone stairway they dragged him, manhandling him extra roughly for all the trouble he'd caused them. "Let me go, you clowns!" he roared. "I am the Prince of

Wales! God, you'll sweat for this. Let me go, I say! Take your . . . beastly hands off . . ."

"I told you to shut up!" the guard snapped, swinging Edward around and striking him across the face. Dazed, the prince clutched his head and staggered senselessly before the arched doorway of the palace. The guards scooped him up and dragged through the doorway and up a flight of stairs toward the palace gate.

Now the prince realized that his disguise had worked all too effectively. Struggling wildly, he screamed at the top of his voice. "Let me go, fools! I am the prince, I tell you! Edward, Prince of Wales! Let me go!" He managed to get one arm loose and threw a punch at the face of the guard who'd struck him.

Enraged, the guard threw him to the ground as two other guards opened the gate. "Crazy rubbish, I warned you!" Edward, knees bleeding, struggled to his feet, turning his back to the other guard, who had produced a heavy leather belt. The guard brought it down on Edward's back with all his might, flattening the prince. Two more blows on his back and shoulders sent cries of agony into the evening air.

Edward managed to get to his feet, staggered, and pitched down the stairs into the crowd of beggars who perpetually hung around the gates hoping for a crust of bread or a benevolent nobleman's farthing or simply a glimpse of royalty.

Edward wobbled to his feet, quivering with rage and shame. "You scum!" he cried, shaking his fist at the guards. Hot tears boiled into his eyes. "I am the prince, I say!" He made one last assault on the gate, egged on by the rabble who, in the absence of bread or coins, were delighted with this novel entertainment.

But the guard Edward had struck, wiping a trickle of

blood from his nostril, dealt Edward yet another vicious blow, sending the boy reeling back into the arms of the rabble, who pushed him back for another round of punishment.

"Now get away!" the guard shouted, "or we'll take you in and trice you up and flog you to bloody rags."

And with that, the guards slammed the heavy gate shut with a resounding thump that for Edward sounded like the sealing of his doom.

"But it is true!" Edward whimpered, imploring the crowd with outstretched hands. "I *am* the Prince of Wales!"

As might be imagined, this declaration was greeted with hoots and jeers and catcalls, and if Prince Edward truly wished to learn more about his subjects, he now had a golden opportunity. For if there is one thing the English peasant would not tolerate, it was "one of their own" pretending to a higher station in life, and "putting on airs".

"Cock-a-doodle-do," shrieked four or five of the mob in falsetto voices. A sluttish wench sidled past him, mocking him with, "Can't I be your pretty princess, dearie?" And one ruffian, a burly scoundrel with stained teeth, shouted, "Yeah, an' I'll crown yer royal 'ighness," and brought a pint pot crashing down on Edward's head, driving him to his knees.

This incited the crowd to an almost murderous pitch, and the unruly beggars began to kick him while he was down, hurl garbage at him, and shout abuse in language Edward had never heard in the sheltered chambers of Westminster Palace.

But the prince struggled back to his feet with a fortitude that surprised even his tormentors. "I tell you again, you pack of unmannerly curs, I am the Prince of Wales!" Then he remembered something as he cast about in his mind for some way to prove his claim. He fumbled inside his shirt and produced the seal on its gold chain.

"Look," he appealed to them tearfully. "Here is my seal! The royal seal of England!"

It caught the glitter of torchlight, and so dramatic was this revelation that a hush fell over the crowd. A number of faces leaned forward for a closer look, and in the flicker of flames in the cressets beside the gate, their evil, greedy eyes glowed.

"Now—will you believe me?" he demanded, hauteur returning despite the blows and humiliations he had suffered.

But he'd misjudged the crowd, for the effect of this display was not so much the gaining of their respect as it was the stimulation of their avarice. The same ruffian who had struck Edward with his ale pot now shouldered through the mob for a closer look at the seal.

"Gawdstrewth!" he gasped, blinking. "Bleedin' diamonds! Nay, that's too pretty a trinket to hang 'round a madman's dirty neck!" Edward fell back as the horrible man lunged for the seal.

All at once the steel blade of a rapier caught the glint of torchlight, and the ruffian found his hand not upon the seal but upon the point of this rather menacing weapon.

"And that's too dirty a hand to lay even on a madman," came a voice from behind the rapier. The crowd sucked in its breath as one man, and turned to see who it was that fancied himself the deliverer of this ragged pretender.

They saw a tall, trimly built muscular man. His doublet and trunks were of rich material, but faded and threadbare, and their gold lace adornments were sadly tarnished. His ruff was rumpled and damaged, and the plume in his slouched hat was broken and had a bedraggled and disreputable look. At his side swung a rusty iron sheath for his rapier. Indeed, the only object on his person that seemed to have been well cared-for was the rapier.

Without taking his eyes off Edward's assailant, he said to Edward, "Put it under your shirt—quickly. Get behind me."

Edward did as he was told, ducking behind his savior as the mob muttered a torrent of ugly abuse and began to close threateningly around them.

Edward's protector flourished his rapier dangerously close to the nearest offender. "One more step, you animated offal, and I split you like a goose. Back off! Let the poor idiot alone."

"I am the Prince of Wales," Edward insisted to his protector as he took a back-to-back stance with him.

"Yes," sighed the other, "and I am Ivan the Terrible." This was most frustrating for the prince, who couldn't even convince a friend of his true identity, let alone an unfriendly mob.

"Back off!" the soldier growled at the ruffian and his ragtag contingent.

"Who's 'e to interfere?" shouted one withered crone.

"Sling 'em both in the horse pond!" cried another, brandishing a knobby wooden staff. The crowd stepped menacingly forward.

The cavalier's eyes were distracted by this surge and he did not notice the burly leader producing a long knife from his belt. Eying Edward's jeweled seal, he grinned at the cavalier and said, "You don't want it all to yourself, captain. Share an' share alike, eh? Come on now, we'll split with . . ."

As the cavalier's attention returned to the leader, a blackguard on his left struck him with a cudgel. The cavalier began to turn in that direction, but realized that this was probably a ruse to distract his eyes from the leader. He whirled around just in time to see that unmannerly lout removing his knife and lunging. The cavalier's rapier blazed across the space between them like a comet in the night sky, parrying the knife thrust. Then a perfectly executed lunge, and the leader keeled over, clutching his bowels.

The mob fell back a moment, gaping stupidly at their writhing hero, then surged forward shouting vengeance and brandishing ugly clubs, knives, and swords. The cavalier unsheathed a dagger from his belt and, making sure the boy stood close to his back, began parrying the assault with both hands, slicing with his rapier here, menacing with his knife there, and kicking a shin when able to. The prince marveled at the man's skill, remarking to himself that it was such men as this who accounted for the glory of England, and not the scum that now assailed him.

"Get to the wall!" the cavalier ordered.

The prince sprang to the wall, the cavalier closing the gap between them quickly, before the snarling curs could fill it and separate them. The cavalier's retreat was as magnificent as his attack, a noble display of thrusts, parries, slashes and cuffs with both hands, forearms and elbows that left three men stunned or wounded on the cobblestones. The cavalier seemed almost to be enjoying himself in this lopsided contest, and actually bellowed with merriment when one snapping assailant left himself wide open to an immense kick that sent him groaning to his knees, clutching his groin.

Glancing over his shoulder, the cavalier noted a stairway at their backs. "Down the steps—quick!" he instructed, removing his cloak and swirling it across half a dozen blades, fouling them momentarily.

Edward darted onto the steps, holding close to his protector as they inched along the balustrade, descending with painful slowness as the exchange of swords, knives, clubs, and curses continued, sending up an awful din. One opponent tackled him around the legs, and he almost lost his balance, but managed to disengage his legs while pinking another assailant in the shoulder.

However, he tripped over the body of the first, and, grasping for the balustrade, struck his knuckles against it and dropped his rapier. The savage mob bayed with delight like a pack of mad dogs closing in for the kill. The cavalier hovered over his sword, slashing with his dagger in the hope of creating an opportunity to pick up the weapon.

Out of the corner of his eye he saw the glint of a sword aimed at his throat and realized he'd neglected his left flank. In a fraction of a second all would be over and his blood would spill over the cobbles of a squalid London street.

But that moment never came. Something deflected that sword, and when the cavalier turned to see what it was he saw his young friend getting a lock on the attacker's arm, and indeed sapping the limb with furious strength. The boy then picked up the victim's sword and, with an expertise that amazed the cavalier, parried another thrust aimed at his protector's throat. The cavalier was now able to snatch his own fallen sword, and, shoulder to shoulder with this ragamuffin, took the offensive. The front of the attacking line crumbled and the whole mob fell back in disarray. The cavalier leaped to the bottom of the stairway, admiring the classic pose the boy struck as he executed the complex offensive and defensive tactics of swordsmanship as if tutored by an expert. He determined to ask the lad about this if they ever got out of this battle alive. But this was certainly not an appropriate time.

Observing the mob pause to regroup, he cried, "Now—run, boy!"

The boy took off like a hart, but one pursuer managed to

slip past the cavalier's guard and caught up with Edward.
The boy stopped in his tracks, whirled, and attacked with
the ease and grace of one raised from childhood with a
rapier in hand. The astonished attacker tripped over his
own feet and took a prick on the wrist for his troubles,
dropping his weapon. The boy now looked up at the rabble
seething on the steps, and all signs of his abjectness had
fled. His eyes glowed and his jaw thrust out in defiant
triumph. "Rabble! Traitors!" he cried, shaking his
weapon at them. "Only wait, and tomorrow I build a
gallows for you." He whipped his disarmed opponent in
the seat of the pants and the fellow went whimpering into
the night. "Aye, run!" Edward shouted after him. "But
my justice shall find you!"

The cavalier was a professional soldier, but every good
soldier lived by the maxim: Discretion is the better part of
valor. Turning to the boy, he said, "Meanwhile, may I
suggest we run ourselves?"

The boy seemed almost reluctant to flee, now that he
was in command of the situation. But that command, the
cavalier knew, was fleeting and illusory. As soon as the
mob got its second wind it would attack again. The boy
didn't realize it, but the trinket that dangled from his neck
(if it be genuine and not a paste imitation) was worth
hundreds of sovereigns, enough to feed every soul in that
crowd for a year. It was worth their risking life and limb to
secure it.

The cavalier nudged the boy, then hustled him off into
the night. "Gallow's bait!" the lad cried over his shoulder. "Carrion! Assault the prince, will you?"

The cavalier sighed loudly. Now that he had rescued
this pathetic, deluded little baggage—what on earth was
he going to do with him?

CHAPTER VI

Tom Canty stood in the chamber of the Prince of Wales, trembling so violently his teeth clacked like two pieces of ivory. He was alone, thank God, but just the brief skirmish he'd had with the Duke of Norfolk moments before had convinced Tom he would be crazy to remain another moment.

After the guards hustled the Prince of Wales out of the palace, the duke had stepped into the room where Tom stood in the prince's finery. Tom was certain the nobleman would take one look at him and cry, "Guards! We've arrested the wrong lad. Bring back the prince! Arrest this imposter!"

But the gentleman merely bowed deeply to Tom and said, "Good evening to your royal highness." As the sounds of the prince's struggles echoed through the corridor, Norfolk glanced out, then looked apologetically at Tom. "A small commotion, of no matter. I trust your grace was not disturbed?"

Tom opened his mouth to speak, but even if he'd been capable of uttering a sound at that moment, he realized that his voice and cockney accent would certainly give him away. He therefore gave a helpless little gesture. Whereupon the duke bowed again and retreated, never turning his back upon Tom, a form which the boy allowed was as peculiar as anything he'd ever witnessed. 'Twas a wonder that the king's courtiers weren't perpetually bumping into each other, scurrying about hind-end first in the presence of the royal family, he thought.

As the duke retreated, Tom acknowledged his bows with awkward little bows and nods of his own, then closed the door and collapsed against it, bursting into a fit of the shakes which threatened to unhinge his very bones.

It must have been fifteen minutes before the quake subsided and Tom was able to think clearly and determine what he must do.

What he must do, naturally, was get the devil out of the palace as soon as possible. The logical thing was to bluff his way out, striding confidently out into the corridor while guards and courtiers bowed and scraped, and simply step out through the gates and into the night.

But there were two things wrong with that plan. First and foremost, Tom had no confidence whatever in his ability to bring it off successfully. Having observed the prince's regal bearing, Tom couldn't imagine anyone believing that this clumsy, quivering, terrified waif was the Prince of Wales. Surely someone would stop him and engage him in conversation and determine instantly that something was wrong.

For a second thing, once Tom did manage to get through the gates, he would have to face the crowd of beggars that forever huddled outside the palace walls. How would they react to the sight of one clad in silks and satins, dainty slippers and delicate embroidery and gorgeous plumes? Most likely they'd tear the clothes off his back, and perhaps rend him limb from limb to boot.

He stepped in front of the looking glass and a hot flush of embarrassment sent a tide of crimson flooding up Tom's throat and suffusing his cheeks. How often had he imagined himself in this very role, posturing before his little mates, declaiming nobly in rounded tones as his mentor, Father Andrew, had taught him to do. But now that he confronted the reality of it, he had no desire but to flee.

He must act quickly before his imposture was discovered. Stepping away from the looking glass over the fireplace, he snapped his fingers as a way out occurred to him. He tossed his cap away, then cast off the ermine-lined cloak.

He had just begun struggling with his shirt, cursing the fool who had designed it to fasten at the back (and realizing at the same time that it was not designed for a prince to don by himself), when there was a respectful knock at the door. A wave of panic went through Tom, and he yanked his shirt until the fasteners tore. Then he stripped out of his pantaloons and silk stockings.

A second knock, and Tom dove headlong for the fireplace, trying to get a toe- and fingerhold on the smooth glazed bricks. A shower of soot settled over his head and shoulders as the door opened and the prince's chamberlain, De Brie, walked into the room.

"Your highness!" he gasped, blinking.

Tom gave up his efforts to ascend the chimney and crept miserably out onto the hearth. "No, I'm not," he said, defeated.

"Highness?"

"I'm not what you think," said Tom. "I mean, I'm not the Prince . . . of . . . Wales. I'm a pauper." He opened his hands in a lame gesture, gulped, and prepared to be delivered into the hands of the guards.

Behind De Brie, several servants stood awaiting his orders. He and they exchanged puzzled looks. De Brie picked up a pomander, sniffed its perfume, and stared once again at this bewildering spectacle.

Then the chamberlain realized what this charade signified. Beaming sycophantically, he clapped his hands with delight. "A pauper! Indeed you are, royal highness! I see what it is—this is your improvised costume for the ball! Oh, a delightful conceit!"

Turning to the servants, he gestured with his hands for them to join in the applause. They followed their master's lead as De Brie returned to his young charge. "Oh, but in exquisite taste! Such felicity of . . . ah, arrangement." He touched Tom's sooty sleeve gingerly. "Truly authentic!" Then, dabbing Tom's sooty cheek with a wet finger, he said, "Your highness permits?" and marked a streak on Tom's face, stepping back to admire the effect.

"Such divine squalor," the effeminate churl swooned. "Not that your highness can ever look anything other than truly royal, but . . . the masque has already begun, and His Majesty waits." He fluttered a hand at the doorway, and a servant opened the door, bowing deeply.

"But you don't understand," Tom protested. "I'm not the prince!"

Tom's protest fell on ears as deaf as his royal counterpart's had outside the gates of the palace. "But of course not!" De Brie said archly, winking at the servants. "A mere pauper. But of such a truly *ragged* royalty. Lead on there!" he ordered the servants. "Make way for his highness!" He bowed, the servants bowed, and Tom, as if listening to the whisper of the executioner's axe, skulked miserably out of his chamber.

CHAPTER VII

Preceded by the dainty De Brie, Tom and his entourage of servants wound their way through the cavernous corridors of Westminster Palace; Tom averted his eyes from greetings of uniformed and powdered servants and guards at every turn.

As they rounded a corner Tom heard the strains of music and the shuffle of dancing feet, and presently was led into the Great Hall of the palace, a room so grand Tom could not comprehend what prevented the vaulted ceiling from collapsing. It was lit by countless candles that illuminated the room almost as bright as day. Hundreds of brilliantly dressed lords and ladies swirled majestically around the floor in measured, stately steps.

Tom stood almost paralyzed at the entrance absorbing a scene almost beyond his comprehension, beyond any tale Father Andrew had ever told, beyond any story he'd ever read, beyond any dream he'd ever dreamed. It was impossible for the lad to grasp that a mere few hours earlier he had been mingling happy-go-lucky through the crowds of fellow peasants in the marketplace. Had not De Brie supported him at one elbow he surely would have collapsed.

After a few minutes the dancing ceased and a silver-haired nobleman bade the throng to turn its respectful attention to a raised platform where the masque was about to be performed. A hush descended and the assembled courtiers pressed around the stage to witness the evening's entertainment.

Presently some twenty young men and women garbed in fantastic costumes representing nymphs, satyrs, gods and goddesses of myth and history, danced out upon the stage and sang a song accompanied by a little band of flautists, mandolin players, drummers, and a tiny lad shaking a tambourine. The song, as far as Tom was able to hear it, was a celebration of the descent from the heavens of the Goddess of the Cloud.

Just as the song was almost finished, the goddess actually did ascend from the scaffolding above the stage, a vision of truly divine loveliness, the most beautiful girl Tom had ever seen. From the murmurs and applause Tom gathered that this was one Lady Jane Grey. She sat on a wooden platform slung on pulleys and decorated with brightly painted silks and back-cloths, forming a sort of silver throne. Several handmaidens, almost as lovely as their mistress, paid obeisance to her in mute accolades.

On a sumptuous couch set on a raised dais, King Henry sat at an angle, his bandaged leg held in the lap of a pretty maid of honor. At his foot sat a gaily garbed jester, clapping his hands in rhythm to the music. At the king's side sat the Princess Elizabeth, a happy smile on her face, for she loved dancing and entertainment as much as her father.

The corners of Henry's mouth were pulled down in a frown. "The flutes are all flat," he growled to his younger daughter. "I could blow better notes on a rusty kettle." Elizabeth moved as if to do something about the discord, for her father was a splendid musician and was physically pained by disharmony or poorly tuned instruments. He had once half-joked that he could tolerate a treasonous minister, but never a musician with a poor ear.

"No, let it be," he said, restraining Elizabeth. "They know no better nowadays. Modern musicians! Ha! Modern mountebanks!"

"It was very different in your majesty's young day," the princess said dutifully.

"By God, it was!" he roared, eyes lighting with happy memories. "We knew how to carry a tune in the old days."

The king returned his attention to the performance, but soon his eyes shifted to the sight of the Duke of Norfolk, mingling with some courtiers on the far side of the floor. From him, Henry's look jumped to Hertford, who stood not far from Norfolk watching his majesty's eyes like a faithful dog awaiting his master's command. Henry gave the command with a nod so subtle that only he and Hertford were aware anything had transpired between them. Hertford inclined his head ever-so-gently, then motioned to two yeoman warders, who sidled behind the unsuspecting Norfolk.

Lady Jane's platform had not completely descended to the floor when Henry made a sign to the Master of the Music, who abruptly waved his hands. The music died as if a blanket had descended upon the players. The king then nodded at a minstrel in the gallery, who in a sweet high voice sang a song the king himself had composed for the occasion. Except for Hertford and his co-conspirator St. John, no one other than the king himself realized the treacherous double meaning of the lyrics:

> "The hunt is up, the hunt is up,
> And it is well-nigh day.
> And Harry our king is gone hunting,
> To bring a deer to bay."

Just as the minstrel finished his song, Hertford clapped his hand on Norfolk's shoulder. "In the king's name," he declared.

For an instant Norfolk was so startled he jokingly said, "Henry, I believe." But the king's name was being used for a far more ominous purpose and, as the wardens took their place at each elbow, Norfolk realized what was happening and gave a resigned sigh. "Oh, you are arresting me. Well, I have been at the court of the Tudors for forty years, so I suppose it is about my turn. May I ask, on what charge?"

"High treason, my lord," Hertford replied sternly.

"How flattering. With a belted earl to arrest me, a guard of yeomen to convey me to the Tower—and thereafter, to the block? These are royal honors."

"Sir?" said Hertford, eyebrows knitted in puzzlement.

"I thought such distinguished treatment was reserved

for his majesty's unfortunate wives.'' He turned and
bowed deeply toward the king, who regarded the arrested
man with a baleful smile. Norfolk has served him well,
but like so many other loyal men (and women—thus his
reference to Henry's wives), he had been caught up in
treacherously shifting political winds, and at last they had
snapped him like an old tree that no longer bends for the
breeze.

"And Harry our king is gone hunting,
To bring a deer to bay,"
the minstrel repeated as Norfolk pivoted and, with a pleasant nod to the courtiers, allowed himself to be led out
peaceably. Many of the courtiers dropped their eyes in
shame. Close to him as they were, they dared not express
compassion while the gimlet eye of the king was upon
them: that way led to the Tower.

This inconvenient matter arranged with a minimum of
fuss, Henry settled back in his couch and signaled for the
musicians to take up the tune, and for the masque to
continue. Caressing the neck of the maid of honor supporting his lame foot, he breathed harder when his eyes fixed
lustfully on Lady Jane. Her platform at last descended to
the floor of the stage. The song was concluded and the
players took their bows. Henry thumped the couch in avid
appreciation.

Lady Jane glided off the stage, helped by two maidens,
and was escorted to the beckoning king. "Well performed, my child," he said, eyes twinkling in an expression that was something considerably warmer than paternal. "Come, a pretty goddess need not stand on her divine
dignity with a king." He grasped her arm with a bearlike
paw and hauled her roughly to his lips for a noisy kiss on
the cheek. She smiled with mock gratification, but managed gracefully to duck away and hide behind Elizabeth,

who eyed her father rather caustically. She knew what a lustful brute he was, a man who did not discriminate between young and old, pretty and ugly, friend or even blood relative when his blood boiled with passion.

Henry now tossed his head from side to side. "And where's the Prince of Wales?" he bellowed.

St. John stepped out of the crowd of fawning courtiers and stooped to whisper in his ear. Henry's eyes widened. "As a pauper, you say? In rags?" He let out a guffaw. "D'ye hear that, Bess? Our sober-sided Edward! No! But this I must see!"

"Then look, your majesty, and see indeed!" Elizabeth said grandly, pointing at the great door.

All eyes turned to the great door where Tom stood, flat-footed and fatuous, gaping at the awesome assembly. His clothes were shredded and filthy with soot from his attempt to clamber up the chimney. His drooping mouth and awe-rounded eyes gave him an idiotic aspect, and there were murmurs of "Perfect!" and "Brilliantly conceived!" as the crowd parted for his entrance. "He couldn't be better if he'd been a pauper all his life," one courtier whispered to another.

Tom stood stone-still before the alley the throng had opened up for him; he required a nudge by De Brie to begin forward motion. De Brie skipped and minced in front of him, clapping his hands in exultation, taking credit for the "prince's" costume.

Tom staggered forward half a dozen steps, then stopped, as if his slippers had been filled with lead. He trembled violently. His heart thundered like an immense drum.

King Henry stared at him in amazement. Princess Elizabeth shook her head. Lady Jane gazed with love and admiration ablaze in her eyes.

Somehow Tom found the strength to lift his legs. He ran

the rest of the way to the king's couch and threw himself upon his knees, hands outstretched in a gesture of supplication.

"Your majesty—I am *not* the Prince of Wales."

Henry continued to stare in wonder, and from the crease in his brow and the curl of his lip, it was clear that Henry was considering if this declaration was true. His eyes narrowed to a squint, and Tom could feel the king's eyes penetrating to his very soul. Then a grin broke on the king's face. His great body began to heave with laughter. His mouth twisted obscenely and gusts of evil breath swept over the poor boy. In moments the laughter had spread throughout the assembly as the courtiers, eager to please their king, took up his cue.

Henry guffawed so heartily that tears came to his eyes. "You never looked less like him, truly! Get up, boy! Get up, before I do myself a mischief! Come here."

Tom approached nervously, and flinched when the king reached out to ruffle his hair. The king's hand was more like a bear's paw than a human appendage.

"Oh, a very proper pauper, on my soul. I never doubted your intelligence, Ned, but I never suspected you had wit! As ragged a rascal . . ." The king's mirthful laughter brought on a fit of hacking coughing, and he wheezed for a minute before recovering. "But such a peacock must lead the ball, eh, Lady Jane? Will the goddess dance a galliard with the pauper?"

Lady Jane was positively radiant to be thrown together with the prince in this fashion. "Very gladly, sire," she said, expressing but a fraction of what she felt in her heart.

"But I cannot dance the galliard," Tom protested. "I don't know how . . ."

"To be sure!" said Henry, wagging his head. "What pauper does? Go on, boy!"

Tom took Lady Jane's hand like a man in a trance. She led him to the floor, her silver raiment catching every candle's glitter and reflecting it a thousand-fold. Henry chuckled, but Princess Elizabeth looked slightly puzzled and a bit concerned. She thought she knew her brother well, but apparently there was a side of him making its debut this evening, for she did not think him capable of extending a prank this long. Surely any moment now he would stop this oafish clowning and assume once more the dignified identity of the Prince of Wales.

But no, he carried the sham out ot the dance floor, where he made a dreadful hash of the lively, chicken-like steps of the galliard. Where Lady Jane led him left, he went right; where right, he went left. Several times he tripped over her feet or tripped her over his. Naturally, the king thought this the jolliest entertainment imaginable, and the toady-like courtiers joined him in gales of hilarity. Part of the dance was to swing Lady Jane off the ground, but Tom performed this maneuver so poorly he almost dropped her on her noble behind.

Lady Jane smiled through her teeth, but it was clear that she, like Elizabeth, had begun to think the joke had gone too far. The mockery reached its climax when Tom made one last effort to swing her off her feet. He missed his hold and fell sprawling at the king's feet. The king's stomach quivered like a bowlful of suet, and tears streamed down his eyes. "Enough, pauper. Ye dance like a pregnant pig. We've seen your galliard—what next?"

Next! Tom said to himself. They expect a *next*? His mind worked feverishly to produce something to satisfy the king's expectations.

"Er . . . um . . . Gathering Peasecods, your majesty?"

King Henry leaned forward, eyebrows knit together in perplexity. "Gathering *what*?"

"Peasecods, sire. It's a country dance—of the common people," said Tom.

"The hidden talents of the Prince of Wales!" the king said good-naturedly. "Well, to it, then. Master of the Music! Strike up . . . Gathering Codpieces, or whatever it is."

The Master of the Music, a red-faced man in shiny satin pantaloons and ruffled jacket in the French style, looked blankly at his musicians, who in turn looked sheepishly at each other, then at their leader. Then one of them, the little boy with the tambour, dredged up from memory a little melody he'd heard in a marketplace once, and after hastily conferring with his colleagues, he led them in a lively dance in round form.

Here Tom was at home, and he launched into the dance with a vengeance, clapping and stamping and completely forgetting where he was. The courtiers looked confused and astonished, and not a little embarrassed to be witnessing so plebian a dance. Henry, noting this, decided it would be great sport if the rest of the court joined in, and he made a gesture with his hand for some of the noblemen and ladies to join in. This they did with pained looks and groans, and Henry launched into another fit of coughing laughter as the courtiers blundered through their steps.

Meanwhile, Tom had expertly initiated Lady Jane into the mysteries of Gathering Peasecods, and a pretty sight they made. Tom, ecstatic, forgot where he was and led Lady Jane masterfully around the floor while those courtiers who had not joined them stood in a circle clapping their hands in rhythm.

King Henry clapped loudest of all, but suddenly his laughter tailed off into spasmodic coughing, and he clutched his heart, gasping. Princess Elizabeth was the only one to note the king's seizure, and kneeled at his feet, clutching his hand and asking what she might do to relieve

his distress. After a moment Henry's pain-contorted neck
and facial muscles relaxed, and he nodded for the ball to
continue.

On the floor, as the dance ended, Lady Jane bowed at
Tom, her eyes filled with laughter and adoration. The
courtiers, who had finally mastered the dance, applauded
and shouted vociferously, and when one of them cried,
"God bless the Prince of Wales!" the shout was taken up
around the great room and was soon on the lips of every
Englishman in it.

"God bless the Prince of Wales! *God bless the Prince
of Wales!* GOD BLESS THE PRINCE OF WALES!"
they cried.

Suddenly the glow faded from Tom's face, and that
haggard, haunted, hunted look came back into his eyes.

"But I am *not* the Prince of Wales!" he sighed.

CHAPTER VII

"But I *am* the Prince of Wales!" Edward sighed,
perhaps precisely at the moment that his counterfeit in the
Westminster Palace was protesting the very opposite.

Edward stood in the middle of his rescuer's poorly
furnished room at an inn off London Bridge. The furniture
was almost monastic in its austerity and simplicity: a small
truckle bed, a rude wooden table, two sturdy stools, and a
wooden stand none too steady, on which rested a cracked
basin. A couple of candlesticks held blunt waxen stubs,
one of which the cavalier had lit upon their breathless
entrance into the room. The candle crackled and sputtered
and emitted a sooty, noxious smoke.

"Oh, to be sure you are," said the cavalier, humoring

Edward. Tired but stimulated by their fight with the mob, Edward sat on the edge of the bed, studying the man who had come to his aid. It was difficult to place him accurately, for though he was well-spoken and bore himself like a gentleman, his clothes were almost as worn and shabby as a beggar's. His cloak was patched, and the feather in his hat was broken and stuck out at a ridiculous angle, like a ship's mast that has taken a cannonball at its base.

Despite this unkempt condition, the man definitely had dignity, a quality Edward admired. Unfortunately, the cavalier had a sense of humor too, one Edward did not admire as much, particularly when it was used at his expense, as the cavalier had been doing since their escape.

"And this other fellow," the cavalier said, "the one you say fell so obligingly from your royal chimney so that you could change clothes with him—who's he?"

"I'm not sure," Edward said, resentful of the teasing tone in his friend's question. "Ranty—Shanty—no, it was Canty. Tom Canty, a thief, he said, from Offal Court, wherever that is."

"Offal Court is in Smithfield. Or used to be," the gentleman said, musing with chin in hand. "Then what?"

"Then? Then we were mistaken, one for the other, and the guards seized me . . ." Edward brought the memory sharply into focus, and his lips began quivering. ". . . and they beat me! They beat *me*! And flung me into the street!"

Now that he was safe, he could endure the humiliation no more. The floodgates of misery opened and he began to sob into his hands. "And there . . . you came."

The cavalier started to get to his feet to comfort the lad, but decided to let him purge his unhappiness. At length the wracking sobs abated. The boy sniffed, wiped his eyes, and blinked. "But it is a nightmare. I must wake . . . before I go mad."

"Yes," said his companion, sliding a mug of ale across the table. "Drink. It's the best medicine I know for an overheated imagination—or lunacy."

Edward pounded the table so hard the mug jumped up in the air, sloshing ale on both of them. "I am not a lunatic. I am the prince!"

"Of course," the gentleman said, trying hard not to condescend.

Edward looked up at him ruefully. "You—you, who-ever you are . . ."

"Miles Hendon. Soldier," the cavalier said with a mock flourish, as if indeed presenting himself before a true prince.

"If you don't believe me, then why did you rescue me from that rabble?" Edward asked. "What was I to you? What profit could you hope for, risking yourself for me? Unless you *knew* I was the prince?"

Miles Hendon regarded the lad steadily, admiring the boy's amazingly gifted performance even as he pitied him his delusion. "That is certainly royal reasoning," Hendon replied. "I saw one man—standing up. Alone, unarmed, not afraid, saying what he believed. It was all one to me whether he was Emperor of China or a moonstruck mad-man." He poured himself some more ale and raised his mug in a good-humored toast. "Health."

Edward scowled. "You do not sit in my presence."

Hendon's brows knit sharply over the rim of his mug, then he slapped the table impatiently. Leaning menacingly across it, he fixed the prince with a squinting gaze as if spitting him on a sword. "Now look you, my master. I am not a patient man but you saved my life, when I was down on the steps. And who keeps steel out of Miles Hendon wins a friend for life. But do not presume on my friendship," he said, dropping his voice to a sinister growl. "Telling me I may not sit in my own room in my own lodging or stopping my ears with drivel about being a prince will not preserve my amicability. God save the mark! D'ye see?"

But the boy was vexingly persistent. "But I *am* Edward, Prince of Wales. Look." He reached under his shift and produced the seal, waggling it in Hendon's face. Its jeweled crust caught the glint of the candle and sprayed golden beams around the walls and ceiling of the rude room. "Do you not know proof when you see it?"

Hendon batted it away with an impatient hand. "I told you to keep that damned thing out of sight," he said angrily. Then, suddenly, he took it in hand; he fingered it, examining it more closely. He'd wondered if perhaps it was imitation, cunningly wrought by a master artificer. But no, this was the real thing or his name wasn't Miles Hendon. "You could swing ten times over for this. Where did you get it?"

"It is the Prince of Wales's seal," Edward answered forthrightly.

"Then the sooner you give it back, the better," Hendon answered, just as forthrightly. "Or lose it. Don't tell me how you came by it." He rose from the table and paced around the little room, visibly annoyed. "Ah, but wait. This amazing fellow who sprang out of your palace chimney—Tom Canty?—was a thief, I recall. Well, Master Canty, you may lie here tonight, but tomorrow you go back to Offal Court, and take your daydreams with you." Edward opened his mouth to argue, but Hendon, almost violently, declared, "That is what I said. And on my oath, that's where I'll take you!"

Edward stared at him angrily for a long moment. If only

this varlet believed him, he'd fall to his knees and kiss his very rags begging for mercy. But Edward had exhausted his arguments: if Hendon did not even believe the seal, then nothing else he could say would make a difference.

"I am very tired," Edward said, an immense weariness all but overwhelming him. "And I ache. I shall sleep." He got up from the table, crossed to the bed, and lay down. It was hard as an oak plank compared to the downy delight of his bed at the palace. Yet such was his exhaustion that he could feel sleep sweeping over him even now. He waggled a finger imperiously at Miles Hendon. "You will sleep across the doorway, since I have no other guards. With your sword drawn."

Hendon's jaw dropped. Leaping to his feet, he came around the table and marched to the bed, as if to pounce on the "prince" and toss him unmannerly on his royal rump. "Will I, by God!" he snarled. But he stopped abruptly. The poor beggar was already asleep. Out of his mind or not, the child had been through a terrible ordeal and it would scarcely be meet to kick him out of bed. The soldier cocked his head, frowning thoughtfully. His eye fell on the seal, which lay partially exposed around the boy's neck. Hendon reached down and fingered it, musing. Then he shrugged. "Mad as a hatter." He reached for his doublet and spread it over the ragamuffin. "Poor friendless little rat."

Retreating backwards from the bed, Hendon bowed. "Good night, your ragged highness."

As Hendon was spreading his cloak on the floor to sleep upon, the boy muttered sleepily, "Good night." Hendon glanced up sharply, then lay down on his cloak after snuffing the candle. He too was quite worn out with the evening's swordplay, but just as his eyes were closing like vault doors, the boy, in sleep-slurred voice, spoke again.

"Master Hendon?"

Hendon rolled away with his back to the boy and ignored him. But the child persisted.

"Master Hendon?"

"Yes?" Hendon sighed.

"Your clothes are very shabby, but sometimes you talk
like a gentleman. What are you?"

"A soldier," Hendon intoned drowsily. "Of fortune."

"Ah, that probably explains your barrack-room manners," said the lad, making Hendon clench and unclench
his fists. "Still, you have shown me great kindness. For
your brave service, is there any honor that I, Edward
Tudor, can bestow on you?"

Hendon shook his head disgustedly, fed up with the
lad's lunatic delusions. "One thing, if 'your highness'
will be so kind," he said, knowing the boy would not be
able to see his satirical grin in the dark. "Since I detest
discomfort, may I and my heirs forever be granted the
privilege of sitting down in the presence of English
royalty—and dropping off to sleep if necessary?"

"It is a great deal to ask," Edward said sleepily, "but it
is granted."

Hendon rolled his eyes and sighed as he settled as
comfortably as he could in his cloak. Then his eyes
blinked open. He frowned, sat up, and reached for his
sword. Glancing at the bed, he sighed and shook his head
at his own folly.

Then he lay down and, naked sword clasped upon his
chest, fell soundly asleep.

CHAPTER VIII

The next day found the king in one of his awe-inspiring dudgeons, the tremors of which were felt, if not actually heard, in the remotest corners of the palace. In addition to suffering from the usual effects of overindulgence in wine and food, he had suffered another of the heart seizures that had been plaguing him of late. Though he would not admit it to himself, it was quite clear to everyone else including his doctors that he would not last long if he did not modify his wanton appetites.

But what had fouled Henry's mood above all was the information that had reached him that his son Prince Edward had continued his charade of the night before, and was not only insisting he was not the Prince of Wales but was behaving in a manner that gave credence to these denials. It was one thing to pretend to be some Smithfield pauper at a masque; quite another to carry this affectation over to the morning.

It first came to the attention of a lowly page, who had found "the prince" cowering under his bed when he'd come to bathe and dress his highness. The page had shrugged and, as ordered, retreated from his highness's chambers and closed the door, but the moment he'd left he'd told the other pages who stood outside bearing the prince's clothes and breakfast. They in turn had spread the news to guards, maids, kitchen help, servants, butlers, and the rest of the help, so that within hours the palace staff was abuzz with the rumor that the prince was, to use their expression, "orf 'is noggin."

Princess Elizabeth had then entered the prince's

chamber, and she too had found the boy trembling like a
whipped puppy under his bed. Hauling him forth by his
shirtfront, she'd asked him the meaning of his behavior
and been treated to the sort of denials Tom had been
making all day before. But whereas it was meet for him to
do so in costume, it was most peculiar indeed for him to
carry on so in the light of morning.

She had summoned Edward's doctor, and several
noblemen including Hertford and St. John had attended
the physician's examination of the boy. They all shook
their heads. Not only did Edward persist in his claim to be
someone named Tom Canty of Offal Court, but actually
imitated the behavior of a street urchin to perfection. That
was a grave sign, for it was one thing to *pretend* to be
someone you were not, but quite another to *believe* you
were someone else, and believe it so thoroughly that you
actually absorbed into your brain the modes of speech and
behavior of that other soul.

There was a remedy for the former—oft as not a good
spanking would make children who were overzealous in
their make-believe games return to their true identities.
But for the latter there was no remedy, as it symptomized a
condition of. . . .

The doctor bit his tongue, and Elizabeth and the nobles
in attendance clapped their hands on their ears so as not to
hear the awful word uttered. But someone had to say it,
and finally the doctor, realizing that he was putting his
own head in jeopardy, issued the diagnosis with a rasping
voice.

Madness.

Madness! The word spread through court as rapidly as
it had done through the servants' quarters. Luckily it
stopped short of the king's door: the Duke of Hertford had
forbidden mention of it to the king until a committee of
lords had had an opportunity to examine the lad and

interview him closely. For hours they had questioned and
cross-questioned him as if he were a spy or thief or heretic,
but he was so forceful in his denials, and so consistent in
speech and behavior, that they had to confirm the doctor's
conclusions.

For another hour they debated the best way to break the
news to the king, and who among them, to quote the
ancient children's story, would "bell the cat." Fortunately, or perhaps unfortunately, this proved unnecessary,
for the gossip had reached the king's ears anyway. He had
roared like a wounded lion for his son, and demanded that
his trusted Hertford and St. John, his doctor, and several
other courtiers and servants produce themselves in his
chambers in one minute or it would go very poorly for
them, however high-born they might be. When they'd
finally assembled before him, they'd stammered and stut-
tered, looking at one another dumbly like cattle. The king
was sprawled on a couch and, despite his fine gown and
robe, looked very poorly indeed. His red beard was
streaked with grey, his rosy cheeks were drawn and their
flesh loose, and great blue pockets hung under the man's
red eyes like the fleshy rings under a hound's. His breathing came in great wheezes, and his breath, for those
unlucky enough to get that close to him, was vile and
rancid, the product of some internal indisposition having
to do with diet, the doctor had said. Henry's bad leg was
bandaged and lay upon a hassock, and one could plainly
see how much pain it gave the king to move it so much as
an inch.

It was to this ill-tempered, dangerous creature that one
among them was to state that the Prince of Wales, the heir
Henry had longed for so desperately that he'd overturned a
religion and sent countless good souls, including his own
wives, to their dooms—was out of his mind.

At length Hertford had the fortitude to mutter something delicately introducing the diagnosis, whereupon the king exploded with rage. "Not the prince? Not the prince? Do I not know my own son?" he ranted. Pointing a pudgy finger at the boy standing timidly by the window, Henry's face grew apoplectically red. "Is he not there, before my own eyes? And will you humor him in his wild tale that he is an imposter? D'ye mean me mad then, that I do not know my own flesh and blood?"

"No sire," Hertford cautiously allowed, "*your majesty's* mind is clear enough. We have spent some . . . four hours now? . . . in fruitless persuasion. There stands the prince, but he denies himself, even to your majesty." He took a deep breath and stole a glance at his cohort St. John, who nodded encouragement. "At first," Hertford continued, "I confess I thought he played with us—a poor and cruel joke. But it is not in his nature. No, it is no joke."

"What then?" the king demanded.

In the long interval that ensued, Hertford looked at St. John and St. John at the doctor and the doctor at Hertford, and they all looked at Tom, each waiting for the other to speak, knowing that the king's rage could reach such a state as to cost them their heads.

Finally Hertford came out with it. "My lord, your son is . . . mad."

Henry's eyes rounded like great buttons, and had his chest not been suddenly constricted by a violent seizure, God only knows what terrible curses would have issued from his lips. Instead he coughed and sputtered, "No! No!"

"There is no other conclusion, sire," Hertford continued, taking advantage of the king's momentary inability to speak. "Dr. Buttes tells me that such delusions have been known before, men one day as sane as you or I, and the next . . ."

The king at last caught his breath, and his ire was magnificent. "The Devil damn Dr. Buttes and all of you. I'll not have it! My son? Heir to England, and you call him mad?"

Hertford, at jeopardy of his neck, pushed on. "My king, there is no other way. What else?"

The king's fury reached speechlessness, and the doctor, despite the poor favor in which he found himself with the king, moved to offer relief to his majesty, who looked as if he were about to choke on his own bile. Then the king slumped, his rage deflating like a punctured bladder. Miserably, he said, "How do I know? No, Hertford, no—call him yet again, let me talk with him."

All eyes focused on the boy standing by the window. "Your highness?" said Hertford.

"The prince" turned to face them, despair written in his sunken eyes. "I am not highness, sir."

Hertford gestured for the boy to come before the king, and this Tom did with utmost reluctance. He dropped to his knees before the couch, glancing at the awful sick leg trussed up on the hassock next to him.

Henry, face ravaged with grief, stared at him and in a voice so quiet that Tom could not believe it came from the same mouth that had bellowed just instants before, said, "Ned, my child—you know me?"

"Yes, sire," said Tom. "You are the king. But I am not your Ned. I am Tom."

"Ned or Tom, do I care?" sputtered the king. "It is your old dad, boy! You will not deny me? You will not break my heart?"

"I would not, sir. But I have told you, I am not the Prince of Wales. I am Tom Canty, a pauper. I would not be so cruel as to lie. I have told you how I came here, and how the prince went away—but no one will believe me." He looked around the room at the faces of the nobles and servants, on which were mingled pity, apprehension, perplexity and compassion. "Would I say I was a pauper if I were not?" Tom asked.

Hertford sighed. "Still the same story. He truly believes it, sire."

"Aye," Henry groaned, leaning back on his couch with eyes closed. For a long minute he remained thus, as if allowing his wreck of a body to absorb the impact of this blow. Then he opened one eye and squinted at the doctor. "Is there any hope?"

The doctor wagged his head and shrugged. "No one can say with certainty. I too believe his highness's brain is affected—by some strain, by overstudy, who knows? These delusions are often temporary. With rest and care, and kind treatment . . ."

The king slashed the air with his hand and exploded, "Have done!" He trembled like an oak leaf in a gale. He reached out for Tom. "Raise me! You, Ned, give me your shoulder, boy."

Tom stepped forward and the king managed to reach a sitting position, his bandaged leg still lying upon its hassock. The king embraced Tom, then separated the lad from his bosom and gripped him by the shoulders, gazing eye to eye at him. Then he turned to the others and glared. With great frightening wheezes, he made a declaration.

"Hear—all of you. This my son is mad, but it is not permanent. Overstudy has done it. There are too many books in this land. Even the scriptures are rhymed, sung and jangled in every alehouse. Away with his teachers!"

The courtiers and doctors looked at each other and gulped.

"Let him have sport and wholesome things, so that his health may come again. He is mad, but he is my son, and England's, and mad or sane, still shall he reign," the king pronounced nobly. He released Tom, and, suddenly overcome with weariness, the king waved him away almost disgustedly. Tom bowed and began to retreat, as did the others. Then the king raised his hand and spoke in an ominous growl so low all had to lean forward to hear.

"And mark this: whoever speaks of this . . . this illness of the prince's . . . is guilty of treason, and shall pay for it with his head. No one shall speak of it—not even the prince himself," the kind said, fixing the boy in his baleful gaze. "He will not deny his royalty. He will not call himself a pauper, or speak as a pauper speaks. Now go, all of you."

The assembled courtiers and servants removed themselves as rapidly as they could, except that Hertford and St. John lingered a moment to observe the king's condition. It was plainly very poor, and they exchanged mute glances that said what was generally known and feared throughout the palace: that the king's days were numbered. The king, unaware they were still present, was muttering as he breathed stertorously. "If he were a thousand times mad, yet is he Prince of Wales," Henry murmured. "Give me to drink!" St. John tiptoed back into the room, poured a goblet of wine for his majesty, placed it in his hand, and departed with Hertford.

They closed the door behind them and stood in the corridor watching as "the prince" joined De Brie, who made his usual elaborate fuss, and marched off with his other servants.

St. John put his head conspiratorially close to Hertford's. "Plainly, what d'you think?"

"Plainly, the king is near the end," replied Hertford. "The prince is mad, mad will mount the throne, and mad remain. God help England."

"Aye." St. John looked cautiously down both ends of the corridor. Seeing no other soul, he said at the bottom of his voice, "My lord, have you no . . . doubts?"

With equal circumspection, Hertford said, "Doubts, my lord? Go on—we are alone."

St. John now examined Hertford as if they were not the closest of friends; indeed, as if it had just occurred to St. John that in this day and age, the closest friends became the most treacherous enemies overnight, at one stroke of the king's capricious will.

"You are the prince's uncle, and have known him since birth. But . . . ah . . . it seems odd to me that this madness should have changed him so much. His walk, his speech, most of all his manner. Oh, he is the same, but these are . . . somehow different. He is less . . . less *princely* than he was. My lord, take no offense, but when I hear him swear he is not the prince . . ."

"My lord," said Hertford with a frosty voice, "that's treason."

"No, no, my lord, I meant no harm," stammered St. John. "I . . . I . . . I am doubtless wrong. No, indeed, I was at fault, I confess. Say nothing of it," he pleaded. His deepest fear, that he had misjudged Hertford, had materialized.

St. John drew a deep breath of relief when Hertford said, "I shall not. We must all forget such doubts. Think now—if he *were* an imposter, and swore he *was* the prince, that would be natural and reasonable. But would any imposter, accepted by king and court and everyone as the prince, *deny* his royalty, and claim to *be* an imposter?"

The reasoning was brilliant and unarguable. "Ahhhh . . . no," St. John said as he reflected on it. "No, no my lord," he said more forcefully as the compelling logic filtered into his mind.

"Precisely," Hertford said triumphantly. "Madness is . . . mad, and made up of strange contradictions and follies. Why, I knew a man once who swore his head was made of Spanish glass, and would suffer none to touch it in case it broke. Our prince is not as mad as that, and will recover. For he *is* the prince, and soon will be our king, even if in his own mind he is no more than a pauper.''

The two exchanged significant gazes, then parted, each deeply thrust in heavy thought. A madman for king!

The prince would need wise heads about him, if England was to survive this crisis at all.

CHAPTER IX

The following morning, Miles Hendon woke the boy at cockcrow. They dressed silently, except for an occasional wince as the lad accidentally bumped a spot on his body still tender from last night's affray. ''Tom Canty'' inquired as to where Miles was taking him, and the cavalier replied that he was taking him to his home in Offal Court. The boy protested violently that that was not his home, that Westminster Palace was, whereupon Hendon threatened to put the lad across his knee if he persisted in the same vein as the night before.

They broke fast with a simple meal of bread and jam and porridge, then proceeded to Smithfield, winding their way through the narrow, noisy, evil-smelling lanes until at last they came to Offal Court. Several little boys and girls, who had oft sat enthralled as Tom Canty wove one of his fantastic stories for them, shouted greetings at Edward, who awkwardly acknowledged them, feeling somewhat foolish and fraudulent. At the same time he observed that this Tom Canty must be well respected and liked here.

Just as they were about to inquire as to the whereabouts of the Canty home, a burly, unshaven man with yellow eyes stormed out of a door across the court, followed by a

tearful woman in frayed skirts and apron, obviously his
wife. He strode, almost charged, toward Edward, and
pinched him nastily on the ear. "Where the hell have you
been?" he ranted, face red as an apple. "Crawling in
some sewer, by the look of you. Or have you been rutting
after some slut in the stews?"

Edward whimpered and looked at Miles Hendon for
rescue. But Hendon stood uncertainly, for though he
would gladly risk his life against an unruly mob of stran-
gers, it was quite another thing to interfere with a father's
disciplining of his son.

"You dirty little ape!" Canty went on, tugging the
boy's head back and forth by the ear. "You want to break
your mother's heart?" The woman now caught up to her
husband and began sobbing uncontrollably at the sight of
her son. "Sharrup!" Canty barked at her. He pulled the
boy's face close to his own. "I told you to bring me five
shillings by supper. Well, you missed it, but you're just in
time for breakfast. Nipper!"

Canty looked up to a balcony overlooking Offal Court,
where a loathesome creature with cropped ears, a henchman in Canty's gang of thieves, tossed a coiled whip down
to his master. Canty caught it, unfurled the braided leather
thong, and drew back to strike the cowering child. But
when he tugged on the handle, nothing happened. The
whip seemed to have been snared on something.

He turned to discover the tip of the lash held by a shabby
gentleman with soldier's cloak, heavy boots, and a hat
with a broken feather. "Is this your son?" he quietly
asked Canty.

"I'm his father, whatever business that may be of
yours," Canty growled.

"My business is with his welfare, which is why I am
restoring him to the bosom of his loving family," an-

swered Hendon, putting a somewhat ironic emphasis on
the word "loving". "I think he is a little mad—which is
no wonder." Hendon quickly surveyed Offal Court and its
disreputable inhabitants. "But even if he is your son, he is
no common boy. So—look you use him kindly." This last
he addressed to Canty with a throaty rumble of warning,
like a lion protecting its cub.

Canty squinted at this impertinent stranger, then jerked
the lash free. "I'll use the bastard as he deserves—so look
you mind your own affairs!"

He swung the whip at Edward, who managed to spring
just beyond the range of its hissing tip. Hendon pounced
on the man and, with an astonishing display of brawn,
hurled him bodily through the air atop a rickety shed,
which collapsed in a shower of splinters. Canty attempted
to struggle to his feet, but took a boot toe in the face for his
troubles.

"Kindly, I said, remember?" Hendon reminded him,
wagging a finger at him. With which he kicked Canty in
the face once again, sending him flying back into the
remnants of the shed. Hendon then raised his hat politely
to Mother Canty and turned away.

But he had misjudged the blackguard. A rusty pair of
tongs whistled past his ear, and he whirled to find Canty,
mouth bleeding, gamely circling him, looking for a soft
spot to attack. "Nipper!" he roared, holding a hand up.
Canty's henchman flung down a broad-bladed shortsword
from the balcony, which Canty caught deftly.

The sight of a blade usually was instant provocation for
Miles Hendon to draw his rapier, but as this was Tom
Canty's father, Hendon felt it would not be meet to run the
fellow through, however worthless he may be. Hendon
therefore backed away unarmed, hoping to reason with his
antagonist. His antagonist, meanwhile, had snatched up a

billet of wood and was advancing on Hendon with both
weapons raised menacingly. "Go to bed, friend," Hendon advised him.

"I'll give you a bed, bully!" Canty said, lunging at him
with his sword. Adroitly Hendon caught the blade in his
cloak, grasped Canty's other wrist, stepped in and slapped
Canty right and left quickly, then leveled him with a
tremendous blow to the chin.

But now Nipper and two more of Canty's rabble came
tumbling out of their houses with swords and clubs, and
rushed at Hendon. The cavalier sighed. Two fights with
riffraff within twelve hours was rather tiresome, but what
could one do? If they insisted, he had to oblige them, did
he not? Drawing his rapier and dagger, he said to Mother
Canty, "Good wife, we shall need bandages and hot water
presently." But as the ruffians bore down on him, Hendon
realized he would have his hands full. This Canty fellow
apparently employed ex-soldiers who knew a thing or two
about holding their own in a quarrel. "Ah—clean bandages for *me*," he smiled at Mother Canty.

Then he flourished his rapier just as one of the ruffians
hurled himself at Hendon's chest. The tip of Hendon's
weapon punctured the man's arm, sending him staggering
with a yelp against a wall. Hendon spun away from him
and engaged Nipper and the third cutthroat, but now Canty
himself was back in the fray, bellowing "Kill the bastard!
Diccon, come at his back!" As Canty and Nipper closed
with Hendon, keeping him well occupied, the weasly cur
known as Diccon slipped behind, looking for an opportunity to run the cavalier through.

For the second time, however, Edward gallantly came
to Hendon's assistance, leaping on Diccon and clinging to
his neck. Spying this out of the corner of his eye, Hendon
lunged violently at his two opponents, driving them back

long enough for Hendon to turn to take care of Diccon. "Out of the way, boy!"

But Edward's body shielded Diccon from a proper sword thrust by Hendon, and Hendon realized he must once again occupy himself with his other two opponents. But it was too late. Canty had leaped nimbly back after his retreat, and struck Hendon a vicious blow on the skull with his billet of wood. At almost precisely the same moment, Diccon fetched Edward a knock on the pate with the handle of his sword. The boy wobbled dazedly out of the fight, and was quickly attended to by Mother Canty.

Hendon was in a poor spot now. He had lost his rapier after the conk on the skull by Canty, and was now confronted by three roughs with blood in their eyes. Hendon backed up cautiously, placing his hand on a heavy wooden chair standing beside a well. Diccon ventured in first, and Hendon swung the chair effortlessly, splintering it on the weasel's head and shoulders. Glancing over his shoulder, Hendon saw an open door and headed for it posthaste.

He found himself in a squalid room occupied by several beggars and dogs. It was furnished with a few sticks of rickety furniture and fouled with refuse of every imaginable sort. A pathetic fire glowed in the hearth, suspended over which was an iron pot, its contents bubbling and steaming.

Seeking a weapon desperately, Hendon fixed on the pot as some slattern leaped for it, trying to rescue dinner from these rampaging gladiators. But Hendon got there first, seized it by its chains, swung it round his head, and flattened Nipper with it, spraying scalding soup around the room. But in these close quarters Hendon was at a disadvantage, and Canty rushed over Nipper's body and struck Hendon squarely on the head, driving him back against a low window. A second blow on Hendon's head

sent him crashing through that window and rolling down
the steep bank of the Thames River. Canty leaped after
him and caught him one last blow as Hendon tumbled
down. He came to rest beside the majestically flowing
water, staggered to his feet, then fell flat on his face and
lay inert. His head bled profusely and face looked lifeless.

Nipper and Diccon joined their chief at the top of the
bank, and in due time a crowd of beggars, women and
children gathered beside them, looking down at the still
figure of the cavalier sprewled at the water's edge.

"Sweet Mary, ye've killed him," Nipper said in an
awed voice.

Canty stared, breath laboring, his own arms and body
covered with blood, grime, and sweat. Then he looked
about him at the silent, accusing faces. "Killed him?" he
yelled. "Killed him, have I? Well, didn't he ask for it?
Didn't he beg an' bloody well pray for it? *You* saw him!"
He grabbed Diccon by the arm. "He struck the first blow,
didn't he?"

But Diccon jerked free and moved back, and the crowd
backed away in a semi-circle from Canty, leaving him
alone and guilt-stricken. Then a familiar voice cried,
"Murderer! Murderer!" Canty looked up and saw Father
Andrew, Tom's tutor, standing on the opposite bank of the
river.

"John," Nipper urged, "it's gallows for supper unless
you get out of here. Come on, man! Stir yourself! The
priest'll peach on you, even if no one else does!"

Canty looked dazed. "Eh? What? How d'ye know he's
dead? How . . .?"

Nipper shook his arm. "He's stiffer than the Pope's
conscience! Come on, quick, afore the word spreads." He
prodded Canty in front of him. "You'll have to run for
it—out o' London."

Nipper pushed his boss back into Offal Court, where

they found "Tom Canty" in the arms of his mother, who sponged the boy's face and wept quietly over him.

"Huh? But . . . where can I go? How'll I live? What can . . .?"

"Join up wi' the Ruffler's gang for a while, out Hendon way. He'll hide you up. Take *him* with you," Nipper said, pointing at the boy. "He can steal enough for both of you." Canty still hesitated. "Man, will you wait till the sheriff's men nab you?"

Canty stood uncertain for a second, but with Father Andrew's imprecations still echoing in his ear, he realized he had no choice. He advanced on the lad. Mother Canty clutched him tightly and shrieked "No, no!" But she was no match for her husband.

CHAPTER X

Tom Canty's interview with King Henry had been one of the most depressing experiences the lad had ever had. After slamming the door to his chambers behind him, he had slid down to the carpet and sobbed for several minutes.

It was not homesickness any more, or fear of being discovered and punished. No, it was something else.

It seemed that the expectations of the king, the court, indeed of the entire kingdom of England, rested upon his shoulders. It was clear that the king was a sick man, and, foreseeing his end, had invested all his hopes and aspirations in his son. And see how his "son" had broken the poor man's heart! How could the king rest easily, knowing his kingdom would be inherited by this babbling dunce, or worse, would be run on the mad prince's behalf by protectors such as Hertford, a man Tom decidedly did not care for?

Tom realized it was futile to go on denying that he was the true prince, and had decided to give up trying. Oh, surely he would pay for it, probably with his life, when the true prince returned—*if* the true prince returned. But until then, the role he had inherited was his to do with as he wished. And what bothered him desperately was the fear that he would botch the job.

In all his dreams and fantasies he had played the role of prince, and had been able to fulfill in his mind's eyes all the requisites of that title: virtue, bravery, compassion, wisdom, mercy. Well then, now that he had an opportunity to exercise these qualities, and actually be of service to people, 'twould be a pity if he turned his back on them and went on whining that he was not the prince.

Furthermore, suppose the king did die before the true prince returned? Suppose the king died and the true prince *never* returned? That would make Tom Canty . . . that would make Tom Canty . . .

Through his tears he managed a giggle.

THAT WOULD MAKE TOM CANTY KING OF ENGLAND!

Well, my boy, Tom asked himself, are you up to it, or will you go on sniveling? Will you take the reins in your own hands, or turn them over to the likes of the villainous Hertford?

The way was clear. It was now a matter of fortitude to bring it off.

By God, I'll do it! Tom cried to himself, rising to his feet, washing the tears off his face at the basin, and walking erectly to his wardrobe to select some garments worthy of the Prince of Wales. He donned a number, paraded and postured before his looking glass, and practiced issuing commands. At first he performed the latter *sotto voce,* so the guards and servants posted outside his chamber wouldn't hear him. Then he realized, Oh bother, they think me mad anyway, so what does it matter if they hear me talking to myself?

He strode about his room in his august finery, barking orders to imaginary servants, courtiers, even ministers. It did not sound totally convincing, for his accent was dreadful and he must remember Father Andrew's instructions about nobility of elocution. Ah well, Tom realized, I will make many a mistake before this sham is done, but the game is worth the candle, and I shall give it my best!

That evening Tom issued his first command in a shaky voice. He told his page to bring him dinner in his room. The page nodded and in moments materialized with a tray piled with delights Tom had never before seen or tasted. He dismissed the lad curtly and imperiously, and with a hasty bend of the knee the page disappeared. Tom giggled and clapped his hands. Surely this was the most delightful sport! As soon as he felt more confident he would have to try something of greater magnitude—order a banquet, a play, a joust or archery contest. Perhaps he would order a war, just to see if they obeyed him!

Tom's overweening fantasies were interrupted by a tap on his door. He bade the visitor enter, and a servant appeared to announce that the king had summoned the prince. Tom gulped and began to tremble again. All that confidence he'd felt a moment before—where was it now, little man? Order a war indeed! Tom was lucky if he could order his legs to raise him from his couch.

He stepped out to discover a group of courtiers and their servants, who fell in behind him as he trod the corridor in the direction of his "father's" bedchamber. As he turned the final corner a gauntlet of yeoman warders snapped to attention, and Tom saluted them with his eyes as he passed through the double line. Two towering guards thrust open a pair of double doors at the end of the line, and a booming voice cried, "His royal highness the Prince of Wales!"

Tom entered the king's chamber, where Henry lay abed beneath a sumptuous canopy of silk and gold threads cunningly woven into a hunting tapestry. At the foot, sitting on the floor, was the king's jester, garbed in his usual garish motley. Surrounding the bed stood a group of brilliantly dressed courtiers. Tom was aware that they regarded him rather differently than they had earlier in the afternoon. Gone was the pity and amazement in their eyes as they fell upon the "mad" prince. Gone, even, was the curiosity. Their expressions were open and natural, and Tom felt less an object of distress. He could not explain why, but he was relieved at any rate, for that put him more at his ease.

Still, the sight of this huge and imposing and formidable man the king sent tremors of fear through Tom's body, and he determined to open his mouth as little as possible until he had a firm sense of what was expected of him.

King Henry's leg was exposed, and the same doctor that had examined Tom all morning long was bending over the leg, prodding it with a sharp silver instrument. The jester was telling a joke to keep the king amused during this probing of his royal limb. "There was a pardoner, an almoner, and a priest," said the jester in an artificially high voice, "and they were all going to Jerusalem . . ."

Henry groaned and swiped the air with a heavy hand. "I heard that story forty years ago, and I didn't laugh then. Ow!" He winced as the doctor's probe found an extremely delicate spot on his leg. "God, my leg! Where did you study medicine—at the slaughterhouse?

"If I might bleed your majesty . . ." Dr. Buttes stammered. Tom imagined that the king was not a model patient.

"I have no blood to spare, you dolt!" He waved his

doctor away, and after covering the sick leg the doctor retreated, bowing all the way.

Henry gestured at Tom, who bowed in the doorway, advanced, and kneeled as Henry said, "Ned, come here, boy, before these rascals murder me. Give me your hand, lad. So."

He gazed into Tom's eyes with that terrifying squint of his. The king's eyes seemed to penetrate to the boy's soul, and he was certain the king would now expose Tom for a fraud. Instead, Henry said through a ravaged smile, "You look well—more like yourself."

Tom studied the king's face: it was sallow, stained with purplish liver marks, and pasty. His eyes were bloodshot and their purple rims sagged. The stertorous wheeze accompanying each inhalation of his breath was almost embarrassing.

"I am ill, Ned," the king said quietly." You must deputize for me at the Guildhall banquet tonight . . ." Tom raised his hand to object, but the king cut him off. "Aye, all men must see you, see that you are well, that the throne will be in safe hands when I . . . am. . . ." He declined to finish the sentence, but a moisture in his eyes spoke louder than words. "Kiss me, Edward," he commanded.

Tom obeyed. Henry clasped his shoulders as the boy planted a kiss on the smooth cheek above the reddish gray bristle of the king's beard. The odor of Henry's breath and body was not to the boy's liking. "You are . . . my boy Ned?" the king asked. Tom was afraid to open his mouth to answer, but in view of his newfound determination to play his role well, he wasn't going to deny the question. He resolved this uncomfortable dilemma by bowing his head silently. This apparently satisfied the king, and Tom was permitted to withdraw.

As he backed away, he noticed Henry beckoning to the

Duke of Hertford. "Hertford," the king rasped, "is the Norfolk snake snug in the Tower?"

Tom hesitated and strained his ears to hear the reply. "Parliament has sealed his doom, sire, with the Great Seal," Hertford murmured.

Henry accepted this news with a smile. Eyes closed, he said, "When it is sealed with the edge of a great axe, I'll go content . . ."

Frowning, Tom backed the rest of the way out of the double doors. Fortunately, Tom didn't hear the king's final words. But all the other courtiers did: ". . . And England shall have a crazy crown, on the head of an idiot." Then, with one last sigh: "But he is my son."

Tom stood outside the doors, abstracted in thought despite the fact that a double row of yeomen gazed at him. The news of Norfolk's imprisonment and death sentence disturbed Tom deeply, doubly so because the Duke of Hertford was behind it, and Tom's feelings about the Duke of Hertford were very plain: the man was treacherous. How he had captured the king's favor was only a little less puzzling than how Norfolk, who struck Tom as the soul of kindness and gentility, had fallen out of it.

Tom walked up to one of his servants, a stout grey-haired fellow in purple livery. "Where is the Tower?"

The servant struggled to keep from smiling. The boy knew perfectly well where the Tower was—at least, he did in his lucid moments. But of course, the servant, like everyone else in the palace, was under the king's command to humor the crazy fellow. He described the precise location of Tower.

"Will you take me there?" Tom asked. It was not quite a command, but when a prince asked a question it had the same force as one. The servant gestured to several other servants and guards, and the procession departed for the Tower.

Not long afterwards, as an officer was reading Norfolk's death sentence to him in his cell, there was a commotion, and guards, officers, and Norfolk himself jumped to their feet and bowed as the Prince of Wales descended the staircase, followed by a trail of guards and servants. The officer, realizing he must fulfill the law by finishing the death sentence, raced through the rest of it. ". . . and for the high treason you have committed, the sentence upon you, Thomas Howard, Duke of Norfolk, is that you be taken hence in the morning, and your head struck from your body. And may God have mercy upon you."

"And upon you too, sir, when your time comes," said Norfolk. The officer bowed and departed, and Norfolk turned to Tom with a cordial bend of the waist. "This is kind of your highness, to come to visit me. I regret that I can offer little by way of hospitality."

Tom was profoundly moved at the sight of his friend Norfolk incarcerated, his clothes already torn and grimed after but one night's stay in this pesthole. "My lord . . . I . . . I. . . ."

But what was there to say? The duke's incarceration had been ordered by the king himself. Tom—that is to say, the Prince of Wales— could not countermand that order. "I wish I could help you, as you helped the pauper boy in the king's garden. And again—when you sent him from the palace without punishing him. That was kind, my lord, to a poor beggarly knave."

"It is just such poor beggarly knaves who hold England's frontier, highness, and win her battles," Norfolk graciously replied. "I have seen them, remember."

The duke paused reflectively, then his expression lightened. "Besides, the older one gets, the more one realizes the necessity of a few good deeds to set on the credit side of the ledger. I've done harm enough in my time, God knows."

"If only I could . . ." Tom stammered, confused. He glanced at Norfolk's face, but when he realized that this very head would be severed from its shoulders before the world was twelve hours older, Tom dropped his eyes. "I am deeply sorry, my lord."

Norfolk laughed. "I'm not pretending that I'm glad myself, highness. But to an old soldier, who has faced it a hundred times, do you know what death really means? A cure for rheumatism. So—God be with your grace." They bowed to each other and Tom began the ascent from the cell, his legs leaden and heart almost as heavy. "My loyal greetings to the king your father," Norfolk called after him. "Remind him that we shall meet again, very soon."

CHAPTER XI

A deputation of nobles and their servants came to call on Tom that evening, to conduct him to Guildhall for the Lord Mayor's feast. The yeomen were particularly resplendent as they snapped to attention to let the prince pass. Tom was helped up into the royal wagon by an Earl Someone and a Duke Someone-Else, and found himself facing Princess Elizabeth and Lady Jane, so close that their knees almost touched his. The coachman touched the flank of the lead horse and the wagon, beautifully festooned with draperies, lurched forward, passing majestically through torchlit streets lined with cheering citizens.

Tom took no notice of them. He sat dully with chin in hand, brooding about Norfolk.

"Is your highness not well?" asked Elizabeth.

"Eh? No . . . yes . . . oh, perfectly well!" said Tom.

"Then wave, you fool!" Elizabeth snapped, leaning close to him.

Tom struggled out of his depressed state as best he could, and began to wave and smile at the crowd, whose cheering there upon doubled. Lady Jane smiled radiantly. Elizabeth lanced her brother with a look of deep sisterly exasperation, then turned her face outward too, waving a dainty kerchief at the mob.

At one point, just after rounding a corner, a disturbance broke out in the crowd, but the wagon passed too quickly for Tom to note what it was all about. It is interesting to speculate on what might have happened had he seen the source of the commotion.

For in that crowd was Tom's father, John Canty, pushing his "son" through the mob. Edward, hands bound before him, looked up at the coach thundering by and, spying the imposter in the window, felt the hot flush of indignation sweep over him. "No! No! That is the pauper! He's an imposter! *I* am the Prince of Wales!"

John Canty was not merely mortified by this outburst but alarmed as well, and wheeled in rage. "Will you hold your tongue, you raving fool?" he said, thrusting Edward against a wall and striking him savagely. "D'ye want us arrested for treason?"

"I *am* the prince!" Edward cried. "That man is——"

Again Canty thrust Edward against the wall, knocking the wind out of him. "Sharrup!" he bellowed. This furor was loud enough to attract the attention of, among other bystanders, a constable, who looked gimlet-eyed at the pair.

"My son, he's a lunatic," Canty said quickly. "An idiot! He means no harm. He has mad fancies!" Then, inspired, Canty took off his hat and waved it wildly. "God bless Prince Edward!" he cried. "God save the Prince of Wales!"

A mighty cheer went up, and the crowd turned away from the spectacle of this street urchin who claimed to be the Prince of Wales. The constable shrugged and moved on. John Canty hustled the boy into the obscurity of night. Edward was almost beside himself with disappointment.

He had had his chance, and lost it.

Tom, Elizabeth, Lady Jane, and their long train of courtiers and guards and servants, were received ceremoniously by the Lord Mayor and the Fathers of the City, in their gold chains and scarlet robes of state, and conducted to a rich canopy at the head of the great hall, preceded by heralds blowing trumpets and reading proclamations. The lords and ladies attending Tom and the girls took their place behind their chairs at the head table, laden with meats, fowls, fish, pies, cornucopias of fruits and vegetables and nuts, a dozen varieties of breads and twice that number of jams, and some delicacies that Tom could not identify and was too reticent to ask about. To one side of Tom sat the Lord Mayor, to the other, Elizabeth, flanked by Lady Jane. At a lower table the court grandees and other noble guests were seated with the important officers of the city, while those of more common degree took place at a multitude of tables on the main floor of the hall.

A servant came around behind the guests of honor and tied embroidered napkins around their necks. As his servant was adjusting Tom's, he examined his and frowned. "No, no, it is sure to get soiled. Take it away— carefully."

The servant, puzzled, did as he was told. And the Lord

Mayor, who had been advised in advance of the Prince of Wales's "indisposition", diplomatically waved his own napkin away. The other guests took note and, though thoroughly dismayed, followed suit. In fact, the entire throng waved away napkins and ate exposing their finery to the juices of meat and stains of wine. Elizabeth sighed audibly but doffed her napkin as well.

A servant poured wine, and Tom reached for his cup. But it was snatched away from him before he could reach it. The impertinent thief turned out to be the Prince's Wine Taster, who quaffed a few drops, rolled them around his palate, and swallowed. The guests at the dais leaned forward, waiting to see if the Wine Taster keeled over dead. When he smiled, a cheer went up, and after Tom ceremonially downed a sip of his wine, all followed.

Tom beckoned to the taster, who stooped beside him. "If you think it may be poisoned," said Tom, "why not try it on a dog . . . or a plumber?"

The Taster stood up and exchanged mystified glances with the other servants. His tongue was tied for an answer, but luckily he was not obliged to give one, for the "prince" turned away to eat. And did Tom eat! He fell upon the food like a cur on a pile of offal, and though table manners of that day were nowhere nearly as refined as they are today, they were refined enough to elicit a tremor of shock among the guests as they observed Tom ripping a leg off a roast goose, picking up a whole pie and shoveling a huge portion of it onto his plate, and grabbing several apples away from the outstretched hands of his neighbors at the table.

All at once Tom looked up and noticed the curious gazes of the entire company of diners. Abruptly he adjusted his manners and appetite, looking left and right to observe how others picked up their food with one sort of implement or another, or actually cut it into bite-sized pieces with a knife before transferring the food to their mouths.

Very curious indeed, courtly life, Tom said to himself, slipping an apple into his pocket in case he needed sustenance later on.

After the banquet, a portly golden loving cup was brought out and Tom, heeding the whispered instructions of the Lord Mayor, drank from it, passed it along to Princess Elizabeth, who sipped and passed it on to Lady Jane. Thence it traversed the general assemblage while a great pageant was put on in which dukes, earls, barons, and other noblemen and leaders of England's armies and navies, dressed in the exotic garbs of Turks and Russians and Germans and Moors, paraded around the great hall accompanied by a hundred torchbearers clad in crimson satin and green velvet. Lords and ladies in astonishing costumes swirled past their royal guest, vying with each other to provoke the prince's delight.

A blaze of color and music signaled the entry of cartwheeling, somersaulting acrobats. Tambours and cymbals clashed and drums pounded their tattoo. The acrobats performed some feats that Tom had never witnessed even in the marketplace, where excellent ones were common enough, and he clapped his hands loudly and pounded the table in appreciation, all the time pocketing fruit and nuts against possible hunger pangs later in the night. Servants observed the boy's bulging pockets but held their tongues, lest the king's awful wrath descend upon them.

But, unknown to them, the king's wrath at that very moment was draining rapidly from his body, with all his other humors as well. He lay in his bed, flanked by Archbishop Cranmer and Dr. Buttes. The latter gentleman had been listening to Henry's heart, and now straightened up and shook his head at the Archbishop. At the foot of the bed kneeled Henry's jester, weeping in a high, reedy voice.

Henry, propped up against a pile of downy pillows, opened one eye and fixed it scornfully on the jester. And here he vented the last of his wrath. "Are you trying to amuse me?" he inquired. But the jester had no witty reply. He merely bowed his head and sobbed yet more heavily.

Henry's eyes swung to the ceiling of his chamber, and in a raspy voice he said, "Norfolk is condemned. Good. It will be a race between us."

His face twisted with pain and his breath came in hideous labored rasps. He struggled to sit higher. "Help . . . help me up." Dr. Buttes assisted him to slide up a bit, but Henry's bulk was such that it left the doctor almost as exhausted as the patient.

"Ah, how short a time . . . life has been," Henry mused, eyes moist.

"Be at peace, sir," said Cranmer. "Try to sleep."

"Sleep?" Henry protested, summoning his last draught of energy. "A priest's advice. Slip meekly into death with a whimpered prayer? No, I am a . . . king . . . of England. I will look God . . . in the eye."

And he began to sing softly:

"The hunt is up, the hunt is up,
And it is well-nigh day,
And Harry our king is gone hunting
To bring a deer to bay. . . ."

Meanwhile, at the Guildhall, Tom was enjoying himself fully, hedonistically taking advantage of the occasion, knowing that tomorrow might bring his ruin if not his death. His head swam with the effect of wine, and he did something he'd wanted to do since he'd first set eyes on Lady Jane: he raised his cup and saluted her. She fluttered her eyes in confusion, but smiled happily. Between them, Elizabeth ventured a withering look but concealed it from the prince. Tom then toasted his sister, and turned his attention to a pretty girl who sang him a charming song which, Elizabeth reminded him, had been composed by the king himself. Tom applauded with double ardor at the end of the song.

As the girl and her musicians departed, a finger bowl was placed before Tom, who raised it to his mouth, examined the clear liquid, and drank it, smacking his tongue on his palate. "An interesting flavor," he observed to the Lord Mayor. "Pretty, but not very strong."

Elizabeth's eyes rolled into her head. She didn't care what the king's wishes were, she was going to make no bones about the prince's disgraceful behavior. The Lord Mayor lacked the princess's courage, however, and at the prince's invitation, hesitantly sipped his own finger bowl. Once again, all the courtier's and guests, gentlemen and ladies of noblest birth, raised their bowls to their mouths and drank. As many of them had already washed the grease and gravy from their hands in the bowls, they found the liquid considerably less "pretty" than their highness did. But not one ventured to express this by word or deed.

All at once there was a stir near the great doors of the hall. An officer entered and whispered something to the Captain of the Yeomen, who pivoted smartly and walked behind Hertford's chair beside the Lord Mayor's. Even as he did, a whisper rustled through the room like a gale rattling the brittle leaves of a forest in autumn: "The king is dead!" "King Henry is dead!" "The king . . . the king . . . the king . . . dead . . . dead . . . dead. . . ."

Elizabeth heard it even before the Captain of the Yeomen, catching the dreaded news directly from the lips of the assemblage. She turned ashen and her hand flew to her quivering mouth. Lady Jane's gay smile turned to instant distress, and she put her arm around her friend to offer comfort.

Hertford took the news from the Captain without a quiver of emotion. He had been expecting it, but more importantly, there was little for him to be distressed about. With the king dead, the administration of the government of England fell into the hands of the man designated guardian and protector to the prince, who was both a minor and a madman.

That man was Hertford himself.

In keeping with the ancient tradition, Hertford rose to his feet. A hush swept across the Guildhall, and Hertford spoke. "The king is dead."

Despite the fact that everyone already knew the news, there was still a gasp, and not a few sobs. Then Hertford turned to Tom, and with a jubilant shout, hailed, "Long live the King!"

The assembly jumped to its feet as one, glasses and goblets raised. Tom was so thoroughly disoriented that he did not believe himself to be the object of the toast, and actually started to rise to his feet when the Lord Mayor laid a heavy hand on his shoulder and pressed him back into his seat.

"LONG LIVE THE KING!" hailed the throng. "LONG LIVE THE KING!"

Tom Canty understood it through the alcoholic buzz in his brain: he was King of England.

Stricken and terrified, he shrank into his chair and began to murmur, "But I am not . . ." Before he could finish, however, he found his left hand clasped by his "sister", Elizabeth, who tearfully kneeled at his feet. She pressed her lips to his hand, then pressed it against her

cheek, resting her head on his knee. Like a man in a dream
Tom slowly put his other hand on her head. She clung to
him thus for a moment, crying.

Tom gazed around the room, awestruck as the entire
throng kneeled before him. Again his lips formed the
words, "But I am not . . ." But the fatuity of it smote
Tom with the force of a cudgel blow. He could not deny
the crown here, now!

In fact, here was an opportunity to do a very kingly
thing indeed. "My lord Hertford," Tom said to the duke,
still on his feet with goblet in hand. "If I give a command,
will it be obeyed?"

"The king's word is law, your majesty," Hertford said.

Tom smiled. "Then send word to the Tower: the king
commands that the Duke of Norfolk shall not die."

Hertford held back a frown as he bowed his head in
compliance. Then a thunder of cheering broke out in the
hall. "GOD SAVE THE KING! LONG LIVE ED-
WARD, KING OF ENGLAND!" The thunder rolled over
Tom like an ocean wave, and Tom sat like a drowning
man, clinging to his "sister's" hand like a floating spar
after a shipwreck.

CHAPTER XII

A very different kind of cheering was going on in Offal
Court, where celebrants cheered profanely and staggered
about drunk.

"Gawd save the King Edward an' all the rest of us
bastards!" shouted one rude fellow, sloshing ale from his
pot on the heads of two cackling maids. "'Ere's to little
King Ned, may 'e dishonor all the maids-of-honor, and

not keep 'is ladies-in-waiting waiting!'' Roars of drunken laughter greeted these crudities, and the beggars of Offal Court refilled their pots and quaffed ale riotously in the streets, looking for any excuse to hoist their brew and refill yet again.

Among the celebrants was John Canty's right-hand man Nipper, who staggered out of a tavern, croaking a song. ''Ow, young King Edward is all my joy, little King Neddy is my delight.'' He paused to shake the muzziness out of his skull, then wobbled over to a dark arch to splash some water on his face from a raised bucket of a well beside the arch. He sputtered as the water braced him. There, that was much better!

Just as he was straightening up, an arm swept out of the shadows and clasped him about the neck. Steel flashed in the dim light penciling out of the tavern window, and Nipper found himself in the clutches of a very strong man holding a dagger to his throat. The face of Miles Hendon appeared next to Nipper's. Hendon's face was black, blue, and bloody, but apparently he'd recovered from his beating with far better effect than John Canty and his gang had believed possible. Indeed, they'd left him for dead altogether.

''Quiet,'' Hendon whispered sharply, ''unless you want a second mouth under your chin. Where's the boy? Where did Canty take him?''

''I dunno! I dunno!'' gasped Nipper. ''Don't . . .''

But Hendon laid the blade of his dagger close to Nipper's gullet. ''Goodbye, master Nipper.''

Nipper squealed. '' 'E's took 'im away! Out o' London! Swear to Gawd! They're goin' to join Ruffler's gang, out Hendon way! It's the truth! Honest!''

Slowly Hendon removed the knife, shaking Nipper as if he were a baby's rattle. ''For your sake, it had better be, or you'll find yourself eating your own Adam's apple.'' For emphasis Hendon tapped Nipper on the throat with the flat of his knife.

Hendon relaxed his hold, and Nipper sagged gasping to the cobblestones. Hendon had hoped that would be the end of it, but he had also provided for the contingency that Nipper was as treacherous as Canty. Thus when Nipper flew up from the ground with a knife of his own, produced from beneath his ragged garment, Hendon was ready. He caught the man's wrist, averting a certain slashing of his own cheek, and pressed the blade back upon Nipper's face. "Your fingernails are filthy," Hendon observed as he butted him violently in the face. Nipper staggered back. Hendon seized his ankles and pitched him headfirst down the well. A despairing, hollow wail echoed through the well, followed by a reverberating splash and waterlogged cries for help. Oh well, someone will come along to collect him sooner or later, Hendon said to himself, picking up his hat and dusting it off. He thumped it on his knees, smoothed the broken feather as best he could, clapped it on his head, and vanished into the darkness, heading for a place he knew all too well.

Far ahead of him, in the Kentish woods near Monk's Hollow, John Canty drove his "son" ahead of him along a dim but perceptible trail that led to the lair of the famed and feared Ruffler gang. Edward, still bound at the wrists, stumbled in the moonlight and fell hard to a pine needle floor, panting. Canty halted and stood over him, gasping for breath. "It can't be far . . . bloody dark." He grabbed Edward by the shirt. "Come on!"

They started on again, but Edward tripped over a root and went down again. Canty turned to him and was about to lay into the boy with the toe of his shoe when there was a blood-chilling shriek. Canty dove for cover over a dead tree and popped up, eyes saucerlike. He saw whence the grotesque noise had come: from the twisted mouth of a bat-like crone, who cackled again. Canty took Edward by the arm and yanked it, indicating a different direction, but when he turned he found himself surrounded by half a dozen faces of equally terrifying visage, illuminated by torchlight.

One of these thrust itself into Canty's. "Where away, friend?"

"Lost your way, friend?" asked a second.

"Frightened of the dark, friend?" said a third.

Despite the cool night, Canty's brow burst into beadlets of perspiration. "I . . . I'm not armed! I mean no harm. I'm looking for the Ruffler."

"Oho, the Ruffler, is it?" leered the first face.

"And what might your business be wi' him?" inquired the second.

"And what might you be?" demanded the third.

"A beggar?" said the first.

"An ambassador?" mocked the second.

"A spy?" menaced the third.

Canty trembled. "No, no—I'm a friend. I need his help."

They chided him. "Oho, his help? Can you pay?"

"Can you fight?"

"Can you steal?"

"I . . . I must see him!" Canty made so bold as to demand.

"Are ye sure?"

"Are ye wise?"

"Are ye ready?"

They suddenly swooped down on Canty and Edward like a flock of vultures and hustled them pell-mell into the underbrush. The branches whipped at the captives' faces. John Canty exclaimed with fear, Edward kept his jaw clamped stoically, as he had been taught to do by his soldierly mentors.

Presently they were flung beside an immense fire inside the largest cave Edward had ever seen. It was actually a disused quarry consisting of three levels, on each of which burned a fire. Columns of stone supported each level, and the flames threw bizarre, unearthly shadows on the granite walls and ceilings.

Edward looked up. Around the fire, and lit weirdly by its red glare, lolled and sprawled the motliest company of tattered gutter scum and ruffians, of both sexes, imaginable. There were huge, stalwart men, faces burnished in the sun, longhaired and clothed in fantastic rags. There were middle-sized youths of belligerent countenance, dressed similarly. There were blind beggars with patched or bandaged eyes, and crippled mendicants with wooden legs and crutches. There was a villainous looking peddler with his pack, a knife-grinder, a tinker, and a barber-surgeon, all with the implements of their trades. Some of the females were hardly grown girls, some were in the prime of their womanhood, and some were old and wrinkled hags. All were loud, brazen, and foul-mouthed, all soiled and slatternly. And most pathetic of all were the babies, sallow, bony, stomachs bloated with hunger, faces scarred with sores. And there were a couple of starveling curs with strings about their necks whose purpose was to lead the blind. Occasionally a piece of finery stood out, a gold chain, a peacock feather, a velvet doublet, a ring, all undoubtedly lifted from the victims of this desperate gang.

"Oho, Ruffler!" shouted one of the ruffians, a lean, swarthy rascal in a high-crowned hat, ragged breeches, and wearing a long rapier. He cast his eyes to the second level of the cave, where the Ruffler sat in state on a sort of throne covered with skins.

He was a large, ugly man with a great tangle of a beard and a scornful twinkle in his eye. A sword-belt was swung over one shoulder. He wore what appeared to be a priest's habit cut down and modified, with a trinkety chain around his neck snatched from some hapless burgher strolling unsuspectingly in a marketplace. His sandals were cross-gartered up his powerful legs, and at his feet crouched a pretty, if ragged, gypsy girl.

John Canty looked up at Ruffler. "We are honest folk," he boldly declared to this prince of thieves.

"Then you're not welcome here," retorted Ruffler. "Now, if you were a thief, say, or a vagabond, or a nobleman, or a lawyer. . . ."

"My son's a thief!" the father of Tom Canty said, indicating Edward.

Edward blanched as several of the beggars darted close to him shrieking with delight. One cart-wheeled, another leaped upon the boy's shoulders, a third bobbed in front of him. They began reaching into the pockets of his garment, producing all manner of things that had never been there to begin with—chains, purses, jewelry, handkerchiefs, even a live crow, which flew off into the cave, squawking. They were better than any magicians Edward had ever entertained at court, and had they not been so devilishly ugly he might have enjoyed the performance.

"Thief is he? Light-finger, cutpurse, drawlatch, pick-pocket! Hey-he-hey?" cackled one.

"Can he steal, can he lift, can he filch?" taunted a second.

"See in his pockets, turn out his pouch, rummage for his goods!" cried a third. "Up and down, in and out, to and fro—oh, a brave thief, a fine file, a very villain!" they mocked, practically crowding into Edward's lap until he hurled them off.

"It's a lie!" he shouted. "I am no thief—and that lying murderer is not my father! I am the Prince of Wales!"

The three tormentors hurled their caps in the air. "Hurray! Long live the honest men! Hurray!" they cheered, capering around the two captives.

"A lying murderer and a madman?" mused Ruffler. Ah, that was more like it! "Welcome, friends," he roared heartily. "Bring them up to my fire. Mandrake." One of Ruffler's henchmen stepped forward and pulled Edward to his feet. Ruffler noticed Edward's tied hands. "Hey —is he violent? We are delicate, fragile people."

John Canty shook his head.

"Then unloose him, Night-Owl," Ruffler commanded. "Linklight, bring food and drink for these worthy unworthies; show them the hospitality of the sturdy beggars. Bat, Moll, Dick-dot-and-go-one, sing them our anthem."

As Canty and Edward were conducted up to the Ruffler's fire on the second level of the cavern, two members of the motley conglomeration sprang forward. One was an ancient one-legged man on a crutch, the other a lean ruffian wearing an eye patch. They were greeted on the first level by the Ruffler's gypsy girl, and the rest of the mob began a rhythmic pounding on saucepans, ale pots, wine bladders, silverware, or on the floor of the cave itself with their hands and feet, as the three launched their song:

"Hark! Hark! The dogs do bark!
The beggars are coming to town!
Some on jades
And some with blades
And some in a velvet gown!
Hark! Hark! The dogs do bark!
To topple the state and crown!
Some wear satin
And some speak Latin
The beggars are coming to town!"

Edward gazed up this scene with mingled disbelief and disgust. He had been taught that the common people of his realm, though poor, were humble, modest, God-fearing, and gentle. Never had he imagined that there existed a breed of human vile and wretched as that which now pranced leeringly before him. Though he had ofttimes wished he could pass through his subjects in disguise, to learn more about their ways and speech and dress customs, he could not believe that he would see the likes of this. Indeed, even as he watched the grotesque performance, he could not believe it, and had to pinch himself several times to make sure he was not dreaming it. Alas, the reality became all too solid when the beggar named Linklight thrust a plateful of revolting food in Edward's hands. This was not a dream but a nightmare, and no amount of pinching would awaken him from it.

While Mandrake, Linklight, Night-Owl, and the gypsy girl Moll clustered around the fire, Canty ascended to Ruffler's throne on the second level. He humbled himself before the thief-prince's throne and said, in a low confidential tone, "Don't mind the boy: he's a good thief, but a little crazy, and he speaks——"

"*The truth*," Ruffler completed the sentence for him. "At least about you. Liar and murderer—oh, you've the gallows look, bully. Sit—and tell us who you killed."

The Ruffler leaned forward with professional interest, like a lawyer interested in a colleague's latest case, while his gang chattered, "Tell us, tell us!"

Canty gulped, hesitant to tell the truth. What if they turned him over to his Majesty's constabulary force? Canty trusted no one, not even his own kind, and held with the proverb that there was no honor among thieves. But the Ruffler's steady, penetrating gaze unnerved him, and he began to stammer. "It . . . it was an accident . . ."

"It always is. We are all here by accident, eh?" Ruffler

said mirthfully to his accomplices, who roared agreement and laughed heartily. Ruffler beamed at them. "We are sturdy beggars!" he said proudly. "Thieves, outlaws, cripples, harlots, runaways—aye, and unfrocked priests, dispossessed monks, banished yeomen and starving soldiers. Maybe even a gentleman here and there, who knows? So—welcome, murderer—and your lunatic." With which Ruffler raised his goblet in a perverse toast.

Canty rolled his cap around in his hands. "He is not a true lunatic," he explained. "And he steals well. But . . ." Canty leaned close to the chief's ear. ". . . he thinks he's the Prince of Wales."

Ruffler cocked an eye. "He's behind the times, then. Doesn't he know the old king is dead—and in hell, God rest him!"

"God rest him in hell!" chorused the others.

Ruffler waxed somewhat reflective. "Though why I should wish him ill, I do not know. He broke the monastery where I was a monk, and drove us out to starve. And yet . . ." He scratched his wildly bearded cheek. "When I was a monk I lived well, took from the poor, and had all the nuns I wanted. Now that I am a sturdy beggar, I live well, take from the poor, and . . ." He gestured at Moll and some other slatternly females. ". . . while they may not be nuns . . ."

"They have not changed their habits," roared Mandrake, eliciting an outburst of bawdy laughter from the mob.

"So," said Ruffler, "as to King Henry's damnation, I am impartial. Drink up, friend."

Ruffler's announcement of King Henry's death had echoed down to the first level where Edward sat, and if someone had clubbed him full on the head he could not have been more shocked. He buried his head in his hands and began shaking as sobs wracked his chest. "Father," he cried quietly, "father. . . ."

"Drink to the new king—Edward!" bellowed Ruffler upstairs. "Long may he reign, and may he look more kindly on dishonest monks, honest beggars, and all poor folk than his father did."

The mob heartily concurred in the toast, and downed its drink noisily, cheering and slapping one another on the back. But a snarling cur named Hodge jumped to his feet. "Why should he?" Hodge barked. "Why should he care? Will he be any better than his father was? You say Henry broke your monastery, Ruffler. You were lucky! I was a ploughman, till they enclosed my land and threw me into the road, with my wife and babies, to be whipped from town to town. Look there!" He stripped off his shirt and exhibited a hideously scarred back, to the gasps of his friends. "So to hell with your kings, Henry and Edward, that let such things be!" Hodge cried, shaking his fist.

"Amen," Ruffler sighed. "It's a cruel world. Drink up, friend," he commanded Canty, who was not reluctant to oblige.

Another rude bumpkin thrust himself forward. "I was a forester," he announced, "till they cut down the trees. Then, when I poached to feed my family . . ." He twisted his head, and a collective moan went up. The man's ear had been cut off.

Yet another stood, stimulated by the testimony of his accomplices. "My wife was hanged," he said, restraining a sob. "They said it was for blasphemy. And if I am caught the law of England says I must burn."

"You will not!" came a high voice from the first level. The mob turned to see John Canty's crazy "son", on his feet, breathing hard. He had listened to these tales of injustice, indignity, and cruelty with eyebrows knitted in dismay. Could this be true? Insulated as he was from the world outside his palace, Edward had no way of knowing. Yet an occasional rumor did reach his ears in the palace, and Edward had glimpsed enough instances of his father's cruelty—the king's treacherous plan to incarcerate Edward's old friend the Duke of Norfolk, for instance—to be inclined to believe these beggars. And now he spoke passionately, aware that the mob regarded him as crazed, yet indifferent. It was as if Edward was making a declaration for himself.

"And that law is dead from this hour," the boy announced. "If the king my father had known of this—and the wrongs you have all suffered, he would never have permitted it."

Needless to say, Edward's statement was greeted first by stunned silence, then by hoots of laughter. But Edward, though shaken, stood with jaw thrust out determinedly.

When the laughter subsided, Ruffler said, "When you refer to the king as 'father', do you speak figuratively—as one who holds that the king is father of all his people? Or do you claim to be one of his late majesty's numerous bastards?"

Scores of heads turned to hear Edward's reply.

"Neither," said Edward. "I am Edward, King of England."

The beggars fell about, holding their stomachs with laughter. John Canty held his hands out pleadingly to Ruffler's gang. "Mates, my son's a dreamer, a fool. He thinks he's the king—damn you, Tom, hold your tongue! He saw the king drive by——"

"That was an imposter," Edward cried righteously. "A pauper who has stolen my throne!"

The laughter redoubled. Some of the beggars could no

longer contain themselves and rolled on the floor of the cave, laughing uncontrollably.

"Then," said Ruffler with mock solemnity, "your majesty had better hasten back to London, for once they put the crown on that pauper's head, it's goodbye to your throne forever."

"Yes," said Edward, not realizing Ruffler had been making sport of him. "Yes, I must go back, before it's too late."

Now the beggars swarmed around him, mocking and hooting. Moll cried, "Don't fret, dearie—we'll give you a coronation."

"Yeah!" joined in the others. "King Tom—King Tom-a-Bedlam!"

"No," said another with a better idea. "King Foo-Foo! Foo-Foo the First, King of the Mooncalves!" They pushed and tripped him, Edward vainly shouting, "Let me go!"

They dragged him towards the "throne" which the Ruffler had vacated. This personage stood and watched, grinning. "Crown him! Robe him! Sceptre him! Enthrone him!" everyone cried as they perched poor Edward, struggling, on a great barrel. Someone stuck a tin basin on his head, another threw a filthy blanket around his shoulders, and yet another thrust a broomstick in his hand.

While a few held Edward in place, the others did a mock-stately dance around him, or groveled before him shouting, "Be gracious to us, mighty Foo-Foo!" "Trample not on your poor subjects, great king!" "Pity your slaves!" "Reward your humble servants!" "Hail to the great Foo-Foo!"

One lout presented his backside, yelling, "Honor me with a royal kick up the arse, great king!" And Edward, lashing out with his foot suddenly, obliged the fellow, kicking him head-first into the fire. The ruffian struggled out, smoldering and swearing. In his right hand was a blazing log, and in his eyes was the fire of hatred and humiliation.

He hurled the log at Edward, who ducked it neatly and yanked his hands free of the restraints of two beggars holding him captive. A great cheer went up as the beggars, who always delighted in a fight, shoved the two antagonists at each other. They needed little prompting. The thieves' champion, Hugo by name, leaped at Edward and took him down in a struggling heap, but Edward managed to get his knees under Hugo and fling him aside. Hugo scrambled to his feet and snatched a quarterstaff out of a spectator's hands. Edward backed away, raising his arm to defend himself as Hugo advanced and made ready to swing. But all at once he tripped over someone's outstretched foot, and when Edward looked up to see who his benefactor was, he met the not-unsympathetic smile of Ruffler himself, who tossed a quarterstaff to Edward. "Here, boy!" He then planted himself amidst his subjects to prevent them from interfering with what was now an equal match. "Let them have a fair fight," Ruffler said. "As foul as they please!"

The beggar and Edward circled each other looking for an opening, then Hugo rushed Edward, slashing wildly. But Edward did not give back wildness for wildness, for he'd learned better at the hands of excellent tutors. He parried each of the blows, then jabbed his staff in Hugo's face. Hugo staggered back and Edward followed up his advantage, beating the man on body and shoulders. Hugo took refuge behind one of the granite pillars holding up the second level of the quarry, but Edward found his mark again and again with well-aimed blows.

The crowd was by no means as partisan as one might

expect; they loved a good fight, and they respected a winner. Ruffler nodded cheerfully and even John Canty seemed impressed by a skill he'd never known his son possessed.

Edward worked Hugo out into the open, and the losing gladiator made one last despairing assault. Edward coolly let him come in, then Edward cracked Hugo's ankle, making him hop ridiculously like a one-legged rooster.

Edward put the fellow out of his misery, dropping him with a clean hit to the crown. The den of thieves erupted with cheers and applause, and Edward tossed away his staff and looked steadily into the eyes of Ruffler and John Canty.

"Now I am going. Let no one hinder me, at his peril."

Canty started forward. "You're going nowhere! You'll . . ."

"When I am crowned," said Edward icily, "my first task will be to build a gallows for you, so that you may hang for the murder of my friend."

Ruffler shook his head. "Children have no respect for their parents nowadays."

Edward turned on his heels and calmly strode for the mouth of the cave. Canty came after him, raging. "You'll stay where you are! By God, boy, if you try to run out on me . . ."

But Ruffler's baritone echoed sharply through the cavern. "Hold there, bully!"

Canty checked his steps and turned. Ruffler wagged an admonitory finger at him. "Don't let paternal affection cloud your judgment. Let him go. Madman or not, whoever he is, he's too good for you."

John Canty knew no superior, and was not going to be ordered about now. With a snarl he turned and raced after Edward, who had entered the shadows just beyond the firelight. "Come back, d'ye hear?" he shouted. Edward broke into a trot, and Canty followed suit.

Ruffler frowned. His command had been thwarted, and no leader could brook such a transgression. He snapped his fingers at an immense man who towered head and shoulders over anyone else in the gang. With remarkable swiftness the giant took off after John Canty. "Prevent him—carefully," Ruffler shouted after him. "And let the boy go."

Outside, Edward picked his way through the underbrush, guided only by the moonlight and the flicker of light from Ruffler's Cave. Canty tore after him, crying, "Damn you, stop, you infernal whelp!"

Edward, looking over his shoulder, tripped and fell, and before he could get to his feet, Canty seized him by the shoulder and began to rain blows on him. Edward struggled as best he could against a man twice his weight but it was futile. Then, mystifyingly, that weight was lifted off him as if a huge bird had carried Canty away in his talons.

Edward leaped to his feet and witnessed a tremendous human being clutching Canty, restraining him with one hand and waving at Edward to continue on his way. But Canty reached into his shirt and the blade of a knife glinted in the moonlight. The giant grunted and swiped the knife out of Canty's hands. Canty dove after it, produced it, and swung at the man obstructing the path to the boy. The blade found its mark in the giant's arm.

The giant flinched and grunted, and for a moment it seemed as if the knife thrust was more like a petty nuisance to him than a serious wound. Then the pain reached his ponderous brain. He went berserk, seizing Canty, raising him in both hands, and heaving him with an enraged bellow against a huge boulder. A hideous crunch of flesh and bone against rock, and Canty's limp body slid to the ground, coming to rest in a twisted heap.

Edward sucked in his breath, horrified—then broke into a run.

The giant stared down at his victim, then picked him up and shuffled heavily up the hill to the mouth of the cave. He lumbered in and up the incline to the second level, where Ruffler had resumed his place on his crude throne.

Like a cat proudly delivering a dead mouse to its master, the giant dropped Canty's inert body at the feet of the Ruffler, then shuffled away, clutching his arm where Canty's blade had inflicted a deep wound.

Ruffler stared speechlessly at the giant's back, then sighed and looked down at the body as Mandrake stooped over it and examined it. "He's dead," said Mandrake.

"Into thy hands, oh God," Ruffler said, shaking his head bearishly. Gloomily he looked at the corpse, then impatiently cuffed Mandrake on the ear. "What did you bring him here for? Now we'll have to bury him."

Meanwhile, in the woods, Edward followed the path whence he'd come, paused pantingly to look back, then turned to continue. No one was in pursuit, but—my God! There before him, a black, menacing figure blocked his path. Edward had no energy left for another struggle after his fight with Hugo, the one with his "father", and an exhausting trek through the woods.

Then the figure stepped forward in the moonlight and Edward saw his face. "You!" he gasped, shoulders slumping with relief.

"Me," said Miles Hendon, embracing the lad. "I've been beating this forest in search of you, and this Ruffler's camp. Where's Canty?"

Edward sucked the night air for breath. "Somewhere," he panted, ". . . back yonder. This monstrous man . . . seized him. . . ."

Hendon put his cloak around Edward's shoulders. "Excellent. Come on!"

He hustled Edward off along the path, supporting him with both hands. "He may have killed him!" Edward protested lamely.

"Better still!" said Hendon, thrusting the lad ahead of him and rejoicing to have the boy, crazy as he was, back under his protection.

CHAPTER XIII

Tom Canty, King of England, sat on his throne, sceptre in hand, a gold and jeweled instrument heavier than an iron skillet. His fur robes weighed his shoulders down, and his crown crushed his skull into his shoulders. If this is what it is like to be king, Tom mused, I can't imagine why anyone would aspire to the honor.

What was worst of all was the distressing obligation which the Dukes of Hertford and St. John had just imposed upon His Majesty. "But I don't *want* to marry the Queen of Scotland," Tom railed at them, trembling with shock. "Why . . . she's only six years old!"

"Royal marriages take no account of ages, sire," St. John explained patronizingly.

"And the alternative could well be war, your majesty," Hertford added.

Tom sprang to his feet, knees wobbling under the enormous weight of state. "All right, let's go to war," he said. "I mean, marriage is a serious affair." He looked up and saw Lady Jane making as if to leave the throne room. "No, don't go, Jane." Lady Jane stopped and awaited his majesty's pleasure, her eyes gleaming with happiness to have been asked to stay.

"Impossible, sir," Hertford was saying. "Any action against Scotland would almost certainly provoke France."

"Oh, devil take France!" Tom snapped.

"By all means, sir," Hertford smiled at the impetuous lad, whose hot temper reminded him so very much of his predecessor on the throne. "But until he does, France will remain a present danger to England."

"Then we'll meet it," Tom said eagerly. "We always beat the French, don't we? We'll fight them——"

"Unthinkable, your majesty," St. John interjected. "We are in no condition for war."

"Which is why your majesty must determine our policy towards Paris and Edinburgh," added Hertford. Indicating the group of nobles standing and buzzing at the far end of the room, Hertford said, "And your councilors are waiting."

Tom paced back and forth, shrugging and shaking his head. "Oh, I don't know! France, Scotland, marriage, policies—can't you and the council decide?"

Hertford masked his gratification behind a diplomatic reply. This was just what he was hoping for, but he didn't want to appear too eager quite yet. "We can only advise, sire. The decisions must be your majesty's."

Tom looked desperately around the room as if inspiration might descend from the heavens in the arms of an angel. "Well, I cannot make them now," he said fretfully. "The council will have to wait." He peered out of a window, then caught the eye of Lady Jane. Turning back to Hertford, he said, "Look, my lord, the sun is shining and my wits are buzzing with all your chatter of . . . of . . . haggis and garlic. So let the council consider all these affairs"—he struck a pile of papers on the table before the throne—"and do what you think best, and come and tell me about it when it's raining."

Hertford's jaw dropped. "The safety and good of the realm, sir . . ."

"I cannot decide now!" Tom barked at him. "I . . . I don't know!"

Hertford nodded, lips tight with displeasure. "As your majesty pleases." He bowed, made a sign to the council, and all retired, leaving Tom alone with Lady Jane.

The doors closed thunderously, and Tom leaned against them, catching his breath. "Phew!" He spread his hands to Jane. "You see what it is to be a king. I don't understand half of what they say. Why can't they make some decisions for themselves?"

Lady Jane rose to her feet. She wore a flowing white gown with red trim, and a delicate lace shawl trailed from her bare, pretty shoulders.

"Because your majesty's word is the law," she said.

"Um? Yes, that's true," Tom said, reflecting on this, almost chewing it as if it were a new delicacy he'd never tasted before. "Kings may do anything they please, mayn't they?"

"Yes, your majesty."

"And a king must be obeyed?" he asked, standing before her.

"Indeed, your majesty." Her eyes widened a trifle as they met his.

"What an excellent arrangement," said Tom, smiling thoughtfully. Then: "Close your eyes."

Lady Jane did so, though it was not obedience but desire that motivated her. Tom placed a gentle kiss on her lips, and her eyes flew open.

Tom drew back, looking at her expectantly. "Well?"

"Whatever your majesty wishes is your loyal servant's command," she said, somewhat breathlessly. "Please . . ."

Tom kissed her again, holding her. They sighed contentedly. "Kings are lucky devils," he said.

"Mm," Jane sighed. "But the council . . . should not your majesty . . . ?"

"Anyone can talk to the council, but there are some things a king must do for himself." And he kissed her a third time.

Suddenly the doors flew open and a yeoman warder's voice started to boom an announcement. "The Princess Eliz . . ." But he was cut off by a flurry of bejeweled blue silk as Elizabeth stormed into the room with blood in her eyes. She slammed the doors behind her, and at the sight of Tom and Jane in each other's arms she blanched and choked. "Pardon, your majesty," she said in a strangled voice. "I had thought to find you alone."

"Why sister," said Tom cheerily, "no ceremony, please."

"If I might seek a word with your majesty," she said through gritted teeth, "in *private*."

"Why, there's only Jane here. What?" This latter was addressed to Jane, who had seen clearly that her presence was not desired and was signaling Tom for leave to depart. "Oh well, then. Wait for me in the garden," he said, disappointed. Jane curtsied, first to Tom, then to Elizabeth, and quickly withdrew.

"Well, Bessy, and what . . . ?" Tom started to ask, completely misjudging his "sister's" mood.

"I could box your ears, by God!" she snarled.

"Hey?" Tom exclaimed, startled.

"What do I find in the corridor this minute? The Privy Council of this realm, chased out like idle schoolboys, so that you can play cupid with that hussy! These, the elders of the state, with vital business to transact, and you've no time for them! Was this what our father taught you? Is this how you discharge the sacred trust of monarchy? God, but you make me mad!''

Tom had begun to find his stride as King of England. ''How dare you talk to me . . . ?'' he gasped.

But Elizabeth had a royal temper of her own. ''I'll dare more than that,'' she blazed. ''D'you think a state runs itself, and that you can wave England's business aside because you are too idle or to peevish or . . . or too hot after that simpering baggage? I shall see to her, God help me, so I will, and you . . .''

Now it was Tom's turn, and he was magnificent in his dudgeon. ''And I'll not be railed at by any royal hoyden who does not know her place—and forgets the respect due to her king!''

''Respect? Respect?'' parroted Elizabeth, almost bursting with fury. She stepped closer, and dropped her voice to a low level that was somehow more dangerous than her ranting. ''Now mark me, little brother, I may forget what is due to you, but I'll never forget what is due to something you seem to have forgotten.''

''And what may that be?'' demanded Tom.

''England!'' Her lip quivered. ''Oh Ned, to see you so changed, so careless of all government, and your ministers waiting like beggars at the door while you trifle away the time—oh, Ned, it is not worthy——''

''What I do is my affair, madam, not yours!'' Tom exploded. ''*I* am the king, and I do not need your advice—or your fishwife tongue!''

This brought Elizabeth, who had been softening, erect as a ramrod. There was a moment's icy silence, then she stepped back and deliberately sank to her knees. ''I have your majesty's leave to go?'' she asked in a cold, small voice.

''Yes,'' said Tom, turning away abruptly. She rose, curtsied deeply, and walked to the door. Tom remained planted in his place, fuming. "*I* am the king, you hear? I'll do as I like and rule as I please! If the day ever comes when *you* are on the throne, then *you* can take care of England."

"My God," said Elizabeth, wheeling towards him as the double doors opened for her, "I will!"

She turned and swept out, leaving Tom Canty breathing heavily with anger.

CHAPTER XIV

As dawn stretched its pink fingers across the night sky, Edward, now atop Hendon's horse, found himself in unfamiliar terrain. He'd thought that Hendon had departed from the path on which Edward had originally been led to Ruffler's Cave, and this confirmed it. The hooves of the horse, a tired grey mare with a slightly swayed back, made a rhythmic clop-clop-clop on the leaf-strewn earth. Hendon, though he'd been walking all night, led the horse at an energetic pace, making Edward marvel at his superb physical condition.

"It's only a little way now," Hendon said.

Edward frowned. "But every moment lost is vital. I *must* get to London. If that imposter is crowned in my place . . ."

Hendon sighed wearily. "Dear God, not that again! Look, boy . . ."

"You do not '*boy*' me, sir. I am 'your majesty'."

Hendon gritted his teeth. If it were not for the lad's eccentricity things would be perfect, for "Tom Canty" was in all other respects an ideal young man and a delightful companion. But this Prince of Wales nonsense was most trying indeed. As soon as they were out of danger,

Hendon resolved, he would take the boy—oops, *his majesty*—to a priest he knew in the hopes this eminent cleric would be able to exorcise the demon that had apparently taken possession of Tom's wits.

"Your majesty's pardon," Miles Hendon said with heavy irony. "Will your majesty be pleased to take gracious note, that your majesty's humble servant is tired and hungry and has blisters on his backside—and my home is just over the hill. We can rest and eat and sleep, and then I swear I'll see you safe to London, and you can be crowned to your heart's content."

They plodded on, the horse's pace dwindling to a pained walk as they crested a hill. Then they descended, passing through a charming village—an ivied church, a wooden inn, a marketplace, some sturdy shops, a smithy's, a bake shop—and they emerged on a crooked, narrow road, walled in with tall hedges. Anxiously Hendon increased his pace, pulling his horse along briskly for a half mile. Then they passed into a vast flower garden through an imposing gateway whose huge stone pillars bore sculptured armorial devices.

A noble mansion stood before them.

"Hendon Hall," Miles Hendon said quietly, as much to himself as to his ward. "Home. The old apple tree is gone. Still," he shrugged, "it's been a long time."

"Since you were last home?" asked Edward.

Hendon nodded. "In that time, I've fought for pay from Poland to Barbary, from the Scotch Marches to Constantinople. For all of which I have got five wounds and seventeen pounds in ready money. And I dreamed of coming home with a fortune. Still, at least that is mine," he said, sweeping his hand across the grey stone façade of the mansion. "And Edith will be waiting."

"Edith?" Edward leaned forward in his saddle.

"A lady whom I shall marry—if she'll still have me

after all these years. But first we'll see how my charming brother Hugh has been looking after my inheritance." Hendon uttered this line with a sarcastic edge in his voice, and Edward inferred that there was probably little love lost between Miles Hendon and his brother Hugh.

They trotted the rest of the way. Excitedly Hendon tied up the horse and helped Edward dismount. Even Edward's heart beat a little faster in anticipation of what Hendon would encounter inside. It was hard for Edward to believe that this shabby fellow, though gentlemanly in his manner and speech, could really be heir to this noble estate. Well, they would see soon enough.

They trod up the broad stairs and entered the manor house. Edward found himself in a large, oak-beamed hall, panelled in elaborately carved oak and surrounded by a minstrels' gallery. To one side, a wide staircase. Leaded windows with stained-glass chivalric designs and coats of arms filtered golden sunlight into the dusky interior. Against one wall stood a massive table and high-backed chairs with velvet cushions. Trophies of arms and the heads of boar, bear, deer, and several species of wildcat adorned the wall.

A door opened and an old servant in rather worn livery shuffled out.

"Why Linder, how good to see you!" Hendon laughed, advancing to greet him with an embrace.

Linder cocked his head. "Sir! I do not understand."

Before Hendon could reach him, another figure dressed in dark clothes and wearing a humorless expression on his round face strode into the room. His frosty gaze made Hendon stop in his tracks. "Who are you, sir? What do you . . . ?"

"Have the wars changed me so much?" Hendon asked his brother Hugh, laughing easily as if this were a momentary misunderstanding that would clear itself up as soon as

Hugh recognized him. "Well, I was never pretty. It can only be for the better."

But Hugh steadfastly denied him. "Whoever you are, you're very much mistaken. I do not know you, sir, nor this fellow." He indicated Edward with a haughty thrust of the chin. "Whoever he . . ."

For a moment Miles Hendon was speechless. Then he said, "Wait. For this fellow," Miles said, thumbing Edward, "he's a madman. That's no matter. But I, Hugh, am your brother, Miles Hendon. Your elder brother—*and you know it.*"

"I know there's more than one madman in my hall," the humorless Hugh Hendon declared. "Call the grooms and put this fellow——"

"Your hall?" roared Miles. "By God, will you deny me?" He took four steps forward and reached out to seize his brother. Then Miles stopped abruptly as he noticed someone standing at the head of the stairs. "Edith . . ." he whispered. He ran to the stairs, his face positively alive with love. "Edith, I've come home."

The lady's brows arched. Her face betrayed no recognition whatsoever. Miles trotted up the stairs, certain that when she looked carefully. . . .

"*Edith*!" Hugh Hendon's voice reported like the crack of a pistol. Hugh followed Miles up the stairs in big strides and looked grimly into the woman's eyes. "You do not know him, Edith. My brother Miles is dead these three years. This is some imposter seeking to——"

"What?" cried Miles, swinging around. His face seethed with anger. "Are you mad? Why, you lying filth, what villainy's this? Dead, by God, I'll . . ." He wheeled around to face Edith. "Edith, you know me! I'm Miles! Dear God, you can't have forgotten!"

Edith's face remained impassive, and Miles's countenance clouded with horror and disbelief. "Why don't you . . . speak? Why don't . . . ?"

"Because my wife does not know you, fellow," said Hugh Hendon.

Even Edward drew his breath in sharply. Miles's face seemed to have drained of all color. "Your wife!" He turned to Edith as three of Hugh Hendon's grooms marched into the hall. Hugh signaled them to wait. "Edith," Miles said in shaky voice. "It isn't true. It isn't true, my dear. I'm Miles." A pause, filled with nothing. "You know I am." Another pause, with no response still. Miles pounded the banister with his fist. "Will you say that I'm not Miles Hendon?" he demanded of her.

The grooms stepped forward in readiness, and Hugh Hendon's hand reached for the dagger at his hip. Edith, dark-haired and deep-eyed, stared levelly at Miles, peering into his eyes in vain.

"This is some pretender, or madman," said Hugh.

Miles ignored his brother. "Edith? Please, my dear . . ."

"I do not know you, sir," said Edith coldly. "Will you let me pass?"

Hugh Hendon smiled, and Edward, who had been debating with himself as to the authenticity of Miles's claim, was inclined to believe Miles after observing Hugh's smile, for it was tinctured with evil and spite.

Suddenly Miles erupted in anguish, grief, and anger, and flung himself bellowing upon his brother. They crashed and rolled down the stairs, fists flying. Hugh scrambled free, seized a rapier from the wall, and brandished it as Miles charged him like a bull. "You lying bastard! You steal my home, my woman, and my name!"

The grooms surrounded Miles and restrained him, but his anger made him bearlike in strength, and he yanked away from them, driving Hugh up the stairs despite the fact that Miles had no weapon but his righteous wrath. Miles managed to parry a thrust of Hugh's rapier with his cloak, then caught Hugh in the face with his fist. The grooms fought as best they could but Miles seemed impervious to pain. He fought like a madman, hurling them about effortlessly.

Then, one of them stole up behind Miles with a cudgel. Edward had stood silently heretofore, but would not brook this dastardly tactic, and rushed the man, tackling him about the knees. But the groom flung him off and swung at Miles twice, the first one bringing him to his knees, the second sending him out of consciousness entirely. A second groom leaped on Edward and pinned him to the floor. These villains looked up at their master waiting for further instructions. From the gleam in their eyes they'd have been happy to slit the throats of the pretender and the boy.

Hugh crossed the floor to where Miles lay, pried a boot toe under his body, and turned him over. He gazed at the rugged face, which, between years of absence, the scars of many battles, the recent beating by John Canty and his gang, and the exhausting trek from London to Ruffler's Cave to Hendon Hall, admittedly had put many a mark on his features. "Amazing," Hugh said, "a crazy fellow, pretending to be Miles. Well, no one will heed his wild claims, will they?" He kicked the body for good measure. "Put him in the village stocks," he ordered his grooms, "so that everyone in the district can look at him and see that he is not my unhappy brother."

Three pairs of strong hands grappled with Miles and Edward, trussed them up and brought them out to a hay wagon. They were carried over a bumpy road to town, then tossed off ceremoniously, and dragged across the village square to the stocks. Hendon's feet were first inserted at the base; then his head was thrust in the semi-circle of the bottom board and his neck laid upon it; then his arms were untied and laid beside his head. The topmost board, with half-circles sawn out to match those on which Miles rested, was then brought down until it covered his neck and wrists. The two halves of the stock were then locked together so that Miles's head, hands, and feet were exposed to a jeering public. Edward was made to crouch on the platform nearby.

"There 'e is," announced the constable of the town, examining the instrument of punishment to make sure its cruel parts were properly adjusted. "Makes 'im happy," the constable announced to the massed townspeople.

A number of leering louts in the mob picked up rubbish, rotten fruits and vegetables, or missiles of a more lethal nature, and began to pelt Miles with them. Edward rose to his feet as Miles, in a stupor still, dodged his head this way and that in futile, feeble attempts to evade the assault. "Stop, cowards!" Edward yelled, rushing the tormentors, but they overpowered him easily, knocking him down, kicking him, and tossing him, half-stunned, beside the stocks. Had there not been an even louder commotion in the other direction, Hendon and Edward might well have been done in.

All turned to look at what the shouting was about, and quickly the crowd drained from Hendon's side of the square to the opposite, leaving the two prisoners with the constable and a handful of others to guard them.

From out of a gate a beggarly woman of middle years was being dragged out to a stake planted on the dirt road at the end of the square. Her screams and whimpers and sobs were quite the most heartrending Edward had ever heard, and in a moment he understood why. The woman's captors tied her hands behind the stake and secured her ankles to its base, then they began to throw fagots of wood and kindling around her. In due time a man kneeled at her feet and set a torch to the pile of firewood. A little girl somewhere at the edge of the crowd cried, "Mother! Mother!" and was restrained.

Yellow flames began to climb upward among the snapping and crackling fagots, and wreaths of blue smoke streamed away on the wind, bearing a dreadful odor and the more dreadful sounds of the woman's cries and moans. A clergyman mumbled a prayer, and an official pronounced something about, "for speaking against the truth of transsubstantiation, death by burning alive!"

The flames rose higher, turned from yellow to orange-red to blue, and the woman's tortured screams rose higher until they reached a blood-curdling crescendo. Edward, eyes bulging in disbelief and horror, heard his own throat shrilling sympathetically. It was the worst sight he had ever witnessed. "Oh God," he sobbed, pressing his face against the stocks when it was over.

"Why d'you hide your face, boy?" asked Miles Hendon hoarsely. "Can you not bear to look on Christianity?" Hendon, face battered, filthy, and swollen, stared ahead, then bowed his head as a shadow fell across him.

"And this, my lord, is the pretender to Hendon Hall," said the voice of Hugh Hendon. "Would you believe it?"

Edward looked up to see Hugh Hendon mounted on a roan horse, beside two other persons, also mounted: a fat, richly dressed man, and Lady Edith, who sat sidesaddle, dressed in hood and cloak. Behind them, some of Hendon's grooms, also on horseback.

"Incredible," said the fat man. "Is he a lunatic?"

"Possibly," replied Hugh. "Either that or a criminal. What is certain is that he is an imposter. No one knows him—do they, my dear?"

Edith shook her head coldly.

But Miles twisted his head painfully around in its

wooden prison. "Wrong, brother. You know—and I know."

"And I know," fluted another voice. It was that of Edward. "This is my friend Miles Hendon."

The mounted gentlemen shouted with laughter. Hugh then signaled to a pair of guards on foot, who seized Edward and hauled him off the platform, kicking and struggling.

"Two lunatics," laughed the fat man, chest heaving. "It must be infectious!"

"Aye, like insolence," said Hugh Hendon. "We have a cure for that, too. Williams—give that noisy cub a taste of your whip. Let's hear him yelp to some purpose."

"Do you dare?" Edward shouted at the guards as they dragged him off. "Lay a hand on me and you'll die for it! Treason!"

Miles looked up at his brother, tears clouding his eyes. "You vermin! Can't you see he's mad? Will you flog an idiot? Stop! If you must lash someone, let it be me!"

The guards dragging Edward away turned in surprise. "Let him alone!" Miles yelled at them. "If you are men at all, whip me instead."

With a glance toward Edith, Hugh Hendon smiled, then addressed the guards. "Very well, take him at his word." He thrust a menacing finger at Edward. "And you—speak up as much as you wish. But for every word you utter, he shall have six lashes more. Begin."

The guards began to flog Hendon, laying the whip on his back with a gleeful will. Miles Hendon, perspiration pouring down his brow, clenched his teeth and bore the blows solidly. Edward stared in silent horror, fighting with himself to shout out his outrage and to contain it at the same time, for Miles's sake. He looked up at Lady Edith, who had averted her face.

The last sound of the whip shattered the air, and Hugh and his wife and companion and grooms rode off. Hendon, his back a bleeding mass of stripes and tatters, hung in his bonds, barely conscious. Edward, tears streaming down his face, staggered up to the platform and put his head near his friend's. "You brave, good heart," whispered Edward. "The king will not forget—*Sir* Miles Hendon." With which he picked up the guard's whip and touched Hendon lightly on the shoulder in imitation of the ceremony of knighting a man with a sword.

Hendon looked up at Edward, who in many ways had been the source of his woes ever since they'd met, and shook his head. "Now God forbid you should ever make me a duke," he said ruefully.

CHAPTER XV

As soon as the sun set behind the wooded hill west of Hendon Town, a chill invaded the ill-clothed bones of Miles and Edward. The townspeople dispersed to their warm houses, and by nightfall the square was empty save the figure in the stocks, the boy attending him, and the smoldering remains of the "heretic" at the opposite end from them. Her ashes still glowed, and a fugitive breeze wafted a dreadful odor of cooked flesh in their direction from time to time.

Hendon, who had spent many a night shivering out of range of an army campfire, managed to doze. Edward, who had never been out of range of warmth a moment in his life, huddled close to his friend but quaked with cold nonetheless. A nightwatchman bayed, "Two o'clock, a fair cold morning, and all's well." Through his clacking teeth Edward smiled to himself: 'twas a fair cold morning, true enough, but all was scarcely well. Indeed, in the last few days he had seen more that was ill with the world than he'd ever dreamed imaginable. Poverty, cruelty, injustice, desperation—my God, if I ever get back to my rightful throne I'll change a few things! vowed Edward. He decided that every Prince of Wales should be obligated to spend some time as he, Edward, had done these last few days, the better to know and serve his people when the time came.

Miles asked for water, and Edward, happy to have a chance to heat up his blood through physical exertion, took Miles's military pannikin and raced across the moonlit square to the town well.

"Now get away and leave me," Hendon bade him after sipping the icy water through cracked lips. "Go on, boy—it's folly to stay here. I shall be well enough."

"I am not 'boy', Sir Miles," Edward said, ignoring the rest of Hendon's sentence. "A knight should know how to address his king."

Hendon groaned and shook his head. He hoped that the poor lad's insanity shielded his body from the cold as well as it shielded his wits from reality.

They had just begun to nod off to sleep when there was a rustle in an alley a few yards away. A whispered "Quickly" and a stamping of hooves. Miles and Edward awoke with a start and cocked their heads. Edward tensed his muscles, prepared to take on whatever this new antagonist might be, at whatever the odds.

A cloaked figure drifted out of the shadows and approached them. Miles peered through the darkness trying to make out the face beneath the hood. A moment later the figure had its arms around Miles's neck and was kissing his face. "Miles! Miles!" murmured Lady Edith. "It is truly you. Oh, God, you're home again."

"Edith!" Miles sobbed, his imprisoned hands fluttering in the stocks like a pair of trapped pigeons.

"I thought you were dead, that you would never come," she said, speaking quickly through chattering teeth. "So many years, and no word from you. And always I waited, and then, three years ago, Hugh showed me a letter saying you had been killed in Germany. And I thought I should die too!" She covered his face with kisses, then signaled to a servant who had been lying back in the shadows awaiting his mistress's sign. He quickly crossed the square and reached the stocks. A muffled jangle of keys on a ring, and the clacking of key after incorrect key in the padlock that held the two halves of the stock together. The servant swore in a low voice, applying each key methodically.

"Letter?" exclaimed Hendon in a loud whisper. "He must have forged it. Bastard!" He looked into Edith's eyes, which glowed brightly in the moonlight with love and tears of joy. "Edith, why did you say you did not know me?"

"My dear, he knew you were coming. One of the grooms saw you on your way here. Hugh said . . . Hugh said that no one must recognize you, that if anyone did, he would kill you. He said everyone must deny you were Miles Hendon. Oh, you don't understand how powerful he has grown! The people here go in terror of him."

A smile of relief spread over Miles's face. Then a stab of anxiety. "You too, Edith? Was it from fear that you married him?"

"No, he held my father's debts," she replied. "You know how poor we were. And then, when I thought you were dead . . ." She started to sob, clutching Hendon's hand in hers.

All at once the servant's curses turned to hopeful mutters as one of his keys penetrated deep to the heart of the padlock. He turned it and . . . it snapped open! Edward rushed to his side to help him slide back the bar and throw back the top half of the oaken fetter. Miles gasped with pain as his feet came free. The three helped him to his feet. He stretched his bones and shook his limbs. Then Edith was in his arms, pressing kisses to his grizzled cheeks.

They led him, staggering, to an alley wall. "There are horses and your sword for you and your friend," Edith whispered. "You must go quickly, before Hugh finds you've escaped!"

"Go?" Miles declared. "I'll go no farther than Hendon Hall. I have an instrument of divorce to serve on Brother Hugh: it is three feet long and an inch wide, and it's made of Italian steel."

"No, Miles, no!" the alarmed Edith begged him. "He'll have you killed, or kidnapped and sold overseas. He can do it—he has the power, and great friends at court. We are going to the new king's coronation tomorrow and Hugh . . ."

"Sir Miles has a great friend at court, lady," said Edward quietly, smiling. "He shall have back his inheritance."

The significance of this vow evaded Edith, who like everyone else inclined to believe that Edward was mad. She stared at him, then returned her gaze to Miles. "What matters is that you are alive," she murmured. "And free. But there's no hope for you here—not now. No one will ever dare to recognize you. Please go, Miles, quickly. For my sake, please."

Hendon moved to protest, but the urgency—and good sense—of Edith's arguments caused him ultimately to yield to her blandishments. He kissed her again, whispering a promise that is all too easily imagined. Then he and

Edward mounted their horses, and with one last look at his beloved Edith, he, followed by Edward, trotted quickly out of the square, heading north to London.

They rode all night, and soon after the sun had risen high enough in the morning sky to shed some warmth upon the world, they dismounted and stripped to the waist to bathe in a forest stream. Edward dipped a rag in the icy water and pressed it to the crusted weals on Hendon's back. He winced with each application of the rag, but fought down stronger manifestations of pain with soldierly fortitude. Through grimaces he spoke. "And I'm to skulk about the country like a thief or a pauper," he railed, angry at himself for letting Edith talk him into fleeing his brother like an arrant coward, and denying his birthright. "Without a name, even, crying from the housetops that I'm Miles Hendon. And no one will believe me? Am I to be a ragged shadow, unrecognized, disinherited, lost? Am I to stare at my face in the mirror and ask myself who I really am? And get no answer? God, there's madness!"

Ah, how well Edward understood *that!* "That is what everyone will say," he said to Hendon, "that you're mad. You may tell them who you are, and they'll laugh and mock at you or beat you or set you in the stocks. But they won't believe you. Oh, I know. No matter how hard you tell them, they will just call you a madman."

Hendon sat up violently, catching Edward by the arm. "Well, I'm no madman!" he breathed heavily. "I *know* who I am!"

Edward pulled his arm loose from Hendon's grip. "Do you? So do I. But no one believes *me*. Why should they believe you? Why should *I* believe you—you, who won't believe me? Where's the difference between us?"

Hendon's brows furrowed as he gazed into the boy's eyes. Edward would not be faced down. He looked as hard in Miles's eyes as Miles looked in his. Miles's stare faltered as, for the first time, the possibility that Edward had been telling the truth all along penetrated his brain. The boy *had* been thrown out of the palace. How had he got in there to begin with? Was it just possible that the other boy, Tom Canty (that is to say, the one that *this* lad was claiming was Tom Canty—oh dear, this identity business could get terribly confusing), looked so remarkably like the Prince of Wales that . . . ? And the way this lad spoke, bore himself, fought; his manners, his haughty air, his familiarity with courtly protocol, the ease with which he ordered and commanded. . . .

There was one other thing that contributed to this turn-around of Miles Hendon's attitude, and as if he had uttered these reflections aloud, the boy reached into his shirt and produced the seal, still hanging around his neck by a gold chain. Now, *there* was a puzzle, right enough! Had this boy, this Tom Canty, somehow sneaked into the palace and lifted the seal out of the Prince's chambers (or off the prince's neck), then been discovered and thrust bodily out of the gates by the guards?

Or had the two lads befriended one another and, for reasons of their own, exchanged identities? If the latter, if everything this boy had been claiming was true, then the young man who was to be crowned King of England this very day was . . . Lord God in Heaven!

"Wait. Where are you going?" Miles demanded of the boy, who, after staring longingly at the Seal, thrust it back into his shirt and rose to mount his horse.

"To London," said the lad. "If I do not, they will crown an imposter in my place. And when I am crowned, you will have your name again, and your lady, and your inheritance. I will do justice—not only for you, but for all this land."

The boy raised his eyes to the heavens, his right hand clutching the seal beneath his shirt. His eyes caught the

glint of sunlight and reflected it with a ferocity that
brought Miles Hendon to his knees. The light that shone in
those eyes could not be the fire of madness, Miles knew in
his heart. It was the blaze of righteousness.

"For all the poor and dispossessed and persecuted,"
the boy continued, holding his other hand aloft. "I have
seen them along the road, and been one of them, and they
shall have right," he swore to the Almighty above.

Scarcely comprehending what motivated him, Miles
Hendon reached out and took the lad's hand and pressed
his lips to it. A great quiver ran through the boy's arm and
body as he looked down at the kneeling cavalier and
realized that at last, someone believed him.

He gestured at Miles Hendon, who rose and assisted
him into his saddle. Then, mounting his own steed and
raking its flanks with his heels, he shouted, "Here comes
the King!" and they shot off up the road to London as if
propelled by catapults.

CHAPTER XVI

Early that same morning, even as Miles Hendon toiled
in the stocks in Hendon Town in the pitch darkness of
night, eager citizens of London awoke and began to descend on Westminster Abbey, which at that hour was just
a dim black smudge against the blue-black of night.
Realizing that they might not see the coronation of a king
again in their lives, privileged and rich men and women
had poured into the abbey, content to shiver all night long
(and all day, too, for the great cathedral never got warm
except for the bodily heat radiated by worshipping
throngs) in the hard benches on the floor and in the

galleries. Commoners shoved in and crowded into every corner, stairway, and cranny they could. They carried squalling children and rucksacks packed with food to sustain them until four in the afternoon, when the great event was to take place. They craned their necks at the stupendous pillars and graceful, fluted ceilings, the carved stone saints, the sarcophagi of famous kings and soldiers, the gilded statues, the immense and gorgeous portraits of saints, disciples, madonna and child, scenes from the passion. And as day broke and the sun ascended over London, the commoners marveled with gasps and groans at the incredible beauty of the stained glass windows, which had hidden itself behind the mantle of night. Here alone was a show! What more could a coronation add?

The north transept of the cathedral stood empty, kept clear of intruders by line of sturdy yeomen. On a richly carpeted raised platform stood a throne, its very emptiness radiating a sort of magical charisma as spectators anticipated the beautiful youth who was soon to fill it. Set into this seat was a rough, flat rock, known as the Stone of Scone. Many generations of Scottish kings had sat upon it to be crowned, and in due time the stone had been removed to London and incorporated into the English monarchical ceremony. Both throne and footstool were covered with gold cloth.

At seven o'clock in the morning the beadle entered the cathedral and snuffed out the torches, filling the air with a disagreeable smoke which soon dispersed. Then, with considerable pomp, the first official guests arrived, adorned in finery so beautiful as to all but blind the eyes of the gaping spectators. A peeress in satins and velvets, all encrusted with jewels, was conducted to her seat by a ceremonial official, as a pageboy trailed behind her, holding her train off the marble floor. The official then placed a footstool before her while she gathered up her train and

placed it on her lap. She was then handed her coronet for
the moment when the simultaneous coroneting of the
nobles arrived.

Now the peeresses flowed into the cathedral in a glittering stream, while before them, handsomely uniformed
officials flitted to and fro seeing them to their seats without
error, according to a protocol extending centuries into
England's dim past.

Perhaps the ensuing hours are best described by a famous recorder of the event:

"After a time, quiet reigns again, for the peeresses are
all come and are all in their places—a solid acre, or such a
matter, of human flowers, resplendent in variegated colors and frosted like a Milky Way with diamonds. There
are all ages here: brown, wrinkled, white-haired dowagers
who are able to go back, and still back, down the stream of
time and recall the crowning of Richard III and the trou-
blous days of that old forgotten age; and there are handsome middle-aged dames; and lovely and gracious young
matrons; and gentle and beautiful young girls with beaming eyes and fresh complexions who may possibly put on
their jeweled coronets awkwardly when the great time
comes, for the matter will be new to them and their
excitement will be a sore hindrance. Still, this may not
happen, for the hair of all these ladies has been arranged
with a special view to the swift and successful lodging of
the crown in its place when the signal comes.

"We have seen that this massed array of peeresses is
sown thick with diamonds, and we also see that it is a
marvelous spectacle. . . . Presently a special envoy
from some distant corner of the Orient, marching with the
general body of foreign ambassadors, crosses a bar of
sunshine, and we catch our breath, the glory that streams
and flashes and palpitates about him is so overpowering,
for he is crusted from head to heel with gems, and his

slightest movement showers a dancing radiance all around him.''

In the throne room of the palace, a frenzied scene of preparation was taking place with De Brie, servants, and courtiers attending to the details of Tom's wardrobe. His gold ermined coronation robe, which felt as if it weighed ten stone, was laid over his shoulders just so. De Brie would step away, examine it, dart at it like a dragonfly, make some infinitesimal adjustment, and jump back to start the cycle all over again. Another attendant on hands and knees polished Tom's slippers, though they would never be seen beneath the immense cloak. A master jeweler was buffing a golden chain encrusted with diamonds, emeralds, rubies, sapphires, and pearls until it coruscated.

The chain was handed to De Brie who fussed a bit more as he placed it on Tom, then backed away to admire his handiwork. He was by no means satisfied, because these coronation robes always had to be cut down when a youth became king, and they never fit as well as they did when assumed by a man of adult stature. But, oh well, De Brie admitted to himself with a sigh, this was the best he could do, and if they didn't like it, what could they do, execute him?

De Brie gulped: maybe they could!

Tom motioned impatiently for all these fussy people to be gone. They fell all over themselves backing away, like characters in an Italian farce. In the background stood Hertford, St. John, and Norfolk, looking pretty much as one would expect after the former two had suffered a setback in the release of Norfolk, and Norfolk rescued from the headsman's ax. Norfolk looked warmly at Tom, and when a voice proclaimed, ''Edward, Sixth of the name, of England, France, and Ireland—King!'' he was the first to drop to his knees in obeisance. The courtiers then rose and retired from the throne room, whereupon Tom broke into the shakes.

He had thought he'd mastered his spirit, but the proximity of the coronation and the actuality of his assuming the throne of one of the most powerful nations in the world—it was almost not to be credited. Surely whoever was spinning this elaborate dream would soon wake him and return him to the comfort of abject poverty, rags, crusts of bread, beatings by his father, freezing winters and stifling summers?

He passed through a side door in the paneling of the throne room and then through Fisherman's Bastion, a corridor connecting the throne room with the church. There, to his delight, he found Lady Jane.

She turned abruptly to gaze on him. Her eyes and smile reflected a combination of a subject's awe and a sweetheart's affection. Tom paraded and postured before her, as he'd done countless times when pretending to be king before the ragamuffins of Offal Court. "Do I look very foolish?" he asked.

"Your majesty could never look that," said Lady Jane.

Tom sighed, mulling over her form of address. "My majesty . . . it's a perilous thing, this majesty." Tom paused a moment, as if mulling over some weighty matter of state. Then he impulsively stepped to her and took her hands. "Jane, I love you and I want to marry you. Do you love me?"

"I have told your majesty so."

"Aye," groaned Tom, "my majesty." The words were spoken bitterly, almost spit out in disgust. "Suppose I were no majesty, but some ordinary fellow. Not Edward Tudor, but Harry, or Dick, or . . . Tom. Would you love me then? Would you be content as the wife of such a man?"

"I could never help loving you," said Jane, closing her

eyes as Tom impressed a tender kiss on her lips. Then, playfully, she added, "But I confess I'd rather be Queen Jane than Mrs. Tom."

Tom turned heavily away. "Ah, I see. Well, that's honest."

Jane came after him, taking him by the shoulders. "But since you *are* king, and soon to be crowned, what's to matter?" She kissed him in return, hoping to send such morbid thoughts fleeing pell-mell. But his gloomy visage persisted, and he hung his head woefully.

The hours preceding the processional were among the longest and heaviest Tom had ever known. Normally of good appetite, he scarcely touched a morsel, dismissed all attendants, and remained ensconced in his room, pacing like a caged animal while awaiting the inevitable tap on the door signaling the dreaded moment.

CHAPTER XVI

Meanwhile, like the many streams that flow into the swelling wash of the Thames River, a number of events were taking place in and around London whose confluence could very well change the tide of the affairs of the British nation.

Rumbling north, in a Tudor wagon-coach drawn by four matched bay horses whose manes and tails had been braided and beribboned, Hugh Hendon and his wife Edith sat apprehensively beside each other.

On Hugh's face mingled suppressed fury and open elation. He was highly annoyed at the escape of his brother, whom he had wanted held for at least one more day, beyond the coronation. After that, when Hendon was

confirmed in his title as Master of Hendon Hall, brother
Miles's claims would be almost impossible to press. Thus
Hugh's elation, for in a matter of hours that very consum-
mation would have taken place and Hugh could worry no
more.

"Inconvenient," he mused, "the escape of that . . .
imposter. Was it not?" He scrutinized Edith, wondering if
she'd had anything to do with the "inconvenient" escape
of Miles Hendon, her former lover. She kept her eyes
averted from his, but a trembling of her lips suggested that
his theory was probably correct. It was to be expected, and
he had only himself to blame for not posting a guard by the
stocks in the town square. "Still," Hugh said aloud, "he
need not trouble us. When we have kissed the hand of the
newly-crowned king at Westminster we shall be nicely in
the saddle. The lord of Hendon Hall will be confirmed
—and so will his lady."

He reached out for her hand, but she moved it away and
he came up clutching only the fabric of her purse. He
frowned and turned his attention to the road ahead, where
a pall of woodsmoke like a smudge on the horizon signaled the last stretch of the road to London. Then he sat
back smugly in his seat. Edith may behave as coolly as she
wishes towards me, he said to himself; in a few hours I
shall have my title, and she will fawn over me like a
pampered dog.

The sound of their approaching coach alerted two
travelers on the road ahead, and they clambered to the
hedgerow bordering the London Road and peered out
through the branches.

"Now remember, boy—uh, your majesty—leave the
fighting to me," instructed Miles Hendon. "It's my
trade."

Edward looked at him with deep irony. "Yes—and in
ten years at that trade you made . . . seventeen pounds, I

think?'' Hendon opened his mouth to protest, but Edward got there before him. ''Forgive me, Sir Miles, but I have seen you fight four times. Once we ran away, and twice—you lost. You must try to do better for your king.''

Hendon growled and gulped back his fury with this impudent snip who also, alas, happened to be King of England and therefore above the Law of Spanking. He turned back to the business at hand, pushing Edward closer to an opening in the hedgerow whence they would leap. The rumble of the coach grew louder and its brightly painted woodwork and glittering hardware came into view around a curve. ''If your majesty will be graciously pleased to lay out the driver, I'll leap in the window. Come on—*sire*!''

They erupted from the woods as the coach clattered by. Edward leaped to the box, taking the driver totally by surprise, and using his weight shrewdly, cuffed the driver out of the box and onto the road in a sprawling, choking pile of dust. Miles was not quite so accurate of aim, and instead of diving through the coach window, crashed headlong through the door panel instead.

Most assuredly this approach was just as effective, for Hugh Hendon was so startled as to be paralyzed for a moment. Also, his boots were pinned down by Miles's rump, hence he was rendered incapable of kicking the invader.

It took Hugh only a moment to recover, and his hand thrust into his cloak while Miles struggled to his feet on the coach floor, and produced a dagger. But Edith stayed his hand just long enough for Miles to take hold of it, and the two began a ferocious grappling in the confines of the coach.

For a minute the two stymied each other, then as the coach lurched around a turn, Miles lost his balance and slid halfway out of the hole in the side panel. Hugh sprawled atop him, pressing the dagger toward Miles's throat as Miles's head skimmed bare inches above the rushing road. "Imposter!" Hugh hissed. "Pretender!" Miles struggled against the ever-descending blade, but it seemed hopeless, for he also had to concern himself with keeping his head above the road or it would be flayed off his shoulders layer by layer.

Then, a stroke of good fortune: the road snaked around a sharp curve in the other direction, enabling Miles to regain a grip on the coach and thrust Hugh back into the coach. Blows were exchanged, then Hugh found himself at the bottom of the coach on his back with his own dagger blade grazing his throat. "No! No! Miles, no!" he screamed.

"Imposter? Miles? Which am I, then?" said the cavalier.

"Miles—Miles, my brother Miles!" Hugh Hendon whimpered.

"You don't know your own mind from one minute to the next!" Miles laughed, knocking the dagger out of Hugh's hands and setting on the villain with his fists. Four solid punches took the fight out of him, then Miles raised his boots as if to crush the man like a worm. "No, Miles, no—you'll kill him!" cried Edith.

"That was my general intention," Miles said, chest heaving. "However . . ." Out of deference to Edith he refrained, and instead set about trussing Hugh's hands and gagging him.

Outside, in the coachbox, Edward beckoned to Edith's servant, the one who had unlocked Miles Hendon's stocks. The servant, riding postillion, clambered over the top of the coach and asked what the lad wished. Edward requested the man's cloak. Gladly, the man untied it and passed it to Edward at the reins, who donned it, concealing his rags. Then, with a shout, Edward snapped the reins. The horses redoubled their efforts and the coach lurched violently toward London.

In the meantime, back in London, the streets along the processional route had become thronged with citizens and people from surrounding towns and beyond, from such places as Wales, Ireland, and Scotland, all come to catch no more than a glimpse of the boy-king as his coach clattered by.

In the grand cathedral, the peers of the realm in their stately robes were assembled and seated, dukes, earls, barons whose names and titles and deeds had been woven into the incredibly rich fabric of England's history. Their coronets were handed to them ceremoniously and set by against that thrilling moment when the protocol of coronation permitted them to don them. The spectators in the galleries and remoter sections of the abbey buzzed continually in recognition of names that had been as inaccessible to them as the myths and legends related to them by their grandparents.

Now the robed and mitred great heads of the church and their attendants filed in upon the platform and took their appointed places; these were followed by the Lord Protector and other great officials, and these again by a steel-clad detachment of the guard. Outside, cannon thundered rhythmically and bells peeled joyously. The moment the entire nation had been waiting for was now at hand.

Tom Canty, in a robe of gold cloth and ermine, gold chains, and several more pounds of clothing that made it well nigh impossible for him to raise his hand to wave at the crowds, rode out in an open ceremonial wagon covered with splendid cloths and upholstered in softest plush, pulled by eight magnificently matched dapple geldings. Despite the weight of his clothes, and the more significant weight upon his spirit exerted by his imposture, he managed to beam and wave at the mass of spectators.

A sturdy line of guards fought back the press of humanity around the main door of the abbey. The throng swayed like closely packed sea plants caught in the crosscurrents of a changing tide. The commander of guards rallied his men to hold the line straight but the pressure was fierce, and at one point a breach was opened. Several people fell to the cobbles just as Tom swung by. "Careful, woman!" a guard shouted at one fallen victim, stooping to raise her to her feet before she was crushed. Tom instinctively reached out too, and as she rose, his face was stricken with a terrifying recognition.

It was his mother.

She stared at him in disbelief, then recognized him as the guards hustled her back into the crowd. "Tom!" she cried, struggling for another glimpse and touch of the son she'd thought she'd lost forever. "Tom!" She stared, confused, not able to provide for herself a glimmer of explanation as to how her son stood robed in the gowns and robes of the king of England, yet certain that this was indeed her own son. She knew not how she knew—how does any mother know?—but she knew that her certainty was bound in hoops of iron. That was Tom Canty or may the good Lord strike her down this moment!

Tom gazed at her, face drained of all blood. His entire life passed before his eyes in that moment, past and future. What did the past offer but crushing poverty, beatings, misery, starvation, and the eventuality that he would one day be caught as a thief and lose his ears or, worse, his life?

But the future? Wealth, power, glamor, comfort, an opportunity to be of genuine service to his nation; to help correct the injustices that had created such villains as his father and such suffering saints as his mother; to lead people as he had dreamt of doing as he paraded around Offal Court conducting his innocent little charades.

Faced with this choice, of extending the past or breaking with it and embracing this glorious future, who but a madman would return to his old ways?

Unfortunately, breaking with the past meant betraying and renouncing those who had created it. And so, as the procession paused before its last lurch forward, Tom looked at Mother Canty and said, "I do not know you, woman."

Unable to look her in the eyes, he turned away abruptly. The train moved on as his mother cried, "Tom!"

"Hold your tongue!" barked a guard at her. "That's the king." Tom, who had dismounted a little way further, could imagine the guard boxing her ear or prodding her back with the staff of his halberd. He froze, stricken with guilt, and moved to turn back as the realization swept over him that he had committed an awful sin.

But before he could, the Duke of Hertford was at his elbow. "Head up, your majesty. Let your people see the king."

Tom did look back, seeking his mother, but she had been absorbed back into the sea of faces, and she was nowhere to be seen. A great cheer went up as Tom acknowledged his subjects once more before entering the abbey.

As he crossed the threshold a triumphant peal of music burst forth. Tom advanced up the north transept towards the throne, his train carried by nobles. A chorus accompanied by an organ sang a thrilling hymn, and the entire congregation rose to its feet with a thunderous rumble.

Tom was conducted up the platform at the end of the transept, on which stood the throne. Ancient ceremonies were conducted with impressive solemnity before the gaze

of countless peers, peeresses, privileged and poor. Tom
kneeled on the steps leading to the throne, waiting for the
crown to be placed on his head. It sat on a velvet pillow, a
golden circle encrusted with gems of surpassing beauty,
size, and value. It looked so heavy Tom feared it would
crush his skull into his shoulders when he donned it. He
grew wan and faint in anticipation of that moment, not
only because he feared the physical weight of the crown
but the more momentous weight of responsibility, which
might well prove impossible to bear.

CHAPTER XVII

Atop the coach hurtling through the streets of London,
Lady Edith's servant, now guiding the horses, whipped
them until they frothed at the mouth and their flanks
glistened with perspiration. Edward cheered and shouted,
hoping the steeds would better appreciate the need for
haste if they heard it from the King of England. Inside,
Miles Hendon struggled into his wicked brother's fine
doublet, cloak and hat, assisted by Edith. Hugh, bound
and gagged, snarled and kicked and tried to loosen his
bonds. Miles prodded him in the back with the toe of his
boot whenever he became a bit too obstreperous.

"Damn the fellow," Miles cursed, trying to fit his
muscular arm into Hugh's sleeve, "is he some kind of
midget?"

"Faster," cried Edward above him, cloak fluttering
like a banner in the wind, "faster!"

They were close to the abbey now, and the servant laid
the whip on mercilessly. The coach rumbled on fearfully,
horses' hooves clattering and sparking on the cobbles.

Pedestrians scattered, not a few diving out of the way as the coach swept by.

At last it pulled up before the abbey door. The Captain of the Guard quickly stepped forward, challenging them. Miles thrust a paper through the window.

"Our invitations, Captain. As you see, we have had an accident."

The officer scanned the papers, then shook his head. "Sorry, sir, you're too late. The ceremony's begun."

Edith imperiously thrust her head out of the window. "Nonsense! This is the Lord of Hendon Hall, and *I* am his lady. You will admit us, sirrah, at once." She glared at him, her eyes mixing contempt and sensuality. The captain hesitated. "You may not know it," she said, "but we are close friends of his majesty—extremely close."

There was some irony in her words, for indeed she *was* close to his majesty. Edward stood only a foot away from her, after opening the coach door in the cloak of a footman. The captain, not wishing to offend a dignitary and a beautiful woman, decided it was best to yield, and murmured an apology.

Miles, in his eagerness, moved to get out of the carriage, but Edith stopped him with a raised hand, smoothed his collar with a wifelike gesture, then gave him a prim, approving nod. He stepped out, offered his hand, and helped her down. Inside the carriage, on the floor, the trussed and gagged Hugh struggled violently, his eyes so bugged they appeared ready to burst out of their sockets. Edward, smiling, slammed the door in the villain's face and cried, "Drive on!" to Edith's servant.

The servant shook the reins and the carriage moved forward a few yards, only to be impeded by the traffic in front of it. And all at once, as Miles and Edith were presenting their passes to an official at the abbey door, they became aware of a heavy thumping coming from the direction of the carriage. It was Hugh, kicking the door with his bound feet!

Both the Captain of the Guard and the official inspecting their invitations heard it, and the Captain strode down the street to investigate. Miles, ill clad in Hugh's garments, which were much too small for him, began to sweat as he tried to edge Edith past the official. He also beckoned to Edward to be prepared to make a break for it. "If you please, sir," Miles hissed at the dawdling official, "we are in haste."

But the official looked to the Captain of the Guard for permission to let them pass, and the captain emphatically denied that permission with a sharp gesture as he opened the door of the coach to investigate. He sucked in his breath as he found Hugh Hendon lying on the floor, arms and legs bound and mouth gagged.

The captain reached for his dagger and carefully slashed Hugh's bonds. Then the Lord of Hendon Hall tore the gag off his mouth. "Stop that man!" he gasped, pointing at the abbey door as Miles, Edith and Edward shouldered their way inside past the shocked official. "He's an imposter, a traitor!"

"Run, boy! In!" Miles shouted, thrusting Edward headlong into the cavernous cathedral. Wheeling, he drew his rapier as several guards rushed him, swords drawn. Rather than run, Miles charged with a flurry of thrusts and slashes, driving the guards back. Then Hugh stepped into the fray after snatching a sword from a guard. "Seize him!" he shouted. "Treason! Strike the villain down!"

Miles crossed swords with his brother now, on the porch of the abbey, holding him and the guards at bay while Edward ran into the cathedral, cloak flying. He tore down the aisle heading for the north transept, but skidded to a halt as several guards came up the aisle on the double, attracted by the clash and clangor of swordplay. Edward

ran back up the aisle to see if he could be of any aid to the
severely outnumbered Miles.

Miles, with great ferocious snorts and stamps, had
driven Hugh and the guards back for a minute. Now,
glancing over his shoulder to see Edward being chased
back, Miles broke with his opponent and charged into
Edward's pursuers, taking both groups of swordsmen by
surprise. He cannoned into one guard, drove another back
with a blow of the fist, then whirled to meet the attack
behind him. Hugh was in the vanguard, sword a blur as
he slashed the air wildly, hoping to catch a piece of Miles
with the edge or point of his sword. This kind of duel was
childplay to Miles, who managed to parry the thrusts
easily and disarm his brother. Hugh wrenched another
sword out of somebody's hands while a couple of guards
grappled with Miles from behind, momentarily pinning
his arms to his sides. Miles shook them off and came out
thrusting, but his rapier was turned and he took a blade in
the arm.

Rallying with one wounded arm, he parried a second
thrust with his bare hand, taking a bloody gash. He looked
over his shoulder for Edward and was exasperated to find
him standing by trying to make up his mind whether to run
or help his friend Miles. "In God's name, your majesty,
run!" Miles shouted. "Go and get your crown!"

Edward reluctantly pivoted and darted away from his
wounded friend, who fell to the stone floor of the abbey,
bleeding profusely from his injuries. Some guards leaped
over his fallen body, but he had enough energy left to trip
the lead one and send them sprawling.

Edward tore down the aisle, only one guard between
him and the platform on which stood the throne. Edward
feinted left, and when the guard committed himself,
darted right. The guard grabbed nothing more than a
handful of shirt—and the chain of the seal hanging around

his neck. It snapped and dropped to the floor. Edward in his haste did not feel it fall away, but continued racing down the aisle, glancing over his shoulder to see his friend Miles, who had struggled to his feet in the confusion, staggering down the aisle after him.

When Edward turned his head back to the platform, he saw to his horror that the crown on its pillow had been raised, and the Archbishop held the crown poised over the head of the pauper, who sat in a gold robe on the throne, orb and sceptre aglitter in his lap.

"Stop!" Edward's high voice echoed through the cathedral. A collective gasp and murmur went up in the audience, and a rumble as all turned their heads to see the arrogant knave who had dared to raise his voice in so solemn a ceremony.

"That head is a forfeit!" Edward said, striding down the aisle in rags ill concealed by his cloak. "That is not the king!"

The Archbishop's hand faltered and almost dropped the crown. Tom Canty's eyes lit up with delight and he half rose out of his throne. Guards came sweeping down the aisle prepared to seize the boy, but after Edward announced he was the true king, they had tumbled to a halt, uncertain what to do. "I am Edward of England," the lad announced boldly. "I am the king."

Hertford, face purple with rage and shock, strode across the platform, almost speechless with fury. "Guards, seize him! Take that man out!" The guards rushed down the aisle amidst a babble of confusion from the assembled peers and peeresses. Several women swooned, others shrieked and screamed, men shook their fists and demanded explanations. On the platform, the Archbishop actually did drop the crown. It bounced like a toy and rolled off the platform to the stairs.

Then another voice cut through the pandemonium. "It's true! He *is* Edward!"

The cathedral dropped to a hush as if a blanket had fallen over the congregation. All faces turned to the throne. Quietly, Tom Canty said, "I am not the king."

"Your majesty!" Hertford gasped, stunned and looking like a man who has just been run through with a dagger. He looked to his friend St. John. "His madness is on him again. He is . . ."

"No, my lord," said Tom. "What I told you all to begin with is true. I am not the king. I never was." He stood before the throne, feeling as if he were desecrating a holy shrine with his unworthy posterior. "I am Tom Canty, a thief and a pauper, from Offal Court in Smithfield. That," he said, pointing at Edward, "is the king."

Hertford gestured at Edward. "Get that fellow away," he murmured to St. John. "Your majesty . . ."

But Tom strode past him, brushing him aside as he bowed low to Edward. "Your majesty."

Hertford, fuming like a kettle about to burst, urged St. John to move, but now it was apparent to everyone that the resemblance between the two boys was remarkable. "Wait!" cried St. John as Hertford moved to throttle the intruder himself. "In God's name, my lord, look at them!"

Now even Hertford saw it, and gulped.

Tom Canty dropped to one knee and swept the air with one hand, pointing to the throne. "Sire?"

Edward looked at Tom without emotion, then mounted the two steps of the platform, heading for the throne. As he passed Tom he stopped and looked down at the kneeling youth. Without changing his expression, he put his hands on Tom's shoulders, gripped him firmly, and raised him to his feet. Tom undid the fasteners on his robe, removed it, and fixed it around Edward's shoulders. As he did, he said in an apologetic voice loud enough for only Edward to hear, "I was not a . . . good king, sire."

Edward smiled faintly and in equally conspiratorial voice said, "I was not a good pauper."

Edward swept past the nobles to the throne, and bore himself with such dignity that not even his pauper's garb could make him look even faintly ridiculous. He seated himself on the throne, and Tom, following him, took a position a few feet away.

However, although the two boys were now in their rightful place, there was still as much confusion as before, for what proof was there that true king and pretender were properly positioned. "But . . . which . . .?" Hertford stammered bewilderedly to Norfolk.

"You have heard us both, my lord," said Edward. "I am the king—that is Tom Canty."

"That's a fact, my lord," Tom assured him. Casting his eyes out into the cathedral, he saw the shocked and confused faces of Elizabeth and Jane. His eyes paused on Jane and he felt a pang in his heart as he remembered what she had told him a few hours earlier: that she preferred to be queen above all else. By relinquishing his crown, he had also relinquished the love of his life.

Further up the aisle was a commotion as Miles Hendon, wavering dizzily, bulled his way towards the platform. Immediately before Tom, a cleric had recovered the fallen crown and was handing it back to the shaken Archbishop.

"But . . . this is not proof," Hertford was saying.

"You have our word, sir," Edward assured him. "What other proof is needed?"

"Something more than the word of a rascal in rags." Hertford stood still a moment, trying to resolve something in his mind. Then he came to his conclusion. Pointing at Edward, he cried, "Arrest that imposter!"

The congregation of nobles had divided in twain, half siding with one lad, half siding with the other. Mutters of consternation broke out in the assemblage, and shouts of "Yes!" and "No!" Edward grew tense on his throne, his eyes filling with cold anger.

Suddenly Miles Hendon broke out of the restraining clutches of a guard. "Show 'em the seal, boy—your majesty—for God's sake!" he yelled across the gulf between them.

Edward's eyes lit up. Of course! He'd forgotten all about that! "If you will not believe me," he said to the Duke of Hertford, "will you believe the Prince of Wales's seal?"

He reached triumphantly into his shirt and . . . gasped. He exchanged a horrified look with Miles. "But . . . but I had it . . ."

Hertford snorted and raised his hand to issue a final command when Edith's voice rang out.

"This is what you are looking for, your majesty," she said, waving the seal over her head. She shouldered through the crowd to hand the object to Edward. "You dropped it in the scuffle."

Edward handed the seal to Hertford. "Proof, my lord?"

Hertford examined it. He had seen it countless times and knew it was all but impossible to counterfeit. "It is the prince's seal," he said humbly. He bent his knees and kneeled before Edward. "Your majesty."

St. John kneeled, then raised his face to the congregation. "God save the King!"

The organs burst forth with an anthem as the congregation took up the cry. "God save the King!" thundered through the abbey. Nobles jostled each other to kiss the new king's hand; Edward acknowledged them with a haughty nod of the head and gracious smile, the product of years of training at the hands of his father and his tutors.

The tight-lipped Hertford, frustrated to the core, decided he would have at least one imposter in the Tower to show for all his humiliations. He summoned the Captain of the Guards, said something to him, and a moment later several guards were rushing Tom. Edward saw what was happening and commanded—his first official command as King of England—"Let him be."

He beckoned to Tom, who came before him and dropped to one knee. Edward extended a hand, which Tom reached to kiss. But Edward clasped Tom's hand friend-to-friend rather than allowing the boy to kiss it subject-to-king. "This is my friend Tom," Edward announced.

The courtiers fell back from the two at the king's sign, bowing deeply. Edward motioned to Tom to stand beside his throne, where the two posed happily before the assemblage.

At this point Miles Hendon, who had been watching with weary glee, swayed slightly, dizzy from loss of blood. Rather than fall, he staggered to the steps before the throne, and with a great grunt seated himself thereon, stretching his legs and nursing his wounded arm.

An exclamation of horror rippled through the congregation at this fearful breach of protocol. Edith whirled away, hiding her face in embarrassment.

The nearest courtier to Hendon was De Brie, the king's chamberlain. "Get up, sir, get up!" he whispered half hysterically into Hendon's ear. "You are sitting in the presence of the king!"

Edward noticed it too, and for a moment reacted with contracted brows. But Hendon, leaning on an elbow, reclining on the step, cast his eyes at Edward, silently reminding him of the promise Edward had made him that night they'd spent in the inn. Edward remembered suddenly, and his face suddenly suffused in a wide grin. "Let him sit," King Edward said, issuing his second command as king. "It is his right."